The Weaving Of Threads

Book Two

Lee E. Eddy

The Weaving of Threads, Book Two

Copyright 2020 by Lee E. Eddy

This is a work of fiction. Dialogue has been fictionalized and is based upon the Scriptures using the following translations:

The Literal Translation of the Holy Bible, third edition, Copyright 1995, used by permission of the copyright holder, Jay P. Green, Sr.

Name: Lee E. Eddy
Title: The Weaving of Threads, Book Two/ By Lee E. Eddy
Identifiers: ISBN: 978-1-952369-62-9
Subjects: 1. Religion
2. Fiction/Historical

Published by EA Books Publishing, a division of
Living Parables of Central Florida, Inc. a 501c3
EABooksPublishing.com

DEDICATION

To the people in the churches where I have been a pastor/teacher and the disciples I have had under my care, who have allowed me to experiment on them in ministry, I dedicate this book. You allowed me to work on things and delve deeply into practical application of the Word of God. Thank you.

CONTENTS

ACKNOWLEDGMENTS

It is my sincere desire to thank those who have watched me and helped me through this process. It has been totally unique to my experience to write a novel and the joy of it was inexplicable. I wish to thank Sarah, Carol, Miranda, Bob, and Roxie for their editorial work and in-depth discussions of matters that few have ventured to explore. Larry and Peter gave me invaluable insight and help in editing. All my other friends just put up with my joyous rantings and indecipherable musing. It was all with Jesus working hard beside us that we got anything done. For all of that, Lord, I am truly grateful.

CHAPTER 1
Setting Up the Pattern

Sheol was next to pandemonium, if that were possible. Lazarus had been raised. They all heard the voice that called him out. What did this mean? How did it happen? Speculation was rampant. To souls who had been dead for some time, some of them for thousands of years, to see someone so blatantly raised caused many to be amazed and perplexed. The angels ministered to them for peace, and that helped. The elders convened, trying to bring some semblance of understanding. The discussions were not that deep considering no one knew any more than anyone else.

Malachi brought the point he had told Shimon earlier that they were only to observe and not do anything. It seemed to make sense, and things were calmed a bit. Shimon had the same question in his mind that many did: if someone can be raised, can we? The question would go unanswered because no one knew. There was no way to know.

Finally, they came to the consensus the only thing to do was trust God, praise Him, wait, and see. Life returned to whatever could be called normal, except the thought was still in their minds.

Things were starting to get interesting among the living. The Jewish religious and political leaders were trying to come up with plans to kill Jesus. They were being fueled by the Dark Spiritual realm. Satan and his creepy horde were working feverishly to stir up these sentiments. Jesus was a threat to the Jewish leaders lifestyles, incomes, power, and prestige. The problem was, though, the people loved Jesus and considered him a prophet of God.

Everywhere you went, there were discussions about Him. The people who believed were solid in their belief, but they were a definite minority. Most of the common people would go with whatever made their lives easier. There were some who wanted to use Jesus for their own political purposes to stir the people up to rebellion against the Romans. One thing was certain: something was about to happen.

Life for Elihu was complicated. He wanted nothing more than just to go follow Jesus, but that wasn't possible with the business the way it was. He was trying to train his son Ezra and nephew Isaac on advanced weaving techniques and still get the work done. He had to force himself to concentrate on weaving.

As he was showing Ezra the new loom and why it was different from what he had known before, Shimei came in with a customer. "Elihu, I have a custom job for you."

Elihu's head popped up from behind the loom on his knees on the floor. There with Shimei was an imposing figure of a man. He was tall and full framed, with a demeanor of grace and importance. His clothing was very expensive, a beautiful pale yellow full-length tunic, with a deep green outer robe, expansive with many folds. His face was pleasant with salt-and-pepper beard and mustache, trimmed neatly mid-length with a full head of rich hair coming out from under the headscarf of a lighter green. His tunic was held together with a sash that matched the robe and the ends hung to his knees. Elihu liked him immediately. Here was a rich man who didn't lord it over anyone. That was very impressive.

Standing up while wiping his hands on his apron, Elihu stood full height looking the gentleman in the face and then bowed graciously asking, "My name is Elihu, Son of Shimon. What may I do for you?"

"My name is Joseph. I have a villa close to Arimathea. I hear you are the one to see for special cloth."

"Thank you for your kind words. I enjoy making unique weaves. What were you looking for?"

Joseph cocked his head back looking up to see the cloth in his imagination. "I'm looking for a cloth 2 cubits by 8 cubits for a special table cloth. I want a tight weave that looks different than most weaves. I want it to stand out."

Being able to see it in his own mind, Elihu was getting excited about what he could do for this man. "I was thinking of a three-to-one herring-bone weave of linen. It would be tight, crisp, and beautiful. We are the only ones around Jerusalem to make it. To get it from Rome or Egypt would take a long time."

"How soon could you have it for me? I need it before Passover. Is that possible?"

"Yes, if I started it right away. I should have it the day after the Sabbath before Passover. Would that do for you?"

"That would be perfect," he said enthusiastically. "What do I owe you for this?"

"You would have to work that out with Shimei." With a smooth glance over at Shimei to transfer the attention, Elihu knew it was going to happen. "I will have to start it quickly."

Shimei and Elihu were brothers who had worked together for a long time, Shimei being the eldest who ran the business, Elihu the best weaver in the shop. They knew how this worked. This customer had the money, the need, and not much time. He also looked easy to work with. Elihu liked him. "Very good, then. Please start on it as soon as possible," Joseph said. "I look forward to seeing what you can do."

"Very good, sir. I will do my best."

"I also need several towels and napkins. Do you have such things available?"

"Yes," said Shimei, "We keep much of that in stock. I can give you some today, if you wish."

"No, I will send a courier. The cloth is the more important item."

"Certainly. Please, come this way. We will let Elihu get things in order." Shimei escorted Joseph out of the shop into the family area to offer some snacks and drink as they negotiated the price.

Allowing them time to leave the shop, Elihu stood by quietly. Turning, he saw Ezra and Isaac staring at him smiling. "Yes, we have a job commission. Yes, it will take the new loom. Yes, you will learn many things. And, no, you aren't going to make this piece. I am. But you will learn from it."

Both of them let out a simple disappointment sigh. "Not to worry, gentlemen. You will get your chance. But first, we have much to do to prepare. Let's get to work."

They all three were deeply involved in getting the linen ready when Shimei walked in.

"That will start yielding us results quickly. He has many projects he wants to be done, and he is quite wealthy. And the really good news is, he is a follower of Jesus. He isn't making that widely known yet, because he is on the Sanhedrin. He and a couple of others on the council are, but they are trying to keep it quiet for now so as to be able to be included in the conversations. They can hear when things are going to happen and what the attitude of the Jews is. That is very tricky. And dangerous. May God shield them from harm."

The atmosphere around Jerusalem was charged. Everyone was on edge. Jesus's reputation was growing. It was difficult for him to travel anywhere since it garnered crowds so quickly. News of raising Lazarus from the dead had spread quickly. The Jews had a very hard time getting support from the people since they held him to be a prophet. The word on the street was he was the Messiah. Rumors were everywhere. The excitement was rising thinking he was going to be the one to deliver Israel from Rome. The rumor had even reached the Romans who had to keep an eye on this possible rebellion.

Jesus was staying in Bethany with Lazarus and his sisters. Since it was so close to Jerusalem, he and the disciples stayed in Bethany and did daily sorties to Jerusalem. They spent the Sabbath with them and just relaxed. The next day was the first of the week. Jesus was getting more pensive, as of late, as if he had something on his mind. But today he was a little lighter. He ordered the guys to go to the next village, Bethphage, and lose a donkey and her colt. The owners didn't seem to mind letting her go when they heard it was for Jesus. As they crossed over the Mount of Olives, they put Jesus on the colt, taking branches off the nearby palm trees and using their outer garments to put on the road. They shouted, "Blessed is he who comes in the name of the Lord! Hoshiana! Save now!" The crowd gathered and joined in the shouting. They came down the slope of the Mount of Olives and headed for the Eastern Gate of the city causing quite a ruckus. Everyone could see it was Jesus they were talking about. The Pharisees and priests were indignant, trying to get them to stop. It jelled the wrath of the leaders to the point where they knew something had to be done and done quickly. They were losing control, and they knew it.

The spectacle was undeniable. Shouting, dancing, covering the road, all this was usually suited for kings coming back from battle victorious. The Pharisees were asking each other, "Is he now their king?" The Passover week had just begun and it was already out of hand. The Jews started to panic.

Elihu had finished the cloth, wrapped it up in a piece of fabric, and tied it up to keep it clean. He headed out the door to deliver it, thinking it would be good to deliver it in person to such a prestigious customer. He was dressed in a good set of clothes, trying to look professional. Arimathea was just north of town a ways, up towards Rama. He was headed up towards the north gate when he heard the commotion. Hoping it was Jesus, he turned toward the east. He was shocked to find them at the top of the Mount of Olives coming down in a full Procession of Victory with Jesus at the center of it all.

Following on the skirts of the crowd, Elihu was amazed at the fervency of the shouting and activity. He didn't recognize most of the people, but some he knew from the synagogue. Those he knew were motivated politically, not religiously. He was very interested in what the crowd had in mind and what they thought they were going to do. Everything wound down toward the Eastern Gate getting quite loud and boisterous. Jesus seemed to allow it for some reason.

As they approached the Eastern Gate, their forward progress died. Jesus got off the colt, smiling and touching people. He walked slowly through the gate and proceeded on to the Temple. The crowd didn't know what else to do and bit by bit dispersed. Elihu could see and sense that many were disappointed. The crowd would be fickle if they didn't get what they wanted at the time they wanted it. Hearing two men dressed in Pharisaical garb, Elihu listened. "Look. We have gained nothing! The whole world is going after him!" It was obvious the displeasure of these two men would eventually be trouble.

Elihu proceeded with the small crowd that continued with Jesus. It more or less was on the way to the direction he wanted to go, so he could follow for a bit.

As they got closer, Jesus could see the money changers had re-established themselves just behind the toureg wall. Now it was his turn to be indignant. "It is too important that the temple be clean for the Passover. Especially this Passover." He walked with purpose straight toward the main body of the moneychangers. On the way, he scooped up a few cords of rope that had been abandoned, tying them into a usable whip. One of the moneychangers saw him coming; he had been here before when Jesus did this the first time. With a quick exclamation and wide-eyed expression, he grabbed his stuff and started to run. By the time others could respond, Jesus arrived, turning over the first table. "I told you, this is a house of prayer, not a den of thieves!" Everyone scattered again, the tables being turned over and the pens opened with the animals being driven away, in no particular direction.

Standing there with his mouth gaping, Elihu knew he was witnessing the authority the Messiah was to wield. As this tirade ended, Jesus calmly put down the ropes, shook the dust off his hands and had a look of accomplishment on his face. He looked up and caught Elihu's eye. Looking straight at him, Jesus smiled a small mischievous smirk. Elihu knew immediately what was being communicated to him. He had real peace come over him as he truly understood that everything was in the plan and he could trust God for it. Elihu smiled back, bowing a little, giving full reign to this amazing man. Things were going to work out, but they weren't going to be the way anyone thought they would be.

As he walked toward the northern gate, a man walked up to him. "Are you Elihu the weaver?"

"Yes, I am."

"I am Asahel, from Joseph of Arimathea. I've been sent to pick up a tablecloth from you. He said it should be ready today. Is it?"

"Why, yes it is. I have it right here."

"Thank you. I have your payment. May I have the package?" He reached into his bag and handed Elihu a pouch with coins in it. "I believe that is the arranged price."

"I am not the one who negotiated with him. I'm sure it is sufficient." The man produced a parchment and some ink and a quill. Elihu counted out the money and signed the parchment. Everything was completed in short fashion. The cloth was handed over, paid in full.

"Thank you. Preparations are being made for Jesus to have the Passover in a room Joseph owns here in Jerusalem. Seeing you here saved me from going to your shop. I thank you very much."

"No, thank you. It saves me quite a trip out to Arimathea. Be blessed in your preparations."

Both bowing, showing respect, the man walked away. Elihu had complete confidence that Jehovah God was orchestrating things. He also had the nagging feeling that things were going to get a lot worse before they got better.

Tuesday was a special day. It was the day of preparation for the Passover. This day was set aside to get all the work done that was needed for the Passover. The Passover fell on Wednesday this year. Since no work was to be done on a Sabbath, that made this Passover a little more difficult than normal. Passover started on Wednesday evening. That night and the next day was the Passover Sabbath. The next evening and day was the first day of the feast of Unleavened Bread. The first day and the last day of this eight-day feast were both Sabbaths. Then the normal weekly Sabbath started on Friday evening through Saturday day, bringing it to three Sabbaths in a row. Since there could be no work for three days in a row, preparation day was extremely important. It was the day for buying everything they would need for three days and setting things in order before the Passover started at sundown on Wednesday. The Passover lamb was offered in the Temple at the ninth hour or three o'clock in the afternoon on Wednesday, three hours before the start of the Sabbath of Passover.

The disciples were instructed to make preparations for the Passover on Tuesday, but they were going to celebrate the feast together on Tuesday evening, one day early. Jesus had something in the works, but they had no idea what it was or why. They found a man uncharacteristically carrying a water jug on his head and followed him. He was part of the crew Joseph had to set up things for Jesus. When they came to the building, they found Joseph there. The disciples said to him, "The Teacher says, 'Where is the guest room that I may eat the Passover with my disciples?'" Joseph showed them a large upper room where everything had been set except the final food preparations. There was one large main table covered with an expensive linen cloth. All the dishes, candles, wine cups, everything possibly needed, was already there and in place.

Joseph bowed deeply, "This is all yours for your master. Blessed Pesach to you all." The entire crew that was there to set up, then all bowed out together and the place was empty for them to use. This night was going to be memorial.

The story was told to the whole shop. Elihu had witnessed the kingly procession that established Jesus's position as King of Judah, but not in a political or judicial sense. It set things in the heart of the people. It also set things in motion against him by the political and religious leaders. They would close up the shop early today as per usual. There would be nothing for work until after the first of the week. All the workers would be blessed with a Passover gift and sent home. However, each of them knew there was something under foot in the nation. This time, it wasn't just the Romans that were the trouble. The rulers of the Jews were up to something, and it wasn't good. One could feel it in the air.

The family was all preparing for Passover. Baruch's brother Chaim and Naomi had come in to celebrate with the family. Baruch and Susannah would celebrate it here with Shemei and his family, and that included Chaim and Naomi. Elihu had his sons and wives and had decided to have their own seder. Shemei and Elihu's brother Uriah had his family and they were to celebrate it at their place.

Since this was Tuesday and the whole day was set for preparation, everyone was busy. Tomorrow would be free for preparations, also, but the sacrifice in the Temple was killed at the 9th hour. That made the day a special day and most of the people had their things done on Tuesday.

Elihu knew that something else was going to happen, he could feel it in his bones. He didn't trust the religious leadership. He decided to talk it out with Ezra. Since they were going to be at his house, Ezra was busy, but available. "What do you think, Ezra? Do you think the Jews will start something before Passover?"

"It's possible. The sentiment around the square is decidedly not in Jesus's favor. The Pharisees and Priests are sowing discontent among the people. All the people at the Mount of Olives could turn on him in a second."

"I wish we could keep an eye on him. There is no telling what they have conspired to do. The whole place feels like evil in the air, and this is supposed to be a holy time in Israel. I am conflicted as to what we should do."

"Well," started Ezra in a way to start planning, "since we don't know where Jesus is, we can't watch him, but we know where the Jewish leadership is. We can watch them."

"That is brilliant! Good thinking!" Elihu had been sparked into action. "Are you willing to do some watching for us? Maybe starting tonight?"

His smile saying everything, Ezra was obviously ready for that. "I think I could be part of that. What are you thinking?"

"Watching the Temple, where the guards enter. If they have an activity, they will use the Temple guards."

"They won't go in the day. Too many eyes. It will be after dark to hide what they are doing."

"Agreed." Elihu settled it in his mind. "You go and watch across the street from the guard entrance. That should keep that avenue covered. If something happens, you can come back here, and we will figure out what else to do. Sound good?"

"Sounds very good." At least they were doing something.

The realm of the demons was extremely busy. They were going all over the place stirring up people in every way they could. The demons would employ the departed spirits of violence and disruption. The demons would get people all worked up until their soul would be open to being inhabited by a departed spirit that would stay and irritate the souls they inhabited. Even the departed spirits like Lachish were used to help get people desiring the alcohol more than usual. The spiritual atmosphere was charged with evil intent.

Lachish was in the area of the Temple hoping to inhabit one of the guards. The leaders needed extra duty and they were letting the extra guards sit around and drink just so they would be available. While he was there a couple of days ago, he watched a man come to the priests who had been with Jesus somehow. Lachish didn't want anything to do with Jesus. That was for sure. This man, however, was important for some reason. It wasn't just demons hanging around, Satan himself was involved here. This man came to conspire against Jesus for personal gain. That was all the opening Satan needed. He entered the man and occupied him. He wasn't trusting this to any other demon. He wanted to make sure of this himself. Lachish didn't like being this close to Satan, but this is where things happened to help him feel what he needed to feel.

Satan's authority in the evil spiritual realm was total. He was fairly unapproachable with a distinct hatred for just about everything. He would be beautiful in form if it wasn't for the darkness that exuded from him at all times. Just like the demons who had a darkness shell around them, Satan had a definite aura of darkness. Fear was like a severe smell about him that permeated everything and caused reactions in everything he came in contact with. He wasn't to be trifled with.

Since his being was greatly larger than the man he was inhabiting, it looked like the man was in a constant fog around him that moved with him. It had to have affected the man in every way. Having a demon was one thing, having Satan himself was quite another.

The man was called Judas, Lachish learned. He was one of the twelve disciples and had chosen to betray Jesus. Satan was all too glad to inhabit him and, therefore, get closer to Jesus. Satan was trying to hide in this man to destroy his Master, but Jesus could see him. There was a power about this man Jesus that none of the spirits could understand. They knew fairly quickly that he had the authority to cast them out and stop them from anything they were doing. That was a little disconcerting.

For the most part, the demons had full reign to do whatever they wished. It was like a party where everyone did what they wanted. There was chaos in the air in Jerusalem. The greatest activity was around wherever Jesus went. It was like the demonic realm was looking for ways to get in and destroy this man. They were swarming around in anticipation of something.

Something masked Jesus from their prying eyes this night. They were left out, swirling around trying to find him. The only thing they knew for sure was that Satan was close to him. They counted on that.

Jesus had Passover with his disciples in the upper room Joseph had for them. Right at the beginning, Judas, with Satan attached, was dismissed to go do their plan, so even Satan couldn't be in on what Jesus did with his disciples. There was a Godly perimeter around them. What they were doing was private and intimate.

Judas came out of there and went straight to the Temple. There he told the Jews that Jesus was going to go to the Garden of Gethsemane later, it was Jesus's normal plan. They conspired to send a detachment of Temple guards to Gethsemane to arrest this man and put him on trial in front of the Sanhedrin. They had to scrounge up witnesses and gather in all of the council that was privy to their plans. It was illegal to have court at night, but this is the only way they could manipulate the law to have Jesus put to death. They needed a foolproof plan so they wouldn't arrest the wrong man in the dark. That's where Judas came in. He knew him very closely. He would take the guard to the right man and signal them who it was with a signal that wouldn't be mistaken: he would give him a kiss of friendship. Satan was delighting in this as it would be the deepest hurt he could think of against Jesus. He was making Judas feel very good about all this. Everything was moving beautifully for all concerned. This night would be remembered as their victory for many years to come. Or, so they thought.

There was heavy activity happening inside the Temple. Ezra knew they had the right place to watch. It was close to the second watch of the night when a large group of guards with torches came out of the guard entrance. They were being led by a man that looked like one of Jesus's disciples. That didn't seem right. The whole group was agitated as if they were being fired up by something. Ezra followed at a safe distance. They weren't hard to follow; they weren't exactly quiet.

They also didn't have very far to go. All they had to do was exit the Temple area and cross the Kidron valley. Gethsemane was right there at the base of the Mount of Olives. Seeing where they were going, Ezra moved quickly so he could see what was happening. He passed them and entered the garden unseen. He had no torch, so it was difficult to see. He saw that he was pretty boxed in. If he was caught, he didn't want to implicate the family. He realized he had clothes on that only the family of weavers would be wearing. Looking around he found a large piece of fabric they used to cover the saplings. Taking it, he took off his clothes and put them in a place by the outer boundary of the garden under some discarded wood and wrapped himself in the cloth. With that being the best disguise he could come up with, he proceeded into the garden at the same time as the mob of guards.

He made it over to them just in time to see them confront Jesus. The disciple that brought them walked up to Jesus and kissed him on the cheek. Jesus looked at him and Ezra heard the first word he could for the night. "Judas, do you betray me with a kiss?" Judas looked stunned and stepped back letting the crowd come closer.

One of the disciples took out a short sword and took a swing at a man coming up to them. His aim wasn't precise, so instead of killing the intended target, he just cut off the man's ear. Jesus stepped up stopping the man with the sword. He then reached out picked up the ear off the ground and touched the man's head who had been attacked. The wound was completely healed. The ear had been reattached with no wound, but there was still all the blood on him from the attack. The mob was struck in awe. Jesus asked them who they had come for. One of the chief guards said, "Jesus of Nazareth."

"I am he," said Jesus. When he said that, the whole group fell backward as if a force had pushed them. The demeanor of the group changed in an instant. Jesus repeated himself. "Who do you seek?"

"Jesus of Nazareth."

"I am he. Since it is me you are seeking, let these go." The disciples felt the need to retreat. They all scattered. The guards didn't know what to do. Their real objective was still standing there. They didn't have orders to arrest them all, just this man.

"Seize him." Their attitude returned somewhat and they grabbed Jesus, tying his hands together in front of him with a lead rope taken by a man in front. As they turned to lead him away, one of them spotted Ezra. He reached out to grab him, but Ezra spun quickly and the only thing the man got was the cloth. Abandoning it, he fled naked. No one seemed to be in pursuit, so he made a couple of turns to make sure he wasn't followed. He quietly made his way around to the place where he stored his clothes. Grabbing them, he ran away from the path leading to the Temple. Ducking behind a small structure there, he stopped and listened to see if he was really alone. Taking a few moments to calm himself, he got dressed and ran a shortcut route to Elihu's home to make a report.

The demons had a great time manipulating he guards and stoking up their minds and emotions. They all went out together to the Garden of Gethsemane. Satan was leading inside Judas; it was starting to be a frenzy. By the time they got to Gethsemane, they were ready for some action.

Soon they came up to Jesus. The demons wanted to kill him right there, but there was something holding them back. Then Satan moved in Judas to betray him with a kiss to hurt Jesus even more. When asked who they were looking for, Jesus said something that surprised every spirit. He said, "I am he." What the spirits heard was "I AM!" A great power and light came out of this man and blew through all the spirit realm with a force that was never felt before. The blinding light had force behind it. The raw faith was more powerful than anything any of the demons had experienced. It set everything in order. All the spirits knew they were touching something greater than themselves. It made them very serious. They all paid great attention.

Satan himself left his little host so quickly it left spiritual scars on his soul. Judas was left thinking of what he had done. Without the spiritual mastermind in him any longer, he was left confused and self-condemned. He knew he had been used to be part of something bigger and nastier than what he had intended. It was destroying his mind. Regret filled him.

The demons didn't leave, but they understood they were dealing with something bigger than they had thought before. There were forces at work here that were to have implications for centuries.

Being motivated by what he saw helped Ezra make good time getting back to Elihu's place. "They have arrested Jesus!" That sentence got everyone's attention. Elihu, Keturah, Boaz, and Ruth were there waiting word. Ezra told them what had happened and it made them all very serious. "What are we going to do?"

"There is nothing we can do," Elihu said quietly. It is in Jesus's hands now. We will have to trust Jehovah God." Elihu got very pensive and thoughtful. "We can't keep this to ourselves, though. We need to tell Baruch."

Getting up and retrieving his cloak and keffiyeh, he told the women, "You stay here for now. Boaz, can you stay with them? If we need you, we will send for you. There's no reason everyone needs to be up at this hour." Boaz knew the look Elihu gave him. He wanted someone around to take care of the women if something should happen. Boaz knowingly nodded at his father.

He and Ezra made their way down the street to Baruch's place. After banging on the door, a light was lit up inside. "Shemei, it is us, Elihu and Ezra. We have word. Open up."

The latch was thrown back and the door snatched open. Shemei was there with a lamp in his hand. "What's going on?"

"Jesus has been arrested." They both walked in and turned to face Shemei. "We think S'ba Baruch needs to know. We have no idea what to do. We probably need to come up with a plan."

Shimei went and got Baruch, their father, up. He came in and together they came up with the idea to take shifts and watch the Temple area. Shimei took the first watch. He left with a dark cloak to be masked in the night. We walked briskly over to the Temple grounds. It was between the second and third watch. There was something going on and that was really unusual. He found out with those going through that the actual trial was happening at the High Priest's residence. He couldn't get in there, but he heard things. There wasn't enough information to do something with, so just after midnight, he went home, and Ezra spelled him. Around the fourth watch, Ezra went home, and Elihu came out. They figured that if something was going to happen, it was going to be early.

Baruch, Shimei, and Ezra joined him just before sunrise. They saw them take Jesus to the Roman Pavement where business and judgments were decided. They couldn't go inside and still stay clean for Passover, so everyone gathered outside at the Pavement. Since this was public, the four men were able to get in and hear what was going on.

Pontius Pilate was the governor of Judea. They got him up early to sit in judgment as to a matter of the people. Going to them, he learned that a Jew was being brought before him in some kind of squabble about their Jewish law. Sitting in the governor's seat, he asked the High Priest, Caiaphas, "Why is this man here? What accusations do you bring against this man?"

"If this one wasn't an evil-doer, then we would not have given him over to you."

With that kind of answer, Pilate knew this wasn't going to be logical to the Roman Law. "Then you take him and judge him according to your own law."

"But it isn't lawful for us to put someone to death. We have to bring him to you."

"Bring him in," he ordered the guards standing next to him. "I'll interview him inside the praetorium." They took Jesus inside. After a short time, Pilate re-emerged with Jesus trailing a little ways behind him. "This man is a Galilean. I refer him to your Tetrarch Herod. Let him decide." They led him off the platform with a fully armed escort of Roman soldiers.

The men were concerned at that. "Herod is a coward and a puppet of Rome. He won't make any decisions. They will bring him back here," Elihu said. "I will follow him. You stay here together. I will come back with a report."

It didn't take very long and the Romans returned with Jesus. Elihu joined the others who were waiting for information. "Jesus wouldn't talk in any way to Herod. He sent him back frustrated that Jesus didn't do what he wanted him to do."

Pilate walked to the edge of the judgment platform and addressed the Jews once again.

"I do not find one single cause of death in this man. He has not done anything worthy of death. However, I know the custom to you that during this time of Passover, that I should release one prisoner to you. Should I turn over this King of the Jews to you?"

Elihu turned to Baruch. "Did you hear that? Pilate thinks Jesus is the King of the Jews. What did they talk about in there to convince him so completely is such a short time?"

Then the totally unthinkable happened. The Priests started yelling, "Not this one! Release Barabbas to us!"

"Barabbas! They want Barabbas instead of Jesus to be released? Barabbas is the worst," said Shemei. "He tried to overthrow Rome and killed soldiers in the process. He is nothing more than a thief and a murderer. Rome hates him. What are they thinking?"

They could see Pilate was in a quandary. He didn't want to kill Jesus, but he was in a very bad position. Maybe if he punished Jesus, they would not need the death penalty. Speaking to the Captain of the guard, he said, "Take him and scourge him. And release Barabbas. Don't worry, we will have him in our hands soon enough."

"Scourging!" Baruch almost collapsed. It was very difficult to believe God had a plan that included scourging. They couldn't go and watch, but they had seen people who had been scourged before. It wasn't pretty. Many died from the scourge alone. They couldn't understand how the Jews had gotten to be this kind of people. They were ashamed of the leadership and what Israel had become. "We need this Messiah. Lord God, I trust you to do what is needed." Baruch's heart cried out in pain.

After what seemed to be an eternity, Jesus was brought back out in front of the people. He looked horrible. On his head was a wreath of plaited thorns in a crown of mockery. His face was covered in blood. A purple cloth was placed around his shoulders, but it was soaked through with blood. His garments were thrown at his feet. It didn't look like he had enough strength to stand. At closer inspection, his face was bruised from fists and slapping he had endured inside.

Pilate came out gesturing at Jesus with his hand. "Behold, the man!" Pilate thought for sure when they saw him, they would drop the accusations and let it be. That isn't what happened.

The chief priests were indignant, thinking they were being ignored in what they wanted. Shouts were coming from all through the crowd. "Crucify him! Crucify him!"

"You take him and crucify him, for I find not even one cause of death in him!"

"We have a law, and according to that law he ought to die because he made himself Son of God!" That word shook Pilate. He took Jesus back in the praetorium. They returned with Pilate visibly affected. He was trying hard to set him free.

The men were shocked at the cries of crucifixion. They were feeling complete horror at the thought. They had seen men crucified before right here in Jerusalem. There was a place already set up for it and used fairly often, a place known as Golgotha, the place of the skull. They knew they had no power to stop this flood of violence. They just stood there helpless.

A new tact was employed by the Jews. A cry went up, "If you release this one, you are not a friend of Caesar. Everyone making himself a king speaks against Caesar!" That blow did Pilate in. He couldn't go against Rome. He had an uprising on his hands that wanted to submit to Rome. His going against them would be taken the wrong way in Rome.

"Bring him forth." Pilate sat down on the judgment seat. It was obvious he was reluctant to do what he really needed to do. Trying one more time, he said, "Behold, your King!"

The crowd all the more cried out, "Away with him! Crucify! Crucify him!"

"Shall I crucify your king?"

Someone from the contingency of the High Priest shouted, "We have no king except Caesar!" The crowd went into a near frenzy with shouts and fists in the air.

From the seat of judgment, Pilate proclaimed, "Take him away and crucify him." The captain of the cohort was given the command. Pilate asked for water and washed his hands in front of the crowd. "This be on you, I wash my hands of this entire affair."

The High Priest said, "Be it on us and on our children." With that statement, Baruch nearly collapsed.

Some Roman soldiers took the purple cloth off Jesus which had coagulated with all the blood on his back starting the bleeding anew. Taking off the crown of thorns did the same thing. They put his tunic back on him and his outer robe. They led him down to the bottom of the platform. The Captain was shouting orders bringing up the cross pieces. He commanded, "Bring up the others under condemnation." It took a while, but soon they were underway.

Jesus was too weak to carry the cross piece called the patibulum. After he tried and failed, they grabbed a large man standing by and forced him to carry it for him; it was legal for the Romans to force someone to carry a load for the soldiers for a certain distance. From there they made the procession to Golgotha.

The spirit realm was incredibly active. Since early in the morning, the demons and their accompanying spirits were agitating people. The whole climate was violence, doing harm, getting blood and it was pointed at Jesus. Satan stayed close to the High Priest, using his authority to cause effect. It didn't seem difficult to whip the people into the bad attitudes and desires.

Before Pilate, it was easy to keep the crowd stoked up. There were spirits whose main thrust was agitation, who were used to great effect. The violent spirits were having a heyday during the flogging. Mockery spirits ran amok in the praetorium amongst the soldiers and then in Herod's court. Satan stayed close to the action around Jesus. He was really enjoying himself.

The demons were screaming at people to want a crucifixion. The air above them was boiling with activity. The departed spirits of violence and cruelty were having the most fun they could possibly have in their condition. Nothing satisfied them, but they continually tried.

When the crowd started toward Golgotha, the spirit realm erupted. It was indeed a dark day in Jerusalem.

CHAPTER 2
The Price is Paid

They dispatched Ezra to go with the news to the family. The men thought it might be a good thing to get everyone together in one place, to console each other and be easier to bring news to a central location. Ezra was to meet back with them up on the flat across from Golgotha. He brought word to the family and Uriah decided he wanted to go back with him.

They made their way back; the streets were jammed with people getting ready for the Passover. It was close to nine o'clock in the morning when they made it over to the road leading out of Jerusalem to the north. It wasn't that far from Fortress Antonia where the Roman garrison was housed. Beside the road the Romans had installed several stipes, upright beams permanently set in the ground for purposes of crucifixion. They put them on the roads so all could see someone was being crucified as a deterrent to rebellious behavior. Ezra and Uriah found the others at a good vantage point where they could see everything easily. Nothing much had happened yet.

The condemned prisoners had been brought to the place that was just in front of a rock outcropping that looked like a skull. There were several stipes in the ground, but it looked like they were to use the first one and the ones next to it. They were close to six feet tall with the top carved to be a smaller piece that entered into a hole in the middle of the patibulum.

They took the first man; a man caught stealing from the Romans. The patibulum was taken off his shoulders and thrown on the ground. They stripped him down to nothing; part of the sentence of crucifixion entailed humiliation. The Romans had no sensitivities to exposure; it was part of the message to others of their seriousness. The took him and put him on his back, dragging him to the patibulum until it was under his head. He was screaming in terror; the soldiers had to fight him to spread his arms out. With two soldiers holding his arm in place, one soldier lying across his body to hold it in place, and one at the end of the patibulum with nails and a hammer, they nailed his arm to the patibulum. They drove the nail into the little notch between the base of his hand and his wrist, causing extreme pain and the hand to malform as the nail pierced the nerve going through the middle of his wrist. They moved to the other side and did the same thing. With both hands secured, they need all four of the soldiers to lift the patibulum with the thief hanging on it high enough to slide it down onto the stipes that was prepared to receive it. The thief was screaming in abject pain as they bent down, grabbing his lower legs, bending them, holding them in place, and they drove a single nail through both feet. He was completed. They moved on to the next man.

The whole time they were working on the first man, Baruch and his sons and grandson were horrified. They knew Jesus was next. Jesus was standing there not moving. He had lost a lot of blood and didn't have much energy to waste. He stood there resigned to his fate, so it seemed. Elihu looked around and saw a small contingency not far from them. He nudged Ezra and pointed them out. "Do you know who that is?"

"Yes, Abba. That one woman is Jesus's mother. The man with her is one of the disciples, the youngest, I believe."

Elihu's heart was broken. This is bad enough, but to see it happen to your child would be a burden indescribable.

There was one soldier with his lance at the throat of the third man to keep him from running. The soldier next to Jesus didn't have much to do. Jesus was no threat. The six soldiers had a commander who was overseeing the whole job. He looked like a grizzled man who had been on several campaigns. He knew what he was doing. He had done this before. He motioned to the ones who had just finished with the first man to move to Jesus.

They took off his outer robe that was a simple, homespun one-piece robe. It seemed painful for him to raise his arms to have it pulled over his head for removal. His undertunic was stuck to the blood all over his back. To get it off they had to cut it open in the front and ripped it off his back, that started the bleeding again. They removed his loincloth that also was soaked with the blood running from his back.

The man who had carried the patibulum for Jesus had dropped it just in front of the stipes, and they had released him. They didn't have to force Jesus down to the ground; he fairly collapsed to a sitting position, they then just laid him back. They had to drag him a little to position him on the patibulum grinding dirt into the open wounds of his back. He grimaced and jerked away some, but not enough to have to re-position him. They got ready to lay across him and pull his arm into position, but he just allowed them to stretch his arm out. He didn't look as they positioned the nail, he could feel the point in the right place, and he braced himself. With a single, heavy first blow the nail went straight through the arm into the wood. A few more hits and it was set deep. Jesus yelled out in pain. His body was trembling in pain and shock.

They moved to the other side and repeated it. Again, Jesus didn't watch. Again he cried out. When he did, the woman Ezra said was his mother buckled and fell under the strain. Those with her moved to hold her and try to comfort her. The man decided to stay on the ground with her.

The soldier's lifted the patibulum with Jesus hanging on it onto the stipes, and it fell into place with a decided jerk. Jesus convulsed in pain. He was having trouble breathing. His back was scraping on the rough-hewn wood of the stipes. All the points of pain at once were overwhelming. He was trying to steel himself for the nail in the feet, but he was unsuccessful. He involuntarily screamed as every nerve in his body seemed to fire at the same time. He lost control of his body urinating on himself with it mingling with the blood and wound at his feet. There he hung with no reprieve.

The third man was summarily hung in the same way, but he had to be wrestled into place. He was totally terrorized by the first two being crucified before him. He watched, knowing he was next. These men, however, hadn't been flogged first. They were shocked at the condition of Jesus.

The commander was handed an object brought to him by a runner from the fortress. It was a piece of flat wood with writing on it. He read it and snickered as if it was an inside joke. He looked at the crowd briefly and turned around to complete a job. Taking one of the nails out of the bag and the hammer, he went to Jesus's cross and nailed the board above his head for all to see. There in Latin, the official language of Rome, Greek, the language of commerce that most people coming through would be able to read, and in Hebrew, the language of the people of Israel, was written: *This is Jesus of Nazareth, King of the Jews.* The High Priest was livid. He immediately dispatched one of his underlings who ran into town.

Baruch and company standing across the way were silent. Each of them was dealing with what they saw in their own way. The only thing they could hear was the screaming and the sound of the hammer on the nails. When all three were nailed in place, and the sign set in place, the soldiers gathered behind the crosses to wait. They had gathered the garments from the three, but the only garment that was full and complete was Jesus's long home-spun outer robe. It was part of what they got for this duty for them to divide the personal effects among them. It wasn't much. They got three sets of sandals and the rope belts of the two thieves. But they decided not to divide the robe, but instead, they cast lots for who would get it whole. They were ignoring the men on the crosses and were actually laughing and playing with the gambling. They were drinking heavily to numb the business they had to do. So it was quite a surprise to them when they heard Jesus speak out loud enough for all to hear without him shouting. Tilting his head back trying to breathe, he said, "Father, forgive them. They don't know what they are doing." That seemed to drain the fun out of it; they became very quiet and serious.

Baruch was sparked by that statement. It helped him realize even in this condition, Jesus was in control of his faculties. He still understood the spiritual surroundings around him. He was doing what he needed to do. His Father was in on it.

They weren't alone. Elihu was watching the others who had come. There was quite a crowd, but up to now, they had been quiet. However, when Jesus spoke, the chief priests and Pharisees saw they needed to gain back the crowd. They had designated some among them to speak, so the high priest himself wasn't implicated. "You who were going to raze the temple and building it in three days, save yourself! If you are the Son of God, come down from the cross!" The whole crowd looked at the man. Some standing close by agreed in mockery. It completely incensed Elihu. He started to say something,but Shimei put his hand on him, shaking his head as if saying, "This isn't the time nor place".

One of the soldiers came and tried to give him some vinegar, but Jesus wouldn't take it. He hung there quiet, trying to gain breath. He had to lift himself up on the nails in his hands and feet causing stabbing pain to shoot through his limbs, just to get a full breath. Every now and then he would look out at the crowd; it seemed to make him sadder.

The mockery continued from the same men, and some new ones joined in. "He saved others; he is not able to save himself. If He is the King of Israel, let him come down now from the cross, and we will believe him." This last statement was directed at the crowd, who sounded like they were in agreement. The underlying current was mean and unfeeling. It felt like it was crushing the Mother of Jesus. Jesus looked up and saw them in their little group of the faithful. They were just across the road in front of him.

"Woman," Jesus spoke out to her. She looked up at him. He nodded toward the disciple with her, "Behold your son!" Looking at the disciple, "Behold your mother!" In very few words he gave responsibility to the disciple to take care of his mother. This really touched Baruch.

The thief on Jesus's left started yelling at him , joining the mockery. "IF you are the Messiah, save yourself and us!"

The thief on Jesus's right cried out at the thief that spoke, "Do you not fear God? You are under this same judgment. We are being punished justly, for we are receiving things worthy of what we did. But this one did nothing wrong!" Then turning to Jesus, he said, "Jesus. Lord. Remember me when you come into your kingdom."

Jesus turned as best as he could toward the one on his right. He smiled under the crusted blood and the swollen, bruised cheeks, and split lip. "Truly, I say to you; today you will be with me in paradise." That exchange filled the Baruch company with great hope.

Time slowly marched on. Conversation between the men was minimal. It was close to three hours that Jesus had been on the cross. Everyone knew crucifixions could last for days before the victim died. They didn't know what else to say; the ambiance was somber. Little had happened. There was still mocking happening. The runner the high priest had sent returned. Ezra sidled down to hear what was happening.

"What do you mean he won't change it?" The high priest wasn't used to people not doing what he wanted.

"All Pilate said was, 'What I have written, I have written. The sign stays.'"

Ezra nearly giggled. "What's the matter, Caiaphas? Not going your way?" he thought to himself. For some reason, it felt like a huge victory. He went back to his group with a good report.

Almost directly at midday, the sun started getting dimmer and dimmer. Everyone was silent, including the mockers. They all looked around trying to comprehend what was happening. It became as dark as midnight. They couldn't see Jesus or any of the crosses. They heard some sobbing coming from over in the direction of the crosses. Then in a loud cry of despair, they heard Jesus cry out between sobs, "My God, my God. Why have you forsaken me?" Everyone watching was shaken to the core. Something extremely deep was happening and no one could witness it.

Torches came from the city. It was some of the priesthood. Ezra snuck over to eavesdrop again. "Master Caiaphas, you need to come quickly. It is only an hour before the Passover Lamb is to be killed. You need to come. Something else has happened. The veil in the Temple has torn! It ripped from top to bottom. All the priests who were in the Temple are scared beyond help. It is dark throughout the land. We need leadership." Caiaphas went with some of them. The rest stayed with their torches for the others who stayed.

This news was beyond comprehension. Ezra made his report quietly, almost as if his speaking out loud would cause something else to happen.

More torches were coming out of the city. One group that had been standing off to the side was now illuminated by the torches that came out. It was Joseph of Arimathea and another man dressed like someone important. They had a small contingency of servants. One of them took a torch down to Jesus's mother. Their torch shed light on the crosses. The Commander sent one of the soldiers back to get some for them. The tone was one of quiet, almost fear. What was happening? Who was this man?

In the group of men, the mood was a little different. Baruch and Shimei were quietly talking about the suffering Messiah their grandfather Shimon had taught them. Since

Jesus's cry, it stuck in Baruch's head what he had said. "He distinctly quoted a Psalm as if it were currently happening. That Psalm talks about the suffering Messiah. It is as if it were writing about this as it is happening. Isaiah the Prophet also wrote about the servant of Jehovah God and the disfigurement that would happen to him. He would be like a shoot out of dry ground who would be pierced for our iniquity and crushed. Is this not what is going on right now? All this is happening so we can be brought closer to Jehovah God. This is for us!"

"It never occurred to me that we would live to see scripture fulfilled. It also didn't occur to me that this would be the price." As Shimei spoke, Elihu broke his stoic stance and started crying. Ezra standing next to him was affected by what his father was feeling.

"What all is needed?" Elihu whimpered, " Why does it have to continue? Isn't it enough?"

"We will have to just watch and wait. We will see. What a privilege to be here," Baruch whispered through a gravely voice of tears. "It is so humbling."

As the three o'clock hour approached, the darkness started to fade. It became lighter every minute; slowly, but surely. They could soon see the forms hanging on the crosses. Jesus was still alive; they could see him struggling to breathe. He said, "I thirst." One of the soldiers took a flask of vinegar and poured some in a sponge, put it on a reed, and offered it to him. When Jesus tasted it, he didn't want any more.

With a loud voice, Jesus cried out, "It is finished! Father, into your hands I commit my spirit." He convulsed heavily once, then slumped down to the end of his arms, his head sagging forward over his body. He didn't move again.

At that moment, the *shofar* of the Temple blew, signifying that the Passover Lamb had been slain. That wasn't lost on Elihu and the men. The Lamb had been slain. Then, starting slowly and building momentum, the ground began to tremble. The earth shook violently for a couple of seconds. Everyone had trouble staying on their feet. Then it was over.

The commander was standing in front of Jesus's cross. Looking up at him he said, "Truly this was the Son of God." All mockery had stopped. Everyone present was shaken in every fiber of their being. God was present. And they had just killed His Son.

Jesus's mother broke down sobbing. Elihu took a few deep breaths, trying to gain control over his emotions. He looked around at the crowd. There was very little activity except across the way with Joseph. Elihu decided to go over there and talk to them. As he approached them, Joseph looked up and recognized him. "You are the weaver. Elihu, isn't it?"

"Yes, sir. Thank you for being here for Jesus. I think he just died."

"We agree. I am going to go see Pilate and ask for the body. My family tomb is nearby. We just had a new portion carved out of the stone. We are going to try to bury him there. Most crucifixion victims are just thrown out in the valley of Gehinnom and burned with the trash. We don't want that for him."

"Thank you for doing that. Is there something we can do? There are four of us here," Elihu offered.

"Possibly. This is my friend Nicodemus. He also is on the Sanhedrin. He is going to go get as many spices for the body as possible. We will need help preparing the body, if you are willing. It will make you unclean for Passover. You need to remember that."

"That is no problem. We just saw the real Passover Lamb sacrificed. We need to do what is needed for him. That is the real Passover." The look of knowing came over all the men there. "We will stay here and await your word. Be blessed." Joseph took a couple of servants, and Nicodemus took the rest. Elihu returned to his party with a renewed reason they were there.

Time passed slowly. The climate had changed somehow. There was peace underlying the mood now. It felt like something had been accomplished, completely finished, just like Jesus said.

The spirit realm was frantic with activity. They were killing Jesus! The demons were there in full representation. There was nothing as important as this. They were giddy to the point of drunkenness at the aspect of taking down the Son of God. Now there was no doubt to their power. They did almost anything they could think of. There were demons strongly driving men to violence, departed spirits of violence greedily lusting for the opportunity to see open bloodshed, sneering spirits of mockery and disruption trying to inhabit every man they could.

When they crucified the first man, the spirits were crazy, lusting over every piece of damage done to the man. Fear spirits were being fed a feast of emotions. When they crucified the second man, however, things were different. They had the violence, the blood, the screaming agony, but they didn't get the terror. Satan was enjoying it, though. This is the Messiah, the Son of God, and we are killing him. This should end it. We will win this world, wrestle it from the hands of Jehovah God Himself. Darkness and sin have overcome! Holiness will be besmirched forever!

The third man restored the spirits of fear again. They still fed off the first man and this man just added to it all. This is a glorious day.

The departed spirits of violence have had many opportunities like this one. Wars, plundering, rape, have all been part of human history. Full fields of men killing each other, but it just filled the air with more violent departed spirits. Today was different for some reason. There was an importance to it, a spiritual quality. It was like they were spiritually empowered to do this here and now. There was a cloud of demons swirling above and around the crosses, especially the one in the middle.

Lachish entered one of the guards when he was still at the fortress. He was there to enhance the soldier's desire for wine. He was there at the cross helping get the man numb to the trauma. The more the man saw, the more he wanted wine. That was good for Lachish. What Lachish didn't count on was how close he would have to be to this Jesus person. He tried to just focus on the wine.

Then something happened that was totally unexpected. Darkness came. Normally darkness was welcomed by demons and evil spirits. This felt different. They went on their frenzy, swirling and screaming, but it was hollow. Even Satan wasn't at rest about it. It bothered him somehow. He couldn't put his finger on it. His eyes were also kept from seeing what was happening with Jesus. It was private. Then Jesus called out, "My God, My God, why have you forsaken me?" It should have been a good thing for him, but it wasn't. Why was Jesus quoting scripture? "Just die! Let us have this victory," Satan thought. It wasn't coming fast enough.

The light started to return. The surrounding air was not the attitude Satan wanted. Mockery was silenced. Satan's core was in knots. He was feeling turmoil inside him. Then Jesus died. This is what he was waiting for; it was everything. But it wasn't full. It was an empty thing. What was wrong with this? It isn't what he thought it would be.

Joseph had gone to Pilate who was very surprised that Jesus had already died. He sent word to the Commander to see if he really was dead. That burned a little time, but word came that he was really dead. Then he did something that was totally unusual; he officially gave the body of Jesus to this man who wanted to bury him. It was pleasing to Pilate to do something for the man he wanted to save, but couldn't. With his official writ in his hand, Joseph went by the upper room and secured the table cloth he had made special for Passover. Now he could use it for the burial shroud. It made him sad to know what had transpired, but he will do everything he can for this man. Had he done enough for him while he was here? Was he a coward that didn't stick up for him in front of the council? May God help him do what he can now.

It was getting late in the day. Just over an hour or so, the sun will go down starting Passover and a Sabbath. He hoped he could get Jesus in the grave before then.

Nicodemus had been successful too. He had been able to get his hands on a good supply of aloes and spices that were usually used for burial. It came to about a hundred pounds of spices. His servants were carrying it out to the place of execution. He hoped Joseph was getting his things done.

Both of them were headed back out of town against the crowd of people coming into Jerusalem for the Passover celebration. Then they arrived pretty close to the same time. Elihu met them.

"Greetings. We have had some excitement out here while you were gone," he explained. "A runner came from Pilate to see if Jesus was already dead. We figured that was because of you, Joseph. It seems the Priests wanted them all dead before the Passover. They sent word to Pilate also. They came to the men and broke their legs so they would die quicker. When they checked Jesus, he was already dead. But to make sure, one of the soldiers stabbed with a lance. He was truly dead. He didn't bleed much and there was no response."

"I have a writ for the commander. Let's get his body down." Joseph took the paper to the commander who was obviously surprised. He turned the body over to them. The soldiers waited for the other two to die and then very unceremonially jerked their arms off the nails and the feet also, dumping the bodies on the ground. Elihu tenderly worked the nail out that was holding Jesus's feet. He and Ezra took one side, Shemei and one of Joseph's servants took the other, and they lifted the patibulum up and off the stipes. They gently laid the body down on the ground. They worked the nails out freeing him from the cross.

Taking a cloth towel Joseph brought from the upper room, they sopped up the blood on his face and head. Laying the tablecloth out they put his body on the bottom half of it leaving the top to be folded over him. Elihu was taken aback. "I know this cloth," he said. "I made it!" He was overwhelmingly blessed that he was part of the honoring of the Messiah through his workmanship. He made the cloth for the King.

They put some of the spices around his body before they took the top half of the cloth and lay it carefully over his body. Cutting off a strip from the full length of the cloth, they made wrapping pieces to tie the shroud together. Joseph had sent some of his servants over to the tomb, which wasn't very far away, to prepare it. Since no one had been laid in that portion, there was no need to remove any bones.

The four men took positions on either side of the body and picked it up. They treated it with great reverence, honoring the man who had died. Walking slowly and carefully they followed Joseph to the tomb. The entrance was narrow, so they had to squeeze in and duck down. They laid him there, putting the rest of the spices around him. Nicodemus took the cloth they had used to sop up the blood at his head, folding it in honor.

The men left the tomb. Nothing was said between them. Each had taken the opportunity to look back at the body in repose to burn the image into their memories forever. Outside, they had quite a task ahead of them. It took all of them to roll the huge stone disk down the trough that had been cut for it until it completely covered the door. The stone went to the end of the trough, perfectly setting it in place. The tomb was closed.

They stayed there for just a moment, it was getting very close to sundown, and they all needed to get home. This day had been a day to remember. They all had to deal with their thoughts and would do so for quite a while. How does one tell anyone else what had happened here? They greeted each other and hugged each other. They were now brothers in bond. With tears and deep emotion, they separated from

Joseph and Nicodemus and their people. They all went home. None of them would ever be the same again.

CHAPTER 3
After Death

They had done it. They killed the Son of God! Satan was so pleased with himself. The demons were focusing all their hate on the body on the cross. They knew something people seemed not to know: death isn't the end. The living see death as the end of it all, but it's really just a transition. Now they have him in their territory.

Lachish was right there. His host was standing right behind the cross. The body slumped. Then Jesus came out. He was standing there with his head held high, wearing a light tan, mid-calf length, robe with a sash.

He stepped forward looking around.

It was like a challenge to Satan and the hordes of demons. Satan moved over to stand just in front of him. They stood facing each other looking in each other's eyes. Satan was trying to be superior like he had just won the victory. "I killed you."

Jesus smiled a little knowing smile. "Yes, I died. Now I am in Sheol." Satan smirked at the statement, thinking it was conceding to him. "But my death was planned before the foundation of the world, not something you did. I died the death of the guilty. I died for sin. I wasn't guilty. I wasn't a sinner. I paid the price for all who would believe into me. I even went to Sheol. All is paid. It is truly finished. I don't have to stay here any longer."

As soon as he said that, his garment started to change into pure white, then it started glowing and growing in light. The light was more than any of them could withstand. They all moved away in the intensity. Jesus laughed a little being filled with joy. He took a step and another as he moved further and further into the ground still shining the light. Satan followed at a discrete distance, stunned, shocked, and unable to understand or speak. Angels joined him one at a time forming a procession of light and music as they sang to him.

Satan was deflated. There was nothing he could do. His victory had no substance. He obviously didn't understand what was happening. Jesus did not inform him. He is a defeated foe, cast out a long time ago.

Lachish followed as best as he could amid the throng. Every demon was silent, just watching. The crowd of departed spirits followed because they also had no idea what to think or do.

The procession went through all the regions of darkness of Unrighteous Sheol where departed spirits of the ages were fighting, hating, trying to do all manner of vile things to each other. The light disrupted them all as if a flood of peace emanated from Jesus. They came to the barrier between the Unrighteous and the Righteous Sheol. Jesus and the angels passed right through, everyone else had to stop, being unable to continue. As the last of the procession passed through, the light was no longer seen. The huge assembly was left standing in the dark, in total silence.

Lachish felt the peace, and then he felt it leave. The turmoil in his soul leapt up in a painful boiling up of emotion and thoughts as if everything that had been held back was suddenly released. His knowledge of the futility of his existence became horribly blatant. The hollowness of his soul was agonizing. He cried out in despair, needing to find a host for the minimal relief of wine lived out in a human. He wasn't alone. Jerusalem was just about to be inundated with departed spirits.

Life in righteous Sheol was normal, the way it has been for millennia. There were a couple unique things that had happened, but for the most part, things stayed the same. Now, something was happening that had never happened before. The angels who ministered to the souls here and the angels who escorted people here after death were bursting into service for something else. All attention was drawn to a certain direction following the way the angels were going. All of them had ignited into brilliant light.

A trumpet sounded that was heard throughout all Sheol. It was a victory blast, a triumphant tone that announced the coming of the King! All the internal angels formed an entrance of spectacular proportions as they made concentric rings, each larger than the last, expanding out. Each angel was shining their glory as they bowed in honor as the King of Glory entered. Jesus came in with all his brilliance beaming. As he set foot down in Sheol, the angels all broke forth in full choral glory of every kind of harmony possible. Jesus stood there smiling. The angels spiraled into a display of stunning patterns and colors giving honor to the King of Kings. Jesus let them go on for a few moments and then raised his hands in a triumphant salute. It all subsided slowly for several moments until Jesus was left standing there in a white robe smiling at the people. The angels all dispersed to their various duties.

"Peace to you all," Jesus said. He walked forward touching people, caressing their faces, touching their shoulders, giving hugs. No one knew how they were all able to see his entrance. Then everything was back to normal, except Jesus was here.

He knew every soul. Each felt he was there to see them, and they were personally touched by his presence. Eventually, he came to the elders. Abraham knelt before him. Jesus bent down and lifted him, looking him in the face he said, "My Friend. We have much to discuss. I will address everyone to tell them the news and what to expect. We only have a short time. I still have things to do, but first

I am here for the people." He allowed people to approach him and greet him. It was like seeing long lost buddies with a lot of catching up and laughing about what had happened and letting people know he knew what they had been through. This time was extremely efficient and flowing. David and Moshe had quite the conversations with him, along with several of the prophets.

He alone knew how long he spent doing that. However, at a certain time, he turned and spoke in a voice that all could hear. "Come. I have much to tell you." He floated several yards upwards. He spoke with a commanding presence, yet tenderly. As he spoke, he would turn to look at different parts of the crowd. He would walk in the air, rambling as he strolled over the people. He gestured as he talked; it seemed everyone was close and that he was talking directly to them.

"You are here because of your faith in me. You were looking forward to what I was to accomplish. Your faith has brought you life. Some of you had all of the Law, the Psalms, and the Prophets to tell you of me. Some had only what my Father told them and their relationship with Him. Each of you, though, had to make a decision to believe in me and put your lives in my hands. Some of you believed because of the word of someone else. Some had direct contact with me or my Father. We have had constant contact with those who would believe." As he continued, he would look directly at certain people, making it very personal to each one. Their hearts would light up within them; every word was burning into their understanding.

"Your faith set you apart. Some of you died for the cause. Some of you paid terribly. The price was always your soul. But you could do nothing for your salvation. All you could do was believe into me. Since I hadn't yet paid the full price, all your faith could do was look forward. I am here now to tell you the price has been paid. I have paid for your sin by dying on a crude wooden cross. I paid for your healing with my stripes. I have cut the new covenant with my own blood. I have fulfilled the entire Law. I have paved the road for any man to come to the Father for that salvation. All they must do is believe."

His preaching was effective. Each one knew they were as loved as the next. There was no respecting someone above someone else. Each heard his words as if they were spoken to them sitting one-on-one by a stream in the meadow. "Now it is time for you to put your faith in me fully," he said. "I have accomplished that to which I was sent. I have yet to ascend to my Father, bringing him my blood. I will go as the High Priest before the Throne of the Almighty to purchase eternal salvation once for all. I will take you with me. You will be the first to receive the Holy Spirit making you the first fruits. I will then descend and bring the Holy Spirit to those who have believed into me on earth. Salvation will be given to those who are still alive. They will live with the Holy Spirit in them while still on the earth in bodily form. However, I must be here for three days and three nights to fulfill prophecy. I know you don't know how long that is anymore, but I do. It will all be done at the exact right time. Have peace."

Finishing, he floated down and stood among the people. He spent time with many, even playing with the children for a while. Life was different with him here.

Shimon had been the man God used to prophecy over His son, Jesus, when Jesus' mother brought him to the temple after his birth in Bethlehem. He had died shortly after and was now in Righteous Sheol. He had been the first to report the Messiah had come to earth, that was just over thirty years ago. He had gotten quite used to life here but was in contact wonder at the activities, especially with the raising of Lazarus. He and his wives were with Malachi and his family when the Messiah entered into Sheol. Shimon was held in complete awe watching the Messiah being introduced by a legion of angels in all their beauty. If he had actually been breathing, he would have caught his breath at the sight of the Messiah. The excitement within him was unchartable. Here is the one he had prophesied over as a full-grown man and so much more. The King has entered our realm! He stood transfixed on the sight of the Messiah being brought in with fanfare beyond what men had ever seen. He heard weeping all around him mixed with laughter. It was impossible to express all the emotion each one was feeling deep within them. There were cries of "Hallelujah," "Praise to the Lord God Almighty," and "Blessing to you!" Words were insufficient as the core of each person's being was stirred near to breaking.

They didn't interact with each other very much; their attention was too fixed on the Being before them. The light coming from him was spectacular, more than earthly eyes would have been able to see. Every person knew they were in the presence of the Son of the Living God, God himself, Jesus *ha Messiach*, the express being of the Godhead in person!

The angels broke into a display of extravagant brilliance that was nearly stupefying to behold, yet the attention was not diverted from the center of that display, Jesus himself. As the light diminished in intensity, yet wasn't any less in presence, Jesus stepped on the ground and was walking among the people.

Shimon couldn't understand how he could be so excited and have such peace at the same time. He knew he had acclimated to life in the soul realm, but Jesus knew how to make things work even better. Everyone could see him the same. Everyone could hear him the same. Everyone was known by him the same.

Shimon noticed he was intensely concentrating on Jesus. It didn't seem to matter what else was happening around him. Everyone was raptly attuned to Jesus. Then, inexplicably, Jesus rose up to address everyone, rising above them all so he could be seen. They all heard him as if He were standing right in front of them personally. Shimon felt like he was standing talking to Jesus face to face as if no one else was around. Jesus intimately relayed information, giving hope for a future event and giving peace until it happened. He spoke in great depth about prophesies and how many were fulfilled and others were going to be. He didn't give anything about the future away, no details or specifics, only that the prophecies would come to pass in their own timing. Hearing what had been fulfilled burst hope from deep within them, affecting each one profoundly. How long He spoke was not known. It felt like He had been speaking forever and no one wanted it to stop.

As the message from Jesus came to a close, he landed softly on the ground, turned, and walked among the people. He talked to whomever he needed to talk to and as long as was needed. Shimon saw that he was released from listening to Jesus and could interact with those around him. His eyes caught Malachi's. They were both so deeply glad of Jesus's coming, They didn't know how to communicate to each other. They knew the other felt the same as they did. Extra communication wasn't needed, but they spoke out of the overflow of their souls. "He is here," Malachi said. "It all feels complete."

"How can there be anything else to think about? He satisfies all my longing," Shimon whispered. Rebekah and Joanna joined them in this celebration of glee. They laughed at each other, shook their heads trying to understand, and tried to take it all in. But in Shimon, a thought that he had entertained before came back as an echo in the back of his mind. "Can we go back like Lazarus did?" The thought stuck in his mind like a burning ember that wouldn't go away.

As the four men came close to the house, they knew they were supposed to be starting Passover. Baruch hadn't touched the body, so he was the only one that wasn't unclean. He could still lead the *seder*. "Why don't you all get your things and come to the house and join us. We will make do." Elihu and Ezra conceded the point.

"Good plan, S'ba," said Elihu. "There is so much to think about. We should probably all be together to help each other process what has happened and report it to our families. That way we can hear what each of us saw."

At that moment Shemei's wife, Jerusha, came out of the house in a great hurry to talk to them. "There you are," she said. "Where have you been?"

"It's a long story," Shimei sighed. "We will tell you everything. Elihu and Ezra are bringing their families over for Passover. We are calling in Uriah and his family to also join us. We all need to be together tonight."

"Did you feel the earthquake?"

"Yes, most certainly. We were where it started."

Some of the families who were coming into town told us that the tombs had been cracked and some of them broken open completely. Shimon's tomb is open! They even saw his bones!"

Shimei looked at the other men. "What else can possibly happen today? Elihu, Ezra. Go get your families. I will send word to Uriah. We will deal with this issue." The two men nodded and left. Shimei turned to Jerusha who had that look every man knows to look for. This woman had questions. "S'ba Baruch is the only one clean to do the Passover service. The rest of us buried Jesus's body. It is a long story we will tell later. Uriah and Elihu are bringing their families and provisions here. You will have to oversee the activities."

Jerusha was trying to get a grip on all that was being said. "That's okay. Susannah and Naomi are here to help. We have Dinah, also. We will make it work. What about the tomb?"

"I've got a plan. I will take care of it, but you probably won't like it. Go. There is much to do."

Shimei looked at the sky. There was only about a half an hour before sundown, not a lot of time. He ran into the house letting Baruch fend for himself. He knew he would be good. "Phinehas! Phinehas! Where are you?" He heard the boy answer from the far rooms. "Come here, son. I have a job for you."

They met in the courtyard amid a lot of people doing a lot of things. Blocking out all the other activity, Shimei got down on one knee, holding Phinehas by both shoulders looking him straight in the eye to keep his attention. "You know where S'ba Shimon's tomb is?" The boy nodded with his eyes wide open, wondering what could possibly be needed there. Did you feel the earthquake?"

"Yes, sir. It knocked me down."

"Well, it broke open the tomb. Shimon's bones are exposed. You don't want some dog to drag them away, do you?" Phinehas vigorously shook his head no with a nearly disgusted look on his face. "Then it is your job to guard the tomb. Take a blanket and a pillow to sit on. You will have to be there a while."

Now the expression was surprise. "You want me to go to the tomb by myself? Alone? During Passover?" His mind was starting to run away with him.

Shimei squeezed his shoulders a little harder to get back his attention. "Absolutely! No one better. You are given the huge job of keeping this family from defilement by animals. We will make sure you have food and water, and anything else you might need. But I need you to be strong and brave like Joshua! You can do this." They had a moment for Phinehas to be persuaded and steel his emotions and attitude for the task. Shimei could see the process happen and the look of determination gel in the eyes of his eight-year-old grandson.

"Yes, sir. I can do this. Don't you worry!"

"Very good. Now, go get a coat and a blanket and anything else you think you will need." He helped turn his grandson and gave him a little pat on the behind to get him moving. Then he smiled in pride at his grandson. His smile faded quickly as he turned to see Jerusha standing there in the doorway of the house with her hands on her hips, glaring at him.

"You are sending an eight-year-old boy to stand guard over a tomb? On Passover? What are you thinking?"

Slowly standing to his feet, thinking of what he needed to say to his wife and the grandmother of the boy he just sent out to be alone in the tombs, he took a breath. "Yes, I am. He will help all the families that have no one to send. It will make him stronger for doing something no one else has done. Don't worry. He will be alright." Telling a grandmother not to worry is like telling the tide not to turn. She also knew she had no say right now.

"We will talk about this, you know." Having the last word, she spun to go back into the kitchen.

He wisely didn't answer out loud, but to himself, he said, "Oh, I know. And I know who will be doing most of the talking." Getting back into being in charge, he yelled out, "Isaac! I need your help! I need you to go to Uriah's."

Everyone barely made it for sunset. Elihu had talked to Baruch about being unclean. "It might have been a dead body, but it was the body of the Messiah. That body cannot make me unclean! We need to go on as if none of us are unclean. This goes beyond Moses!"

Baruch and Shimei were in agreement. They would go on as if it were a normal Passover.

There were a lot of people in the house and courtyard. The lambs, there were several households represented here had been slaughtered, no bones were broken. The blood had been gathered. Candles were lit, Baruch stood before them all with the customary blessing of the household. They had a small cup of wine each to dedicate the beginning of the meal, everyone who had already had their bar-mitzvah (or bat-mitzvah for the girls) was old enough to partake of the wine. Baruch explained to everyone the story of the first Passover and blood on the doorposts and lintel. As he told of the plagues that were brought on Egypt, they diminished their second cup of wine by ten drops with their fingers, so they were sad for the Egyptians who had suffered by not believing the Lord. They took a loaf of the unleavened flatbread and divided it amongst them, dipping it in bitter herbs to remind everyone of the bitterness of slavery. They used a little sprig of garnish dipped in salt water representing tears to remind themselves of new life that also had some sadness to it. They all ate some egg also dipped in salt water representing the sacrifice for their sins.

At that point, Elihu couldn't stand it any longer. He began crying.

The mood at Passover is always quiet, but this was different. As he tried to explain what was happening in his heart, the other men who had been with him earlier joined him. They had not had time to tell everyone what had happened to them. It could be contained no longer.

"He was the Lamb!" Tears poured out of his eyes as he tried to speak in between the sobs wracking his chest. "The Priests officiated at his sacrifice. He died at the moment of the lamb in the Temple. He died so that death could not touch us. It passes over us if we believe in him." He looked at the lamb they were just about to eat. "No bone was broken, he died before they broke his bones. He was silent as a lamb before his shearers is silent. He fulfilled all the scriptures today. He died! We were there. He died! What does all that mean? Why!? Why!?"

The entire family was silent. It wasn't easy watching Elihu in such deep emotional agony. Baruch was unable to continue. Shimei and Uriah were lost in their own thoughts. Ezra broke down and joined his father in deep sobs. The rest of the family sat still, deeply affected by the scene before them. After a few moments, it was understood that an explanation was needed. Elihu gained some semblance of composure, taking some very deep breaths, wiping his face with a towel set beside him. Looking around the room at the faces of his loved ones, he knew he could never explain totally, but needed to try something for now.

"Today we followed Jesus to the Roman governor's place where our priests and Sanhedrin convinced Pilate to crucify him," he said shakily. "They scourged him, shredding his back. They mocked him with a crown made from thorns and a purple cloth on his shoulders. They had beaten his face until it was almost too swollen to see. Pilate tried several times to release him, but the Leadership of Israel wouldn't let him." His sentence stopped in a series of sobs. He covered his face with the towel, his voice breaking too badly for him to continue for a bit.

"Then, they took him to Golgotha and crucified him with two common thieves." The women were now caught up in the emotion all five men were exhibiting. "We stayed out there until he died. The priests mocked him. The crowd mocked him. It got dark for nearly three hours, like everyone knows, but it was because of what was happening at Golgotha. The Temple veil was torn in two from top to bottom. We heard the reports to the High Priest. We were there to take his body off the cross and helped wrap him for burial." Elihu had been starting to speak normally, but when he mentioned the cloth, he broke down again. With a squeaking voice, his face still partially buried in the towel, he continued, "It was the fancy cloth I made for Joseph of Arimathea that we used to bury him. I made his shroud!"

The children had gathered to their mothers for comfort. The mood was somber. Occasional sobs were heard around the room. Ezra was next to Elihu and put a hand on his shoulder in moral support, "It was a cloth fit for a King. God chose you to do it to honor His son with the best."

Breaking the sobbing silence, Baruch spoke. "Let's do this night differently than we have done before. Let us partake of the Passover Lamb in honor of the lamb we saw slain today. This is a greater meaning for Passover than we had before. The men all looked up at him and then each other. A bond was made between them at that very moment.

Taking some of the roasted lamb, Baruch held it up, lifting his eyes upward, he prayed, "Blessed are you, Oh Lord our God, who has supplied for us the new and true Lamb for sacrifice. We take this into ourselves to bind us to him forever." He then took the piece of lamb and broke it for each of them to eat. They took the rest of the meal in quiet reverence, each with his own thoughts. They broke the bread in honor of God's provision in everything.

At the end of the meal, Baruch took the wine, filling the small cups they all had and raised his. "How fitting that this third cup is the cup of the lamb. Blessed are you , Oh Lord our God who gave to us the fruit of the vine. We drink this in Honor of Jesus." They all drank. It was a holy moment.

They all started feeling a little more normal. They ate the rest of the meal. The last cup of wine was to celebrate the coming of Eljah before the Messiah. Ezra suddenly perked up. "Remember when I went to Galilee? They said John the Baptizer was the Elijah to come. We know Jesus was the Messiah. Elijah has come!" They all stared at each other and laughed.

The evening had come to the close. The men had grouped together as the kids were put to bed. It was such an emotional evening; the kids weren't putting up any problems, they went right to bed, even though all the cousins were piled in the same room. There were so many people, they decided just to use the dinner pillows, and everyone was just to find a place to sleep. Baruch and Susannah opened their room to include his brother Chaim and Naomi. Shimei and Jerusha put as many as they could there. Shimei was rather glad they weren't alone, extending the discussion they were to have a little longer.

Since everyone was trying to find a place to sleep, the men didn't want to take much time for talking. The discussion was rather muted. There was so much to say, but there wasn't much to add. Finally, Elihu concluded it all, being exhausted and emotionally spent. "We have all witnessed things today we don't understand. We will have to trust Jehovah God to bring us the understanding as we go along. Let us all be thankful for being included in this mighty work of God. We are so blessed."

They all agreed. It was time to rest and process what they had seen and experienced. Life was going to be different from here on in.

Everywhere Jesus went was a party. He talked with people, laughed with people, answered most questions. The joy exuding from Him was infectuous. There were topics he wouldn't talk about. He wouldn't say what was going to happen in the immediate future or anything with details about that. He would just smile and say, "We will have to trust the Father with that one, won't we?"

He answered all sorts of questions about the fulfillment of Scripture and how the prophecies had been accomplished. There were fascinating conversations with Daniel, Isaiah, Jeremiah, and David. Moses, Isaac, Jacob, and Abraham were fun to watch as they approached him together.

Malachi had his opportunity to speak with Jesus. Jesus thanked him for his willingness to write at a time when few were listening. Malachi beamed with joy hearing how what he had written was impacting the realm of those who would hear.

During that interview, Shimon stood just off to the side captivated by Jesus's presence. He had questions, just like everyone else, but he was content to be close. At one point, as Jesus was concluding his dialogue with Malachi, he turned and looked at Shimon. Jesus smiled a very warm greeting to him. "Thank you for speaking into my life and into the life of my mother. That was something she held dear for many years and actually still does. You were chosen to be that messenger for my Father to speak that blessing at a very critical time. Thank you for being a willing vessel."

The words washed over Shimon like a flood of joy and peace. "It was my honor and privilege." Jesus smiled a bit bigger and cocked his head to the side a little, raising one eyebrow some.

"You have a question. Go ahead and ask it."

The surprise on Shimon's face was undisguised. He looked like the little boy that got caught stealing fruit off the table before dinner. "Well... We have seen some who have been here and went back to earth. Your friend Lazarus, for example. Is that possible for anyone else?"

"Ah, I see," Jesus said. "There are some who will have this experience through the years to come. There will be some quite soon in a unique display of life. Who knows? You may witness more of that sooner than you think."

Jesus reached out and touched the side of Shimon's face. "You are blessed, friend Shimon. You tickle me."

Jesus smiled again and snickered a sly, little snicker. Then turning his attention to others, he moved on.

Standing there dazed, Shimon had no idea how to respond, or even if he needed to. Trying to get a handle on what was said, he turned to Malachi. "What does that mean?"

Malachi just looked at him and started laughing. "Who knows?" he said. "I guess you will have to wait and see, won't you?"

CHAPTER 4
Life and Redemption

No one knew what to do. Passover was over. It was still Passover day since it would be until sundown. However, the ceremony last night was so unusual no one knew how to respond to it. Shimei had come home just after sunrise. Phinehas had fallen asleep in his arms and they stayed wrapped up in the blanket until this morning. They had eaten some of the bread and fruit he had brought with the jug of water. After Phinehas was awake enough to function, Shimei left him in charge. They had chased away a dog or two earlier, but that was the only activity they had encountered in the tombs.

Except the soldiers. What was supposed to be very quiet last night as everyone was having their Passover ceremony, a small contingent of soldiers had come from the city. Phinehas had watched them with great interest as they passed through going to the area of tombs of the rich people. Leaving his post for a few minutes, he watched them go to a tomb that had a large round stone disk rolled in front of it. There, they had set up camp. They were guarding that tomb for some reason that didn't seem to make sense to Phinehas. They had set a seal with crossing bands across the stone disk, then settled into camping there. They had started a fire and had set a guard. At that point, Phinehas returned to his post just outside the tomb of his great grandfather, Shimon.

It was kind of creepy, staying at a tomb. Before the sun went down, he could see the bones laying on the shelf. The door had been knocked off its top hinges and had fallen askew. Part of the right front wall had fallen off so there was a clear view inside. He had been given the job to protect those bones from any animals, big or small. He knew there were many rats down by the valley of Hinnom that would travel further out, but there didn't seem to be any around here for now. Dogs he could throw stones at, but rats didn't care much about that. He would have to chase them with a stick. He found the perfect stick and was well armed. Then the soldiers came. Having them in the vicinity was both comforting and disconcerting. He didn't know how to think about them.

Shimei came late with provisions. He had told Isaac that he wanted to spend time with his grandson and all would be safe. Phinehas loved seeing him come. They were going to have a grand time together. The food was really good. The torchlight was comforting. The company was better. It was really good to have his grandfather out there. He reported the soldiers to the great interest of Shimei, who went over and saw it for himself. He came back quiet, lost in thought. Phinehas didn't understand what was going on and his grandfather didn't have any answers, so the subject was dropped. It was quite late when Phinehas fell asleep in his grandfather's arms.

People were just stirring as Shimei got home. The shofar had blown at the Temple, the day had started, but it being a Sabbath, there was very little activity. The cups of wine had helped them all sleep a little long and, coupled with the emotional draining of the previous day, few were really awake. As he entered, he was very quiet. He found Elihu on his way through the house, he was awake and just staring at nothing in the darkness of the room. "Good morning," Shimei said quietly. "Awake so soon?"

"I have much on my mind. And your floor is hard." Elihu snickered a little as he tried to stand. There was some groaning as he tried to accomplish that task. "And I don't think the wine helped."

"I have a little news, if you wish to hear it," Shimei spoke quietly with a hint of mystery in his voice.

That perked Elihu up in a look of surprise. "Lead on." They stepped carefully through the people still lying on the floor and went out to the courtyard. Elihu turned to face his brother in anticipation of something new. Shimei stood close to speak quietly. "There is a Roman guard at Jesus's tomb. They have sealed the stone."

"Why? Why would anyone do that? That makes no sense at all!"

"I have no idea. They were there all night and are still there with no immediate signs of leaving. Something is going on that we are not in on."

"You left Phinehas out there?"

"Yea, but I'm going to have to send someone to spell him at some point. Is Ezra around? Maybe he heard something about the Romans and the tomb."

"He is still asleep. We had talked well into the night. We can ask him when he awakens. We are all going to have to go home. Good thing we live within a Sabbath's walk from here. Even that doesn't seem that important anymore. Can't you feel the change in the air?"

It took another couple hours before everyone was awake. Ezra was still groggy. Ruth had awakened him so they could clean the main room. He made it to the courtyard, the light was quite bright making him squint. He turned to see his father and uncles sitting with his grandfather. Elihu laughed lightly joined by his kin as he saw his son and the degree of sleepiness that was still evident on him. "Rough night, Ezra?"

"Yeah, couldn't get to sleep. Once I did I didn't stay asleep long. My pillow was lumpy and I fell off of it twice. It was hard to get my mind to turn off from what we saw yesterday."

"Well, there's more. There's an armed guard at Jesus's tomb," said Shimei. "Do you know anything about that?"

"How would I know anything about that?"

"Anything in the teaching Jesus had that would shed any light on it?"

"Not that I can think of. He was pretty private about the things he told his disciples. They had much more information than we did. But at the trial we heard some of the men who had been inside that Jesus said something about destroying the temple and building it in three days. That made the priests very angry. Maybe that prompted this. I don't know."

"Who knows?" Baruch offered. "All we can do is keep an eye open and see what happens."

"Well, we are in good position to do that," Shimei said. "We have established a guard at Shimon's tomb and from there we can observe what happens. We need to spell Phinehas who has been out there since before sundown yesterday. Ezra? Can you go out there for a while today?"

"I might as well. I'm already unclean. We can't work today. I'm pretty useless for anything else. I can go out there today. Let me see if there is anything I need to do for Ruth first. I'll head out there as soon as I can. Phinehas must be spent."

The crew fell into a pattern. Several of them spent some time out by the tomb. There wasn't much to report about the Romans. They just sat there while one of them stood watch. They rotated on an extremely consistent basis. This close to Jerusalem, they were under scrutiny by just about everyone. None as much as the house of Shimon.

Thursday went by without incident. As sundown came, Shimei took the night shift. He tried to stay awake through the night. He walked around, built a small fire, and actually killed a rat. Periodically, he would go check on the Romans. Why they were there fascinated him.

That night went by fairly quickly. Tobiah came by and relieved him in the morning. Uriah was scheduled to stay the night. Friday came and went without incident. Since this was the first day of the feast of Unleavened Bread, it was another Sabbath. No one was doing any work. No one was out in the streets. That is why there was the day of preparation. The next day, starting at sundown Friday night, was the normal weekly Sabbath, three consecutive days of Sabbath, starting at sundown going to the next sundown. The third night came to be Elihu's turn.

By now they had established quite a comfortable camp. A place for the fire, a place for food and water, a torch for moving at night, and even a chamber pot was established. The same was said for the Romans. There were others who had found their tombs broken and had family members camping close. They could see the other camps dotting the area. It felt less forlorn when there are others around.

Elihu enjoyed the time alone. He was trying to process everything they had witnessed. He felt things weren't over, yet. Something lingered in his mind that there was more to come. His night was peaceful. Elihu got to thinking about Shimon and how much he missed him. He was Phinehas' age when Shimon died. It made him think about what Shimon would have been like and what he would have thought about Jesus and all that happened. "Well, S'ba. What do you think about all this?" he murmured under his breath. "You would have been the first one involved, wouldn't you? Oh, how I wish you were here to see this."

Ezra came at daybreak and Elihu spent some of the day with him as he didn't leave too quickly. They talked and rehashed their memories of Golgotha. Elihu finally went home, leaving Ezra to himself. They had all chased away things, protecting the tomb and the bones therein. Tomorrow would be the first of the week. They could repair the tomb then. They would need a guard one more night.

As Elihu stopped by the shop and Shimei's house to check on everything before heading home. He caught Shimei, Baruch, and Chaim in a serious discussion. They were discussing the ramifications of the Priests being so involved with Pilate and the Romans. The topic was going political. They were concerned with how the governing people were going to respond and whether the Romans had been given a situation to take away things from the country. Elihu listened for a little while and he got more and more troubled. After a while just listening, he couldn't resist jumping in.

"I think you are missing the point," he began. "I don't think Jehovah God went through all this for political reasons. I think He is working to bring his people closer to

Himself. I think redemption is involved. I don't think we can understand what we are talking about. There is more to come that will change the whole discussion. We will have to wait and see what is coming."

They all looked at him thoughtfully. "Why do you think that?" Shimei asked.

"I had a lot of time to think last night and feel that the Lord God of Israel is wanting us to be patient and trust him. Right now is not the time for action, but rest and trust. That is what I intend to do."

Phinehas walked in quietly, looking pensively at the group. "S'ba, may I talk to you please?" Shimei turned to him and smiled, receiving him to speak. "I want to go back out tonight to the tomb and stand guard. Everyone is doing it and I want to be part again."

Slightly surprised, Shimei responded to him, "Why, I don't see why not. You want to do the night shift?"

"Yes. You came the last time. I want to do it by myself. I want to do it the way the rest of you did. I can handle it. Really, I can."

That made Shimei smile. "Of course, you can. I have no doubt. You are brave. I will clear it with your parents." He held Phinehas arms beaming his support for him. I will make sure you are there at the end of the Sabbath. Okay?"

The look of satisfaction came over Phinehas' face. "Thank you, S'ba. I will do it well."

"I'm sure you will. Is that alright with the rest of you?" Scanning the faces of the rest of the men in the room he received an affirmative vote from them all. They were pleased at his request. "Go make sure you have everything you want. You can go out there to take Ezra's place just before sundown. Okay?"

Phinehas just beamed at the men. He stood as tall as he could, a broad smile plastered all over his face. He would do his best.

After he left to get his stuff together, Elihu addressed Shimei again. "I know Chaim is getting ready to return to

Joppa. Could Keturah, Boaz, and I dine with you all tonight? Tomorrow we will have to repair the tomb before we can get back to work. I wanted to spend some time with them before they leave."

"Certainly. I will tell Jerusha. We would love to have you."

Shimon also felt the change in the air. Having Jesus around made a huge difference in the atmosphere of Sheol. There had always been hope, but now the hope is near to being completed. No one knew the plan. Everyone, however, knew something new was coming. The anticipation was palpable.

Jesus moved to where all could see him. He wanted to address the entire crowd again, just like he did when he first came. Every eye was on him, each heart was on fire to hear him.

"Blessings to you all," Jesus began. It has come time to finish the work my Father sent me to do. I must go to Him. I will return and complete what has been started in your lives. Your wait is to be rewarded beyond your highest dreams." Shimon looked around. The faces around him had the same feelings he had. There was nothing anyone wanted more than to be right there and in alignment with Jesus. "First, there are some things that must be accomplished. Some of you have been chosen for a special task. There are representatives among you to witness to the power of life. You will accompany me for this first stage."

All through the crowd, individuals started to rise up, floating above the rest. Shimon was startled to see he was one of them. He was elated beyond his imagination. He focused on Jesus with glee running rampant through his heart. His level of excitement could not be explained.

"You have been chosen to go into Jerusalem. Your bodies will be prepared to receive you. Your memories of this place will be limited. What you will know, is that you have been deemed worthy and will be there to witness what is about to transpire. Be open to those you talk to and keep your focus on me. I will be busy for a while. Then I will return to those of you still here. Be patient for a little longer. Your redemption is drawing near."

As he spoke a beam of light beyond intense burst through from above. A voice that permeated everything and rattled the very being of each person there came through. It was the Father God. "It is time. Come forth to life, my Son!"

Jesus turned to face the light with a look of extreme joy. "Yes, my Father!" Those who were called out quickly formed a procession behind him. With blinding speed they all followed Jesus up as the beam pulled them all away. An exclamation of praise rose from those left behind and continued to grow to a fever pitch of praise. The celebration was vast and across the board throughout all of Righteous Sheol. The anticipation was extreme. Sheol would never be the same.

There was something happening in the tomb Jesus had been given. The body was flooded with light but it wasn't from the outside. Inside the body, the glory of Jehovah God was doing a work. The light shone out of every pore of the skin as an intense individual beam blasted out from within. Even the hair had light coming out of it. As soon as the light hit, every fiber, every molecule was rewritten. All the damage that had been purposed on this body was being healed. The Spirit of God manifested in the body submitting it to the spirit realm. The body came up through the cloth leaving it laying there on the shelf undisturbed as if a body was still in it, but now flat. It was as if all the air had been suddenly taken out of it. The winding bands were still around it, at the neck, the waist, the feet.

Jesus was in his body as it rose through the cloth. He was totally healed in every way except there were still holes in his wrists and feet from the nails and there was still a gash in his side from the lance. No blood came out of the wounds, but the wounds were there nonetheless. The body was clean, no defilement or dirt was on him. He stood on his feet as his righteousness was manifested in creating new clothing on him. The tomb was filled with light.

An angel came and rolled the stone back, breaking the Roman seals, as other angels joined him. The light poured out of the tomb invading the space where the Roman soldiers were. When it came on them, they were stunned to the depth of their being and were overwhelmed by it. Each of them fainted dead away and would not rouse out of it until morning. It had been three nights and three days, completed at sundown. Each day was a full Sabbath, night and day and now fulfilled. It was now several hours past that for completion to be totally verified.

Jesus walked out of the tomb, bending slightly to duck under the top of the door. As he stood up erect, the angels all fell to their knees, bowing prostrate before him in compete honor to the King. The worship was intense as they poured all their being into exalting the Lord of Glory. Jesus received the worship. He was no longer living as a man, he was fully the Son of God, The Creator of the Universe. The joy in him was powerful as he looked to his Father in victory. What a blessed time as the ages were coming together for fulfillment. Jesus looked back down at the angels who were basking in the honor of worshipping him. "Come," he said to them. "There is still more to do. I need some of you to stay here and greet those who are coming. I will be ascending to my Father here in a moment. What a beautiful day this is!" Jesus had always loved the beauty of his creation. He took a deep breath of air into a body that was now full of glory instead of blood, had full properties of spirit realm, and could be used in the physical realm. This body could not be killed. It housed life itself. Jesus stepped away from the tomb, walking in the garden that surrounded it, loving the flowers and trees. He was waiting for something.

Before sunrise, a group of women came out of Jerusalem toward the tomb. As they were coming, they were discussing how they were going to roll away the stone.

They had more spices and aloes with them to prepare the body better. They had heard the preparation from the other day had been rushed. They wanted to clean it again and put more spices around it and in the shroud. They had water and cloths with them. As they approached the tomb, the sun was nearing broaching the horizon, it was getting lighter out. As they rounded the last corner, they were stunned seeing the tomb was already open. The soldiers were laying around where they fell. They ran to the tomb, two of them went inside. There they saw the cloth but no body. Not knowing what to do they just stood there with their mouths gapping. Suddenly, they realized they were not alone. There were two men standing there in very bright white robes. The two women instinctively stepped closer together, eyes wide and mouths open.

"Why do you seek the living among the dead?" one of them said. "He is not here, but was raised. Remember how he spoke to you, yet being in Galilee, saying, 'The son of man must be delivered into the hands of sinful men, and to be crucified, and the third day to rise again'?"

The women were startled by the words. Looking at each other, they giggled a little as the words produced joy in them. They walked around the two angels who were smiling and letting them by. They ran out of the tomb to the others standing there. "He is risen! Two angels just told us!" One of the women there was named Mary, from Magdala. She exclaimed, "We must tell the disciples!" and turned running toward the city.

Coming to the upper room where the Passover had been for them, she ran in and up the stairs, yelling for them. "Peter, James! We've been to the tomb and he isn't there. Two men there told us he is risen. Do you think that is possible?"

Peter jumped up, "What? You were there?"

"Come, see for yourself!"

The young man who was at the crucifixion came up quickly, totally interested in the conversation. "I'm going with you," he said emphatically.

"Let's go, John. We have to see this!" They ran out with Mary close behind.

Arriving at the tomb, Peter, who was older and slower, got there second. John had made it to the door first, but stopped. Peter didn't hesitate, he went on in. John followed as he went. Inside, they saw what all the others saw, the cloth with no body and the head cloth that had been placed at the head at burial. There was no one there. Peter was visibly shaken, he was feeling skeptical, afraid. John was also emotional, but in a different way. He was excited at the possibility of Jesus being raised. They both turned and left, heading back into Jerusalem.

Mary didn't leave. She stood there weeping. The emotional strain was getting through to her. She stepped closer and stooped to look in. She saw something the two men hadn't seen. There, one at the head and one at the foot, sat the two men dressed in brilliant white. "Woman, why do you weep?" the one at the head said to her.

"Because they took away my Lord, and I do not know where they put him." She backed out to the outside, trying to control her breathing. She turned and saw a man standing there. She thought it was one of the workers in the garden. Hoping he was in charge, she looked at him.

"Woman, why do you weep? Whom do you seek?"

Hoping for an answer, she told him, "Sir, if you carried him away, tell me where you put him, and I will take him away." She was speaking through her tears and sobs, trying desperately to find answers.

"Mary."

That one word jarred her to attention. She looked up and saw it was Jesus himself standing there. *"Rabboni!"* she exclaimed with passion. As she spoke, she began to move forward, but Jesus motioned her to stop.

"Do not touch me, for I have not yet ascended to my Father. But go to my brothers and say to them, 'I am ascending to my Father and your Father, and my God and your God.'"

He smiled a comforting smile to her eradicating her weeping with joy. He turned and walked away. She had orders and needed to fulfill them. She got up and ran toward Jerusalem. Her heart had been satisfied. It was true.

Jesus had to wait for that exchange so the information would be given about what he was doing. Now he turned his face to the task of being the High Priest of all time for all time. His faith clothed him in amazing garments of stunning light. He had full clothing the high priests were to wear that was only a type and shadow of what was to be real. His turban on his head was white with blue ribbons holding a gleaming golden band on the front that had *Holiness unto Jehovah* written on it. He had a tunic of brilliant white under an ephod of blue and an outer robe of stunning colors: red, blue, purple, and white, held together with a sash of the same colors. On his chest there was a breastplate. Unlike the one the high priest of Israel had, this one had twenty-four stones. These represented much more than just the tribes of Israel. The stones were of great value of intense perfection.

He was resplendent with radiant glory. Nothing on earth would be able to withstand the power of the brightness coming out of Him. Even then, though, his joy was the brightest as he beamed with delight at what he was doing. Angels beyond count shined everything they had in amazing patterns around him, forming a corridor of praise leading directly into the throne room of God the Father. The sheer volume of triumphant music was staggering, as harmonies beyond imagination were performed in honor of the High Priest coming into Heaven.

Walking straight to the Throne, Jesus came before his Father, God himself. Great peals of lightning were flashing all about it as rolling thunder rumbled from everywhere and smoke of incense of the Spirit filled the atmosphere. The Throne was a huge box-like structure of purest gold, with the four Cherubim flying around it. The size was huge while being approachable, it wasn't defined as occupying a space, it just existed. A Presence that couldn't be defined was on the Throne appearing to sit on it, but without having a corporal being to house him or define his shape or location. The Presence commanded attention and awe. Sheer raw power emanated from him. The holiness was extreme, but the love was filling everything everywhere.

Standing with his arms out wide, Jesus spoke loud and clear. His voice permeated everything, it was the sweetest tones ever heard. "Father. I have brought you my own blood to pay the price of sin and obtain eternal salvation for all mankind who will believe into me." As he spoke, droplets of blood came out of the wounds in his wrists and flew straight to the middle of the Throne. There, they were received into the presence of the Father, the payment was accepted in full. A force flashed from that point outward affecting everyone and everything, rippling in waves of pure power from the Throne.

A voice came forth as the Presence stood up in extreme authority, speaking into the Spirit realm, dictating and declaring the judgment from the Throne. "My Son has paid the price. Salvation is now offered to mankind. He has redeemed man from sin, allowing him to have open, intimate relationship with the Triune God. It is complete!"

Worship sprang forth throughout the heavenly realm in spontaneous expressions of every kind and variety. Heaven was replete in worship. Jesus walked toward the Throne. The four Cherubim flew down to form a reception honoring him with cries of "Worthy is the Lamb who was slain!" Jesus stepped up, turning around and sat down as the Presence also sat on the Throne. Jesus sat so that he united with the Presence in the Father's right side. The left side glowed every color in a swirling display of brilliance as the Spirit of God manifested there. The Triune God was united in a display of Glory as the Son took his place at the fulfillment of his assignment.

After a time, as the whole Throne Room erupted in Worship, praise, and homage of every sort as all the angels bowed to the Lord God Almighty, Jesus stood and walked from the Throne leaving an image of him that stayed seated there. The Spirit came with him as it extended from the Throne into him making a permanent connection. Jesus dissolved as he walked back into the physical realm.

He looked like any other man, with the possible exception of his joyful attitude, walking in the garden by the tomb. There were other women there who recognized him and ran to him, falling at his feet, caressing them and kissing them. Jesus told them, "Do not fear. Go tell your brothers that they may go into Galilee, and there they will see me." They left running to the upper room to tell the disciples.

Jesus left there and appeared to a couple of men who were walking toward Emmaus. He talked with them until nearly sundown and revealed himself to them. He then vanished and they ran back to the upper room to report what had happened to them. The disciples were getting reports of Jesus being seen, but they were mostly in doubt and fear. They stayed in the upper room out of fear that the Jews or the Romans would do to them what they had done to Jesus.

Jesus, however, was enjoying seeing different people. He walked up to the house with the upper room from Passover. Climbing the stairs, he walked to the door and didn't stop, but walked through the locked door into the room where the disciples were cowering in fear. When they saw him in the room, knowing it was locked, they thought they were seeing a ghost. Each face was drained of blood as they stared at him. "Peace to you," Jesus said calmly and each of them felt his peace touch them as their fear ebbed away. "It is really me. See my hands. See my side. I am no longer dead. I have risen."

The peace and joy started having the full effect on them as they began to rejoice and welcome him. "Peace to you," he said again as he knew what he had to say next was going to sink into them. "As the Father has sent me, I also send you." They didn't know it until later that they had been called to a life of dying to themselves and living for others, just as Jesus had. As he was the center of attention at the moment, he said to them, "Receive the Holy Spirit." Then he blew on them.

Each of them experienced the Holy Spirit flowing from Jesus into them as their spirit was born from above. The Holy Spirit now lived within them, dwelling in their spirits. Every one of them was changed as they became new creations. Their identities were changed to be the new men God had seen them to be before the foundation of the world. Each one received it differently as it would take time to process what had just happened. All they knew was that they were different. A massive change had hit them.

Jesus now gave them more information about how they had changed. "Of whomever you may remit the sins, they are remitted to them. Of whomever you hold, they have been held." The impact of that statement hit them as very serious, but they didn't understand it to the degree they may have wanted. This was something they would get revelation knowledge about as they grew and matured in their walk with the Holy Spirit in them. As for now, they were overwhelmed with all that had just happened to them.

They reveled in his presence and basked in his light for a while, then Jesus blessed them and disappeared, leaving them alone together pondering the wonder of the evening.

Sheol was still abuzz with what had been done. The anticipation was mounting, the wonderment increasing to a boiling point. They looked at each other for answers, but they knew no one had any. Why were some taken? Now what was going to happen? Everything had been stirred up for a while now, though no one knew how long.

Rebekah and Joanna joined Malachi and his family as they patiently waited for Jesus to return. When? No one knew. How? Again, a total mystery. No one was complaining, just waiting. They had learned to do that a long time ago.

Then, in a burst of light and angels, Jesus returned in a blaze of glory. He hovered over them as every eye focused intently on him.

"Peace to you all! You are above all people highly blessed. Your faith has brought you salvation. Receive the Holy Spirit!" As he spoke, he flung open his hands in a gesture of flinging something from his chest. The Holy Spirit flooded out of him into each of them as the salvation they had been waiting for was given to them. The joy was beyond anything they had ever thought possible. Their eyes were opened to seeing things like never before. Sin that had been in each of them since conception was completely blown away from them, absolutely remitted. They were sinless for the first time. The freedom was indescribable, the ability of mind next to absolute. The extent of emotion was stunning. The thing that amazed them most, as some of them were experiencing, was how much more they could see out of Jesus. Without sin, they could see him in all his beauty. For the first time, they could worship him without hindrance. Their expression of worship was nearly absolute. Holy pandemonium broke out as they united with the Holy Spirit in them in extreme worship. Even the children and babies were laughing with him.

Holding up his arms, Jesus called attention. "That is only the beginning. You have just been given salvation for the faith you put in me. The Holy Spirit is now dwelling within your spirit. Now you no longer have to be kept in this prison. You are to have entrance into the heavenly realm. I am taking you home to my Father!"

No one knew how to respond to that. Jesus turned as the angels made a pathway. "Come with me, my loved ones!" His call pulled them forward. Jesus led them out into the heavenly realm as a portal formed. The walls of Righteous Sheol began dissolving as the millions of beaming spirits and souls transported from where they had been for ages into heaven itself. As they went from Sheol to heaven they found angels beyond count there to receive them, ushering them in as the Father welcomed them home.

Going back to the Throne, Jesus sat down as they were all brought in. The air itself was filled with the essence of worship. Eternity had begun for each of them. What a glorious time.

CHAPTER 5
Full Circle

Satan was stunned. He had killed the Lord of Glory. Jesus was in his hands, executed as a criminal according to both Jewish law and Roman law. He was declared a sinner and died in that sin. He was supposed to be in the realm of darkness forever. Then the unthinkable happened. He didn't stay!

Jesus had died, but he pulled out the godly law of covenant. He had died an innocent on behalf of others. No one else had ever been innocent or sinless. He had become the perfect sacrifice. Then he left Satan's territory and had gone into righteous Sheol. Satan couldn't touch him.

The entire realm was shaken. They had never seen Satan like this. He couldn't function. He didn't know what to do. His rage was intense and leveled at everyone and everything. He slashed at everything close to him. He caught demons unaware by their throats. Spirits can't be killed, but they can feel pain, The volume of his curses shook the Dark realm. He spat his furor far and consistently with great accuracy. This was the terror a fallen angel could inflict but even he knew it was limited by the throne which just added to his intense frustration. Jesus had been in there for three days. "What is going to happen next?" Satan screamed at those around him. "What is his plan?"

The days of darkness reigning as Jesus went to trial and the extreme victory of the crucifixion had been abruptly ended. The demons were in disarray and lacked direction. Everything had gone according to plan, but it went beyond what they had foreseen. Now they were floundering.

The departed spirits were still trying to do their thing, but the entire atmosphere seemed dull. It all was useless and needless. The edge had been taken off the realm of darkness. Demons and departed spirits alike were more or less wandering around. Even those who were normally violent were laying low. It was a complete mystery to the entire realm.

Lachish was included. He was different than when he first died. He knew he looked like everyone else: emaciated, hollow, dirty, and ugly. He had no distinct personality or characteristics. He was just one of the millions vying for some form of input to try to satisfy their yearning desires. His experience at the crucifixion shook him. He had seen that Jesus person, followed him and saw him go into Righteous Sheol. It made him think of that beggar and his conversation with Abraham. He had received quite an education since then. Life is only despair as far as he was concerned.

It had only been three days since the crucifixion, and he had wandered around without finding a host. Now he was out by the tombs, the death felt familiar, for whatever that was worth. He was just meandering through, hoping to get into a Roman guard, but they were serious and not getting drunk for some reason.

As he stuck close to the soldiers hoping for an opening, a light came out of the tomb that hurt him. He turned to see angels invading the space, guarding the area. One came down and rolled the stone back, letting intense light flood the entire area. The soldiers all fell down as if they were dead, but nothing came out of them. Lachish and a few others were left standing there staring at the angels who looked at them, communicating not to interfere or else.

A different Jesus than he had seen before stepped out of the tomb. He wasn't just a man with a holy light coming from him; he was the light! He was power. He was holiness. He was the King! The angels all gave him deference, bowing to him, honoring his existence. He took a few steps away from the tomb satisfied with the outcome of his raising. He walked away with several angels accompanying him in a formal escort. Other angels seemed to be posted in places with a job to do.

Since the light from him caused Lachish pain, he didn't follow him but stayed grounded to the spot in holy terror. He sensed that there was truly no place to flee from this being. Something is changing in the world, he couldn't pin it down, but it was tangible. And it was pervasive. All of creation had been affected somehow.

As he was trying to put his mind on the situation, some women came up to the tomb. The angels spoke to them, they all were able to see him and hear him! They couldn't usually do that. Lachish had seen angels doing things before, but he had never seen the living interact with them before. What were they saying?

One of the women ran back to Jerusalem. She ran as if she were being chased by beasts. The other women heard the news and rejoiced with great glee. They hugged each other and laughed, nearly dancing with each other in celebration. They eventually walked back toward Jerusalem.

One of the soldiers started groaning. He was waking up from a very deep sleep and was groggy. Sitting up, he realized they were all on the ground. It was difficult for him to get his thoughts together, but finally, the seriousness of what was happening struck him. He was having trouble standing, but he started yelling at the others, "Get up! Get up! Wake up! We have all fallen asleep! We could be killed for this! The tomb is open!" The others stirred and slowly awoke, looking around gradually taking assessment of their surroundings and condition. The first soldier got up to his feet shakily, leaning on his lance for support. Stumbling forward, he went into the open tomb.

The other three were still orienting themselves as they heard him cry out from inside the tomb. "Oh, no! The body is gone!" He ran out of the tomb in a panic, eyes fully open, as was his mouth. "If our commanders or Pilate find out, we're dead men! What are we going to do?"

The others were just coming to speed mentally as they heard him talking. Realization struck one at a time as the information filtered its way into their consciousness. Each one scrambled up and into the tomb to verify the truth. They gathered just outside to decide what to do. After discussing the options of running and living like fugitives or trying to blame someone, they hit on an idea. "Let's go to the High Priest. He is the one who had them put us out here. Maybe he can square it with Pilate. That is our only hope." With that, they gathered their gear and moved off into Jerusalem, wanting to sneak into the temple area without being seen.

Lachish almost followed them knowing they were going to get blinding drunk if their plan worked. However, at that moment two men arrived running from the city. One stopped at the door of the tomb; the other ran on in. Lachish was afraid to follow them, there was something still holy about the atmosphere in there, and it bothered him. They both came out, one concerned and the other rejoicing.

A woman came up, the one who had run into Jerusalem earlier. The men mostly ignored her and walked back toward the city. She was just kneeling there weeping when Jesus walked back to her. His radiance was stunning, but she couldn't see it. Lachish could both see it and feel it. He backed off as Jesus's presence made him both inert and in pain.

The woman and Jesus had a conversation, and then she got up and started back to Jerusalem. She didn't see what was happening all around her as a multitude of angels gathered around Jesus. They were there to escort him into heaven. The brilliance was overpowering causing Lachish to turn away and flee the scene. Jesus and his entourage slipped seamlessly into the heavenly realm leaving things on earth back into seeming normal. Every creature in dark Sheol knew, however, that things would never be the same.

Phinehas was keeping his watch. He had slept that afternoon in preparation for the evening work, but he was getting sleepy. He had been here for several hours, keeping the fire going, drinking water, walking around the fire, and singing all in the attempt to stay awake. He had chased away a few animals, which made him think his job was important. He really wanted to prove to his grandfather that he could do this.

He had eaten some more of the figs and dates and a little of the bread they had given him and had sat down with the blanket wrapped around him to rest his feet from trudging around the fire. He sat leaning his back against the front of the tomb. It was almost a mistake as sleep started to overcome his eyes and mind. A bright light blasted from across the way that startled him totally awake. It was from the tomb where the soldiers were. He could see even from this distance that the tomb was open and light was glaring from it. There didn't seem to be any activity over there at all. Were the soldiers laying down? It looked like it from here. It was hard to see what was happening over there, but the light went out. He could see the soldiers fire, but that was all.

He noticed then that there were some people coming out of Jerusalem. It was getting a little light on the horizon; sunrise would be happening pretty soon. Someone would come out and get him in a while after that.

Then he heard a sound behind him. It sounded like it came from this tomb! It better not be a rat! He grabbed his stick and moved into position to look inside. They had built the fire to shine light into the tomb just for that reason. What he saw wasn't a rat. What he had heard was the bones moving. They were lining up with each other into correct anatomical position. Phinehas stood there mesmerized watching as ligaments and tendons appeared. Blood vessels were stretching out into the muscle that was forming. He could see organs growing and setting themselves into place. The man who had been buried here was being put back together. As things were moving, he could see skin start to form and stretch and cover until the entire body was completely covered. Hair grew out of the skin and fingernails hardened on the fingers.

The body jerked a little and shook as each leg and arm had life reinstated, flexing the fingers and joints. Then a sudden gasp, as breath entered it, and a single, low moan. Phinehas stood transfixed on the sight. He could now see the face as the beard grew in rapidly, the breathing coming in steadily with the mouth open. The eyes sprang open, and with another powerful gasp, the body sat bolt upright as one who was quickly aroused from a deep sleep.

The man was looking around the tomb trying to orient himself to his surroundings. His hand found the far wall and he steadied himself. He looked down and was shocked to find that he was naked. And he was cold, sitting on a slab of stone.

As he looked around, he eventually realized there was someone standing just outside staring at him. It was a young boy. The look of shock on his face was evident that he had seen the whole thing. "Hello," Shimon said to him gently. "My name is Shimon. What's yours?"

The new body talking to him was almost more than Phinehas could handle. He didn't know whether to run, or cry, or protect himself. "It's okay. I know this is a little strange, but I need your help," The body said to him.

"This man isn't doing scary things, he is talking to me," Phinehas thought, trying to talk himself into action of some sort. "My name is Phinehas." At least he can answer the man's question.

"Oh, good. That's a nice name. Do you live close to here?"

"A ways over into Jerusalem. It's not far."

"That is good. Who is your father?"

"He is Isaac, son of Shimei, son of Baruch, the weaver."

Now it was Shimon's turn to be shocked. "How do I respond to that?" he thought. "Um, that is excellent," he said. "As you can see, though, I don't have any clothes. Would it be too much to ask for you to get me some?"

Realization hit Phinehas. "Oh, of course. Here, you can have my blanket. I'll run home and get help. Will you stay here?"

"I'll be right here waiting for you. Thank you so much." Shimon reached out and took the blanket offered to him, holding it close in front of him.

"I'll be right back," Phinehas shouted as he spun and tore down the path to the road. He wasn't cold anymore. Shimon knew he didn't have long to wait. That boy was on a mission.

Taking an assessment of his situation, Shimon looked around. He knew this tomb. His wives were both buried here. Their ossuaries were right there in the niches in the wall. The wall attracted his attention. There were cracks in the wall, and the front wall had broken with the door hanging askew. It might not be safe in here. Swinging his legs over the edge of the shelf, he stood and wrapped himself in the blanket. Taking care where he stepped, he moved outside. The fire felt good; his feet were cold, however, so he sat and tucked the blanket under his feet. Then he came to an understanding that none of his joints hurt. He was moving quite easily. He popped an arm out of the blanket and looked at his hand. It was a mature hand, but not aged. His fingers worked deftly. While he was looking down, he noticed his beard which reached down to his chest. It was mostly dark brown, but it had a steak of gray right down the middle. The biggest job he was working on was trying to remember what was happening and where he had been.

He remembered prophecying over the baby Messiah and his mother. He remembered telling his family. He went to bed and saw a bright light. Things got very blurred after that. Some things came to mind like images he couldn't quite retrieve. Colors, sights, sounds, feelings—they came in flashes and bits without sticking in his consciousness. Then he thought of the Messiah and joy flooded his heart in a way that was impossible to describe.

He had been touched by the Messiah. He knew that, but didn't know how or when. His soul clung to the feeling of joy and the almost image of the Messiah. It was like he couldn't quite grasp it, but it shone on him anyway. He knew he had a purpose even though he didn't know how to accomplish it exactly. Why had he come back to life? There is a reason just beyond the borders of his comprehension.

Phinehas ran without stopping all the way home. How was he going to tell anyone what he had just seen? He ran into the house beside the shop. He knew they would all be gathering there for the work day to start. Isaac and Dinah lived just around the corner. Phinehas knew his father would be there at the shop already. His mother would be home with the baby. It was his father he wanted to talk to right now though.

As he ran in, he caused a little commotion since he was supposed to be out at the tomb. His shouting didn't help keep the calm. "Abba! Abba! Come quick!"

Isaac skirted the folks there, coming to Phinehas, kneeling down to receive him, scanning him to see if he was injured. "What is it? Are you ok?"

"Yes. I need clothes!" That put an expression of inquiry on his father's face. "The man needs clothes!"

"What man? Slow down. Tell me what happened." Isaac held Phinehas arm for comfort and help in keeping him focused. "Take a breath."

Phinehas stopped and looked his father straight in the eyes, took a breath and started his narrative as best he could. "There was something that happened at the tomb where the soldiers were. I saw the light and the soldiers fell down, and light was coming out of the tomb. Then I heard something behind me. I thought it was a rat and I went to chase it away, but it wasn't a rat. In our tomb, they were moving!"

"What was moving?" Everybody around was now caught up in what he was saying.

"The bones! They were rattling around. I could see them really good in the firelight and it was starting to get light out. Then things started growing on them! I saw sinew and blood vessels and muscle and organs! And then there was skin and hair and everything! Then the man sat up and talked to me!"

"The bones came alive? It all became a man?" Isaac was attempting to understand the fast ramblings coming at him. "He talked to you?"

"Yes! I got scared and almost ran away, but he asked my name and talked real nice. When I told him my name, it made him act like he knew me." After all the things that had happened over the last few days, no one was willing to dismiss this story. "Oh, and he told me his name. He said it was Shimon."

Elihu was standing next to Isaac listening to this story with growing interest. When Shimon was mentioned, he gasped with an unhindered expression of possibilities. He looked around at the others for some kind of confirmation. Finding Shimei's face having the same reaction, they fixated on each other for a moment.

"And he's naked!" continued Phinehas, breaking the connection with down to earth revelation. "That's why I need the clothes. I gave him my blanket, but he was sitting on that stone shelf and was really cold."

Shemei broke into action. "Got it. I have some things right here. I always have a bag ready for day trips."

"Could you take us back?" Isaac asked Phinehas. "He might be very glad to see you. You are the only person he knows right now."

"Sure! He said he would wait for me." That elicited a light-hearted chuckle from the people around.

"Do you have sandals?" Elihu asked Shimei.

"Right by the door."

"Let's go," Elihu said as he motioned to Isaac and Phinehas

"We'll be right back," Shimei told the crew. "Tell Jerusha where we went. We are going to have a very special guest here today." Elihu led the small band outside and on the road.

Shimon's reverie was interrupted by someone shouting his name. He snapped back to look up and see people running his direction. The boy was back, but there were three men with him, two a little older. They were running at him with looks of joy and astonishment. He stood and almost tripped as he was standing on his blanket and nearly jerked it out of his hands. He grabbed it, holding it together in front of him, both bare arms out in the breeze. One man got there first, elated at seeing him.

Grabbing Shimon by the shoulders and pulling him into a tight embrace, the man said, "S'ba! It's me, Elihu!" Shimon was floored. This grown man was his grandson? It seemed he had just talked to the little boy yesterday.

"Elihu? How is that possible? How old are you? This is amazing!"

"S'ba, I am forty with sons of my own. How is it possible you are alive?" Elihu held him at arm's length beaming at him.

"I really don't know. This is all very strange to me, too. I just woke up here naked, in a tomb, laying on a slab of stone with a young boy staring at me."

The other older man broke in, "Hello, S'ba. I am Shimei!"

"Shimei?"

"Yes, S'ba. And this is my son, Isaac, and my grandson, Phinehas, who I believe you have already met."

"Yes. I seem to have given him quite a start. Uh, do you have any clothes for me? I feel rather exposed out here."

They gave him what they brought, and he stepped into the tomb to get dressed. He came out looking like a normal

Israelite. The sun was up and it was becoming a normal, bright day in Israel. As they proceeded to go back into Jerusalem, Shimon asked, "Do you know anything about that tomb over there? A group of soldiers left there in quite a hurry and there have been people running to it and walking away. It seems a little strange."

Elihu and Shimei looked across the way. They recognized the tomb immediately. Something was different with it. The tomb was open! The stone was rolled away! They looked at each other in amazement. Elihu couldn't resist any longer. "I will be right back," he said as he left the group standing there and ran to the other tomb.

Approaching it, he saw a couple of women standing there. They saw him coming and watched him closely, but without fear. He went to the tomb, ducked in, and let his eyes adjust to the darkness. He saw the shelf. There was the cloth he had made still wrapped in the strips, but there was no body in it. The head cloth was still there, folded, bloody, and undisturbed. His body ran chills and goosebumps covered his arms. There was something unusual about this tomb. He carefully and quietly backed out of the tomb. Turning to the women, he asked, "What happened here?"

"Some of our people came here today to prepare more honor for his burial," one of them said with excitement in her voice as if she were trying to keep herself calm. "Angels met them and told them he had risen from the dead and they would see him again. One of our women said she had talked to him, and so did a couple others."

"They talked to Jesus? He is risen?" Elihu was having difficulty trying to wrap his mind around that information. Looking across the way, he could see Shimon standing there. "There is a lot of that happening today. We are alive in the best of times. Praise be to Jehovah! Thank you."

He walked briskly back to his family completely lost in thought. He had many more questions than he had answers. There was something at work here that was far greater than they had ever hoped would be. He didn't know exactly how to respond to what he had just heard. But the evidence of the supernatural activity was overwhelming. As he got closer, he could see Shimon standing there. How could this be possible, and yet, there he is!

"What is going on, Elihu?" Shimei inquired. "What happened over there?"

"Jesus has risen. He is no longer in the tomb. The shroud we put him in is there, but he isn't. The women standing there said angels told them he is risen and some of them talked to him personally!"

"What? That can't be true! How is that even possible?"

"Shimei. Your Grandfather is standing next to you alive after dying 30 years ago and you are asking me how this is possible? I don't know what to expect next."

Shimon looked like someone had taken all the blood out of his face. Something deep within him was sparked hearing that Jesus had risen. It was like a memory he didn't remember making. "Jesus is here? Can I see him?" He was trying to figure out how he knew Jesus and why he sounded so familiar, yet so far away. He was suddenly very confused as to where he was and what he knew.

Elihu grabbed him and helped him sit down on a stone by the path. "S'ba, are you okay?" Shimon just looked at him as if he were trying to place his face. He felt like he belonged somewhere else, but didn't know where. His thoughts were catching up with him. He wasn't fully oriented to this world. Then it passed. He recognized Elihu and the boy standing nearby. He was shaken out of his reverie with reality setting in.

"Oh, I'm sorry. Talking about Jesus hit me for some reason. I feel I should know what you are talking about, but I really only remember holding him as a baby. That seems like only yesterday. Do you know him? I want to hear everything."

That caused Elihu and Shimei to laugh a little. "Wow. Where do we start? Well, you started it. You told us you held him and prophesied over him. You told us to be on the lookout for him. Abba Baruch never stopped looking. Come.

Let's go home and we will tell you everything we know. It gets a little crazy. The last few days have been interesting, to say the least."

They got Shimon on his feet when he was sure he was steady and headed into the city. It was still early in the day, but it felt like it had been a full day already. They told Shimon about finding Jesus and the miracles they had heard about and witnessed. When they talked about the raising of Lazarus, Shimon got that look again, like he knew something about it but couldn't recall it.

They made it home about that time. The entire house was in shock seeing their patriarch standing there alive and well. When Baruch entered the room, however, everything came to a standstill. The two men stood face to face in abject wonder. Baruch was definitely older than Shimon, it appeared, but seeing each other like this got through to both of them. They held each other in a firm embrace, and both of them cried with deep emotion. Baruch was seeing the father he knew as a younger man, full of vitality and here in his arms. Shimon was seeing the son he had raised and worked with for so long as an older man, mature and blessed. Life had given them a gift. It was deep and valuable.

Then Chaim and Naomi, Susannah, and Uriah came. It was almost too much for Shimon to handle. He hugged everyone and met the ones he had never known. His emotions were flooding in with no way of dealing with them all. He finally just sat down and numbly looked around at the amazing family he was just meeting. Shimei sent Phinehas around to the other homes and brought the wives and children. They all needed to get in on this. He was afraid God would take Shimon away somehow before they could all meet him. At this point anything was possible.

Elihu, however, stood back away and watched with awe at what was happening, but his thoughts were running full speed. The empty tomb stuck in his mind. Now what? How were they going to track Jesus and what was he going to do next? What had changed? What did it all mean? He finally saw that this all was too much for Shimon. "All right, everyone. Let's give S'ba Shimon a little room and some time to acquaint himself to life here. Jerusha, could you give him some food and drink to refresh himself with?"

"Certainly," she said as she went off to get it done.

"Shimei," Elihu continued. "I need to go do something. Will you please stay with S'ba Shimon? He still needs to hear about Golgotha." Those words perked Shimon's attention. He knew what Golgotha was, but he had no idea what had happened there the last few days. "We need to get some of the guys working on the tomb. There are still ossuaries in there that need protecting."

As he got up to leave, Ezra stepped close to him. "Where are you going, Abba?"

"I need to tell Joseph of Arimathea about what happened at his tomb. He should know it is open."

"I'm coming with you," Ezra said without any discussion.

"S'ba Shimon will need to hear what you witnessed."

"There will be plenty of time for that. He already has had more information than he can handle. I want to tell him when it is a little more relaxed around here."

"Okay," said Elihu. "I will enjoy the company." Then to the folks standing around, "Please tell Keturah and Ruth we will be home as soon as we can."

Shimon just looked up and smiled. "Be blessed. I will be here when you return. There is so much to catch up on."

It seemed to Elihu that they should try the closer places before they went out of town. They were coming up to the upper room Joseph had told them about, when they saw Joseph and a few of his servants coming out.

"Good Joseph," said Elihu in a greeting, bowing slightly as they met.

"Master weaver. It is good to see you again."

"Do you know about what has happened at the tomb?" Elihu didn't want to waste any time. This subject is way too important to delay things.

"Yes. Some of the disciples told their people, who told us. We are on our way out there right now."

"May we join you?"

"By all means. You would be welcomed." A couple men stepped out leading the way. Elihu and Ezra walked with Joseph, with the other two servants taking the rear. They walked briskly as they compared notes on Jesus's rising. Elihu told Joseph about Shimon which astonished him so much he stopped for a second to look at them as if he were trying to ascertain their mental state. "Are you serious? Others have risen?"

"I don't know about others; I only know what has happened to us. It is real."

Joseph turned, walking toward the tomb again, but this time his thoughts were even more scrambled. He was trying very hard to get a grip on all that had happened in the last few days. He was not succeeding. They talked about these things knowing they didn't have enough information to come to any conclusions.

They came to the tomb, and all discussions ceased. Joseph entered the tomb first. The full light of day helped them see what they needed to; the cloth was still there without the body they put in it. They could still smell the spices. Joseph went slowly to the shelf and touched the shroud as if making sure it was truly empty. He then picked it up gently as if it were going to disappear in his hand. Ezra picked up the head cloth; it was still bloody, but dry. They looked around and, finding nothing else remarkable, they stepped outside. Joseph untied the strips, letting the spices fall out of it. He opened it up to fold it. Elihu took the foot as they stretched it out, shaking the remaining spices out of it. There was no talking.

As they held it, though, Joseph noticed something. Looking closer he saw an image on the cloth. It was the full length, front and back of Jesus just as they laid him on it at Golgotha. It showed his face with the blood from the thorns, swollen with the beating. His hands were crossed just as they had done to him beneath the cross. The back showed the back as it had been flogged and the blood from the wound in his side. The blood had dried and it all looked very real.

"Look at the image!" Joseph said to Elihu. Elihu pulled it up to look at it better and saw the image the same as Joseph did. He grabbed the bottom of it to pull it closer to examine it. The image was faint, but decidedly there.

"What do you make of that?" he asked Joseph.

"I don't know. Everything is out of the normal right now. Did Shimon's shroud do this?"

"There was no shroud," Elihu said. "It had disintegrated years ago. Phinehas didn't say there was light with Shimon, but there was a blinding light with Jesus. It even knocked out the Romans. I think they were different somehow. This is much more powerful."

Ezra came and looked at what they were talking about. He was equally stunned at what he saw. "Abba. This is proof of his rising. No one has ever done this before. Even Lazarus didn't have this. This is the raw power of Jehovah. Jesus was definitely the Son of God."

They held it for a few moments, standing in awe of what they saw. "Help me fold it," Joseph said in a whisper. The three of them and one of the servants carefully folded it with the image inside to protect it. "I will take this and keep it safe."

"Just a minute," Elihu said as he turned to the tomb. Going inside he came out with the head cloth. He unfolded it and looked at it closely. "No image on this one."

"It wasn't on him when he rose," Joseph said, remembering how things went. "It was only this. Give that to me anyway. I will keep them together."

They solemnly turned to leave. Elihu said what they were all thinking, "What else could possibly happen that is deeper than this." They would soon find out.

The family had come together again. Having Shimon return was a remarkable event. They had just had Passover, but this was different. It wasn't every day you had someone come back from the grave. The day had been unproductive as far as the business was concerned. The employees had come and got some things done, but the family didn't do anything in the shop. They had planned to get the tomb repaired and to get work done, too. With Shimon showing up all plans were thrown to the wind. Chaim, Uriah, Tobiah, and Isaac went to the tomb to repair it for now. They would return someday soon to do a better job, but at least it was sealed up enough to protect things.

Shimei stayed with Shimon and filled in some of the gaps. The telling of the tale of Golgotha brought silence to the whole room. Shimon's eyes were filled with tears the entire time. He knew the Messiah was supposed to suffer, but he didn't realize how much. What a heavy price to pay.

What hit him hard, though, was how much his family was involved with it. It vastly pleased him that Elihu had made the shroud for him. He saw the seed that the Messiah was here had been planted and how it grew. This family had been highly honored. That didn't escape him. Hearing of the resurrection of Jesus, though, had shaken him to his core. There was something about that that sounded familiar. No, not familiar like he had heard of it before, but that he had known something about it that he couldn't nail down.

Elihu and Ezra returned after mid-day with more of the story. Joseph of Arimathea had the cloth in his possession, and it had the image of Jesus faintly burned into it. They were experiencing the supernatural in a natural setting. They didn't know how to think about that.

Ezra told of what he had seen Jesus do and the story of Elezar. That story again burned in Shimon's heart. There was more to it, but he couldn't tell what. As more family came, it thrilled his heart to see them.

The little boy Shimon knew from before was now a grown man. Elihu had come to sit beside Shimon and the connection was nearly palpable. God had connected them before in a spiritual way and now they were together again. "Thank you, S'ba, for giving us such a deep spiritual legacy. You sought Jehovah intently your whole life, and He rewarded you with showing you the Messiah. Now, we have not just seen him, but have been a small part in his story. What a blessing!"

"Yes, my son, but something tells me it isn't over, yet," Shimon said. "I am fully anticipating more to come. Jesus is back. What does that mean? What is he still going to do?" He reached over as he spoke and squeezed Elihu's leg, just like he did so many years ago. The sparkle in his eyes was a joy to behold. Elihu grinned with pleasure.

"Can you tell us anything about what it was like to be dead?"

Shimon laughed at that. "Who asks a question like that? Isn't that funny?"

Elihu snickered, "But who gets to talk to someone who was dead? This is our only chance!"

They all were getting in on this one. Shimon got thoughtful for a minute. "That is a good question. What is bad is, I can't really answer it. I have vague images and feelings, but nothing solid to grab. So many things feel like I should know something about it, but I just can't do it yet. I know my body feels differently. I don't have the aches and pains I used to have. I can see and hear everything. I wasn't even winded coming home. I have been very blessed. I feel I could live another twenty years!" When he said that, something sparked inside him. It didn't ring true completely. "What does that mean," he thought to himself.

The rest of the family showed up including the tomb repair crew. It was getting later in the afternoon. Shimon was still trying to remember who belonged to whom and what their names were. He was thinking he should probably write them down. Pretty soon, there was controlled chaos as the women were preparing the evening meal. There was a lot of people in this house again. Shimon's heart was filled with joy watching everyone. Conversations around the room were lively; the atmosphere was filled with life and laughter. Baruch and Chaim stayed close to Shimon. Neither of them could explain the feelings they were having.

They nestled into the evening meal, everyone trying to find a place close to Shimon who sat at the head of the table, as was fitting. As they were eating, light banter was floating through the room and laughter broke out in spurts in different areas. This was a memory for all of them.

Shimon, however, was starting to feel something different. There was a joy bubbling up within him, an anticipation of something great. Others were feeling it, too. Shimon started to cry with his eyes looking up. Out of his joy, he stated, "I believe in Jesus." As soon as he said that, he felt a change happen within him. He knew he wasn't alone. He was fulfilled. He made a strong gasp. Every eye was on him.

He looked at Elihu. When their eyes met, Elihu also stated, "I also believe in Jesus!" His eyes got a lot bigger as he experienced what Shimon had. He shot a look at Shemei who looked like he was getting in on a joke of some sort.

"I believe in Jesus," Shimei said out loud. Baruch and Suzannah did it next, followed closely by Chaim and Naomi. It was happening all over the room. Uriah, Tobiah, Josiah, Keturah, Ezra, Ruth, they all entered in. Deborah was slow, not understanding what was going on. Uriah took her hand and softly led her, "Do you believe in Jesus?" It took a few seconds for her to reply with a nod. "Say it."

"I believe in Jesus," she said quietly. Then she understood what others were getting. A smile spread across her face and she threw her arms around Uriah in joy. Others who watched that laughed out loud with joy. It was very hard to explain what they were feeling. It filtered down to the kids.

Phinehas was watching with great delight. It seemed he was waiting for his turn when he suddenly shouted out, "I believe in Jesus, too!" He almost exploded with joy, leaping up and dancing. The room was touched by the Spirit of God. Salvation had just been given to the house of Shimon. Eternity had been won. The price had been paid. The Holy Spirit was now indwelling man on earth.

CHAPTER 6
The Pattern in the Fabric

A bomb had just exploded. That was the way it felt in Dark Sheol. The entire foundation of life throughout the realm was shaken. Something had made the fabric of that place quiver. They all felt it. The general feeling turned to fear. What could demons and departed spirits fear? They knew their whole existence was based on fear, but this was different than that. They had no hope anyway, but now something had changed.

The center of the explosion came from the upper room where Jesus had Passover the night their stooge betrayed him. They had thought everything was in hand and going exactly according to plan. Satan was confident of the outcome. Then, after Jesus had died, just when they thought they had him in custody in the realm of darkness, he declared it all paid for and went to Righteous Sheol. They didn't know what to do about that when three days later he rose from the dead!

Directly after the rising, he led all the spirits in Righteous Sheol out of there and took them into the heavenly realm! Lachish watched that parade of glory happen right before his eyes. The realm of darkness seemed darker because the light was gone. He was very curious and went to the place he had talked to Abraham. There was no longer a barrier. He went right in.

It was empty. There didn't seem to be any residue or evidence that anything had ever been there. He was hoping something from that place of peace he had witnessed, was still around, but there was nothing. All the blessing had been taken away, leaving only the curse. It felt worse than the normal places on the surface.

He heard something and turned to see many evil spirits migrating into the place left vacant. They were filled with hopelessness and were drawn here by the frequency of vacant hope that now permeated the space. He felt worse, not thinking that was possible. He meandered back up to the surface passing a throng moving in. He needed a drunk host in the worst way. He came back to Jerusalem on the hunt.

The demons were in total disarray. There was no direction. They tried to stay close to Satan, but that didn't feel good either. He stayed close to the tomb, walking to and fro along the hills and every now and then venturing into the city. He seemed almost bewildered, unsure of what to do or what to think. He had no idea what was happening. He didn't know where Jesus was; he couldn't track him. He finally went to where the disciples were. Maybe he could have them destroyed, his wrath was extreme and lashed out at everything, but it was as if he were truly powerless to stop anything that was going on. He couldn't get very close for some reason, so he hovered close by, watching everything. His closest demons were hissing and spitting, but they knew there was nothing they could really do. They all had to wait and see what was going to transpire, including Satan himself.

Lachish wandered around, but couldn't find anything to inhabit. His day was pretty wasted. He found himself congregating with all sorts of departed spirits watching the demons swarm around the figure of Satan. He would stand still for a while, then burst into ranting and raving in rage. Each time of raging sent the demons into a frenzy of blasphemy against Jehovah, but it was ineffective and hollow.

Appearing suddenly in front of the building, Jesus caused everyone to stop and be quiet. He was extremely radiant, shining brightly. Everything around him ceased. Angels showed up with him, but not physical like he was. Jesus didn't even look at Satan and the horde, he just walked into the building and up the stairs to the room. None of the dark realm could follow or even get close to see better. Something was going to happen, and it would be big.

No one made a noise at all. Satan stood there watching. His main demons stood around him. Everyone's attention was on the building in front of them. That's when the explosion happened. Emanating from the building and moving out in all directions came a power that was unstoppable. The very air itself was changed. The entire crowd of dark spirits was affected deeply.

Satan let out a yelp like he was cut with a knife. His understanding hit him like a hammer to the forehead. He knew this power. It was the power that had been coming from Jesus since his ministry started. This was the Holy Spirit in a completely different way. It was no longer just to be in Jesus. It had been released into the earth. He screamed out in deep despair, "No! It can't be that! We had won!"

He spun around looking for something. He was trying to wrap his mind around the depth of what just happened. Some of the main demons got it when Satan did. The looks on their faces were total defeat and helplessness. "The Spirit of God has just been released to bring the covenant to people. Now, what do we do? How can we stop this?" In a fit of rage bigger than he had ever had before, Satan screamed in absolute frustration with his arms curled in front of him as if he could hold this in his hands. In a blast of fury, he shot up into the air and disappeared.

The demons scattered, none of them knowing what to do or where to go. They just left. The departed spirits were left there in their emptiness with no idea what all that meant. Fear permeated the group. Each was looking around as if expecting something to come and destroy them. The gates of Sheol have been shaken.

No one could explain what had happened to them last night. Shimon knew something drastic had happened, and none of them would be the same. There was a fundamental change deep within him. He had no idea how to know what it was or how to understand it. He did know, however, that he liked it. There was a peace within him he had never known before. It was as if his future was absolutely assured.

He laid there in bed before dawn staring into the darkness. He had slept very solid, waking refreshed and totally aware of his thoughts. He knew he wasn't alone. Even though he had a very excellent family and wonderful relationships, he had always felt alone. Now he wasn't and he didn't know why he felt differently about it. He didn't know how long it was before sunrise, but he was awake.

They had put him in with Baruch and Susannah in his old room. He arose as quietly as possible. He was elated that there was no pain. Wasn't it just the day before yesterday that he went to bed in this room with every joint hurting and breathing hard to come by? Now he was waking up a younger man with all his wisdom and knowledge intact. He wanted to go out to the courtyard.

Reaching down in the dark, he found his sandals. Well, the ones they had given him, anyway. Nothing was familiar. The bed, his clothing, everything was new. So was he. He was starting a new adventure, and the aspect of that thrilled him. He had set a prayer shawl aside for this morning and a robe. He picked them up with no sound and with his sandals in his hand, stealthfully glided to the door, opening it slowly. He stepped out and closed the door gently. He didn't think anyone was disturbed, so he progressed to the bench, laying his things on it. There was a single lamp lit, and that gave him the ability to light others, illuminating the courtyard in a dull, yellow light.

It was a little cool, so he put on his robe and sat down to put on his sandals. As he sat, his attention was lost to thinking of what the Lord God had said to him just the other day. His heart nearly jumped as he remembered the words spoken to him, remembering the deep intimate feeling he had then. He didn't know God would talk to people like that. Now Jehovah was talking to him. The thought occurred to him that his feelings now were the same as when the Lord had spoken to him back then. He spoke out the expression of his heart, "Oh, Lord, how great you are."

He felt, more than heard, an answer. He recognized the voice as the one he had heard before, but this time it was much more personal, within him. He knew the presence of the God Almighty was with him. With words, yet without words, communication from God touched him. "I love you." Shimon was dazed.

"Are you with me, Lord?" He felt the answer boiling up from within. It wasn't words, just understanding, coming to the forefront of his mind. He remembered that the Lord spoke to Elijah in a still, small voice; a voice of relationship. The intimacy was overwhelming; tears of joy poured down his face. He was truly worshipping his God. There was no religion, only a relationship. "How long can I have this, Lord?" His understanding broke in again. This wasn't temporary, but permanent. He could talk with God anytime he wanted. That is what happened last night. They had been given access to God somehow. He didn't understand it, but he did accept it. "Oh, Lord my God, show me your ways."

After a short period of quiet acknowledgment of the presence of God, he knew suddenly he wasn't the only human in the room. Baruch was standing over by the door to the bedroom. He was watching Shimon and hearing the things being said. "It's different now, isn't it?" Baruch asked. "I have always wondered what it would be like to hear from God like you did so very long ago. My life has been changed since last night. I hear him. It isn't like words out loud, but it is still God himself speaking to me. It is beyond anything I have ever expected." He was walking as he spoke, making it to the bench and sitting down beside Shimon. "I don't know how to explain it or even what to do with it."

Shimon lightly laughed to himself with a little of it squeaking out enough to be heard. "So, it isn't only me," he said. "I am so glad. We will have to learn things as we go." He had been looking at Baruch since the conversation started, but now his face softened. "I have wanted you in on this for so long."

"Me, too," Baruch said. "But longer than you. I still don't know how to think about seeing you after 30 years. How are you younger than me?" They both laughed lightly at that.

"I have no idea. This is all strange to me, too. I fall asleep, wake up in a tomb naked, and my whole family has grown up and had more children. I find it difficult to keep track of them. It's only been a day I've been back. So much to understand. I feel I am failing to do that."

"You aren't the only one. This is a very unique time in history we are living in. What is God doing? What's next?" Baruch leaned back against the wall, looking at his hands on his lap playing with each other. "Here we are, two old men, with a house full of family and great mysteries happening all around us and to us. We aren't in control of any of it. But, instead of fear and turmoil in me, I am filled with peace."

Shimon leaned back looking straight ahead. "There is much to consider," he said. "Along with the peace is a knowing that it is all going somewhere on purpose. I have hope for the future. I don't know what is going to happen, but I know we can trust God for whatever it is. I am rather excited to be a part of it all. How about you?"

"I just wish it happened while I was younger. This being old is a pain."

"Well, it was a pain just a couple days ago!" Shimon said with a laugh. "I really don't know what happened to me and why. I just think I am going to enjoy it as long as I can.

"Yes, Abba, but you will have to help me!" They sat there laughing at themselves when others started coming. Shimei and Jerusha came out. Shimei had his prayer cloth in his hand. Jerusha headed straight to the kitchen. Shimei came and stood by the bench. The older men looked at him, waiting for him to speak first.

"I've been praying," he said. "It wasn't the same as before. I don't need this," he said as he dropped his prayer cloth on the bench beside Shimon. "All I have to do is open my thoughts to him and there I am. I don't have to quote the Torah, even though it is still there. God isn't out there somewhere. He's right here. I can feel him, sense his presence. It's been like this for the last hour or so. What is happening to me?"

After a short silence, Shimon said, "That is what we have been talking about. It is the same for us. Last night changed us profoundly. We just don't know how or why or anything about it. We will just have to trust God to explain things to us as we go."

Shimei grabbed a nearby stool and sat off to the side in front of them. "I don't know what to expect," he said. "This is all so strange, but I want it more than anything."

"I understand. None of us expected this, but all of us are experiencing something absolutely outside of anything we have ever known." Shimon paused, and an impish smile broke out on his face. "And I like it." Baruch laughed, but it took Shimei a minute before it sank in.

"Yeah," he said softly, "me too. I guess I'm too used to the traditional religion. How much of it is going to change now?"

Shimon thought for a minute before chiming in. "Who knows? God is doing a new work on the earth. Jesus came and brought the presence of God. Most have rejected him. We have the honor to see and believe. I have no answers, but I do have a lot of questions. I will have to let God sort it out for me."

As they were talking, Susannah came out of the bedroom. Usually she would be walking with a goal of making it to the kitchen, but she wasn't moving very quickly nor heading anywhere in particular. She came over and stood beside Baruch as he sat on the bench. Baruch was looking at her with a puzzled expression. "Are you okay?" he asked.

She looked down at him with a tender, but vacant face. It was as if she were lost in thought or had a deep question to answer. "I'm good," she said. "I just had the most unusual thing happen to me. I was sleeping very deeply when I had a dream. It was different than any other kind of dream I have had. I was walking in a meadow beside a stream. I saw a shepherd ahead of me standing with his back to me, leaning on his staff. As I got close, he turned to me. He was smiling at me and said to me, 'I can care for my sheep. Have peace and let me lead. Do not let your hearts be troubled. You are in my care. And I love you.' It was so real to me. I woke up very peaceful. I feel I need to tell you that."

They all were staring at her with their mouths open. They looked at each other, pleading with their eyes for someone to explain that to them. Baruch was the first to speak. "The Lord is my shepherd; I shall not want. Even the scripture is being fulfilled." What they didn't say, but each of the men thought, was that it came to a woman, not just the men. Their whole world was turning upside down. Baruch continued, as he spoke to Susannah, "We have all been changed somehow since last night. Prayer has changed. Our hearts have been changed. Now even our sleep has been changed. I guess we are in for an adventure of discovery, being led by the Shepherd."

Business still had to go on. The employees all showed for work. Shimei knew they were behind. They had to deal with Passover break normally, but this one was different with three Sabbaths in a row and an unexpected added day to deal with broken tombs and raised dead folk. The people who worked there at his shop were all in on the search for the Messiah and the events leading up to the Passover. The events of the last week were confusing enough, let alone having Shimon show up. Now he had to bring everyone up to speed.

As they all showed up for work early on Monday morning, Shimei gathered them all and tried to explain what had happened with the trial, condemnation, and crucifixion of Jesus. Most in the room already knew most of it, especially the trial. The details of the crucifixion were news to most of them. The burial interested them exceedingly because of the shroud. The broken tomb was interesting as they understood the cultural implications. When he got to the raising of Jesus, every eye and ear was in full attention. As he told about Shimon, they were in shock, especially since Shimon was standing right there.

Shimon really wanted to be there. As the tale was reiterated, he stood there in total fascination. It was very good to hear it all in close succession. Shimei did a very good job explaining everything succinctly, telling the main things without getting lost in the narration. As his name was brought up with the story of how he came back to life, Shimon just looked up to the people and smiled, actually waving at them at one point. Baruch was standing at his side lending him credence. Since all three brothers worked there along with their sons, the principal players were all in attendance giving the whole story weight. Each of them was rather lost in thought as Shimei continued, adding the details in their minds that they had lived. Phinehas was even there at his father's hand beaming a grin as his part was told.

The part Shimei faltered at, however, was the telling of what happened to them all the night before. He still couldn't explain it. "Then last night we experienced something that is hard to put your finger on. We realized that the Messiah died to take away our sin. As we confessed our sin and accepted what he had done for us, ah, we were changed somehow. Each of us that did that have found that our prayers are changed. God seems to be talking to us, leading us. We will be talking about it for some time to come. You may ask us questions, but I'm not sure what we can actually tell you at this point. Everything points to Jesus and his crucifixion and rising from the dead. Other than that we don't have much in the way of answers. But in the meantime, we have a weaving business to run. Let's do what we can, and the rest will be in the hands of our Lord. Does everyone know what their jobs are and what we were doing before all this came along? Let's get back to it and if there is any confusion, let me know, and we will help get it straight. God bless you all today and may His peace be on our business. Thank you."

The people looked at each other not knowing what to do exactly. This was a lot of information that was difficult to process, and this was going to take some time. One by one they slowly headed to their stations and back to work. A few came and greeted Baruch, and some wanted to meet Shimon. He was definitely an oddity; he even thought so.

"Uriah, Elihu. Could you come here for a minute, please?" Shimei said. The two men walked to him, paying close attention. "Uriah, I need you to see what inventory we have, especially the flax. Elihu, could you get back to training the boys on the big loom?" They both nodded in affirmation. "What I really need, though, is that you keep an eye out for anyone who needs to talk about what we told them today. The more ease we can put their minds to, the better. Okay?"

"How are we going to answer any questions when we have the same questions?" Uriah said with a slight snicker. "I'm sure we will do our best."

"Ezra! Isaac! Let's get on that tight piece we had started before Passover," Elihu ordered. Before he went to the loom, he reached out and took hold of Shimei's arm. "You are a great leader. There is more for you than just running a fabric shop. I'll get that piece moving in a bit, but I need to talk to Abba for a minute. Okay?"

Shimei nodded, "Thank you. That means a lot to me." Then he moved off looking for what was needed for today's work. Elihu took a second, then headed over to Baruch and Shimon.

"What are you two going to do today?" he asked.

"I'm thinking of going to the synagogue and maybe the Temple," Shimon said. Glancing over to Baruch he asked,

"Would you like to go with me?" Baruch smiled in agreement. "Why do you ask?"

Elihu was studying the ground for a moment gathering his thoughts. "I just think we aren't the only ones who have seen things or know things." Looking up at the men again, he continued. "It might be good to ask around some. Discretely, if you know what I mean."

"Ah," Baruch started. "We will see what we can find."

"Thanks. It seems I will be stuck here for a while." Elihu smiled and bowed, turning on his heel, he went off to work.

"I guess we have been put on a mission," Shimon said. "Let's tell the women we are going out for a while and get moving. Don't worry; I'll take it slow. Son." Baruch just chuckled and shook his head. What a strange development.

They decided to go to the Temple. Shimon was very interested in how things had changed in thirty years. He was amazed at how easy it was to walk. It was actually painful for him to watch Baruch. He remembered a strong man who could work all day and still be able to play with his family. Now he is old. The hands that worked the looms with such dexterity were now gnarled and slow. Shimon remembered how he had longed to die before the Lord spoke to him about the Messiah. What wonderful changes there are in his life now. If only he could remember what had happened to him for the last thirty years. It seemed to be lurking there in his memory just out of reach, but taunting him.

The Temple area was pretty much the same as it had been. There were some repairs made and new workmanship here and there, but mostly the same. They went into the Women's court and walked toward the stairs. It was right up there that he had an encounter with a little baby and his mother, Mary. He remembered Joseph and his tender protection. That baby had grown up. The Messiah had come and done ministry here. What would it have been like to see that?

He was shaken out of his reverie with a commotion ahead. There was a small crowd of priests, very animated and excited about something. As they approached the group, they could hear what they were saying.

"This can't be Kohath. He died years ago! You must be mistaken," one of the priests was saying. A man was standing there in the midst of the crowd smiling apologetically. His closest family and friends were around him trying to convince the priests who he was.

"His tomb was broken open on Passover. We guarded it for three days. Then he just walked out of it wearing only part of a shroud!" The speaker was one of the priests. "I should know my own father. He has been gone only eleven years. This is him. He was one of the priests in charge of the altar. Now we have him back."

"But this is impossible!" another priest said. "How can this be?"

As Shimon stepped into the group, his eyes made contact with the man who was reported as raised. They both started as they stared at each other. "Do I know you?" the man asked. The feeling of familiarity hit them both.

"I don't know. I think I should know you, but I don't know how." The rest of the men there went silent. "I have a vague memory of your face, I think."

"Who are you?" the Priest's son asked Shimon.

"My name is Shimon." Then to the man again, "Does that sound familiar?"

"My name is Kohath, a Levite. No, it does't sound like I should know you. Your face makes me think I have known you from somewhere. I don't remember anything about the last eleven years. But my body is very healthy. I died of a fever. The last thing I remembered was being in bed with my wife holding my hand."

Shimon snickered. Baruch said to the group and no one in particular, "He died thirty years ago, and we found him at his tomb very alive yesterday morning." Kohath was taken aback.

"I don't remember anything between the day I died and yesterday. I also am healthy now. Before, I was a son of eighty-five years."

Kohath smiled a huge toothy grin, stepped up, and gave Shimon a strong, heartfelt hug. "I thought I was crazy, like this was a dream I couldn't wake up from. I am so glad to see you." Then he held Shimon at arm's length, and they both smiled at each other like they were long lost friends. This was all the evidence the family needed to press the point home that this man had come back from the dead.

They chatted a while, getting to know each other and Kohath's family. Shimon wasn't in the mood for small talk. He waited until he was practically alone with Kohath and got serious for a minute. "Did something happen to you last night?"

"Yes! How did you know?" Shimon just smiled knowingly. "It was after sundown. My family was still trying to get used to having me back. Some didn't believe it. Then I felt something wash over me. It felt like it was vastly important, but I don't know what it was. It has been nagging at my heart ever since."

That statement wasn't what Shimon was expecting. Has anyone told you what has happened over Passover with a Prophet name Jesus?" Mentioning that name took Kohath by surprise.

"Why do I know that name? My heart is filled with joy just hearing it."

Shimon knew for some reason he needed to be careful here. "Just ask your family about Jesus and what happened the last few months around Jerusalem. When you desire, come to the weaver's shop and ask for me. I will help you understand." Shimon patted him on the shoulder in reassurance. "I will let you get back to them, then. May Jehovah bless you."

They joined the rest of them. Baruch had been watching Shimon and Kohath talking. He understood what was being asked. Then they turned to leave their new friends. Kohath asked Shimon, "Does the name Malachi mean something to you?"

Shimon was struck silent. "Yes, but I don't know why. Do you know a Malachi?"

"No, I don't. But it feels so familiar. I just hoped you knew. Thank you again for coming today. Be blessed."

They walked a distance before either spoke. Finally, Baruch asked, "What did he tell you?"

"He felt something last night, but it wasn't like what we experienced. He didn't know about Jesus being the Passover Lamb that takes away the sin of the world. He knows there is something available, but doesn't have any frame of reference to know what. It will have to be explained to him, I expect. He is ready for it, but he will need some help getting there. I told him to come see us at the shop. I hope he does."

Over the next few days they heard about others that had returned from the dead. The rumors were running full in the synagogue. It was all the Rabbi could do to keep up with them. He met with Shimon who told him his story and how he had prophesied over the baby Messiah. The Rabbi had followed Jesus and counted on Elihu and Ezra to keep him apprised. Finally, Elihu asked him if he believed that Jesus was the Messiah. He knew that to do so would be politically tricky, but the evidence was too strong to be ignored. As they explained what happened to them at Golgotha and the understanding of the Passover Lamb that takes away the sin of the world, he grew very serious. When they told him what happened to them that night they confessed their sin and believed, it was all he needed. He talked to the Lord God of Israel and admitted his need for the Lamb to take his sins. He was affected that same way they had been. He sat there and wept in joy. Rabbi Gershom became a follower of Jesus.

The family was learning what was needed in people's lives. It wasn't just those who had been at the crucifixion or had come back from the dead. It was anyone who confessed and believed. Now they knew. They had a new purpose.

CHAPTER 7
New Dye

Telem was getting old. He had worked hard to get where he was, but the price was getting too steep. He had served Lachish well right up to his death. He was the only one who really knew the business. Lachish' widow, Abigail, needed help in every way. Her dead husband had been a tyrant at home and the alcohol had complicated everything. Telem had stepped in and became the steward for the business and under his hand.

The Romans were always in need of something. Procuring everything they desired had become second nature to him. Lachish had been hard to get along with, but he had built quite a sizable list of places and people where things could be obtained. Under Telem, who was much more amiable and gracious, the list grew.

His influence and income grew also. He was making a sizable fortune for his host family, but his own personal wealth had become substantial. Then things started getting complicated. Shemuel, Lachish' son, had grown up. He was becoming more and more uncontrollable. He demanded to be part of the company. Telem brought him to work with him several times as just an observer. He didn't just want to watch; he wanted to run it. He wanted to rule and tell people what to do. He wanted prestige and authority. Telem tried to keep him out, but in reality, he owned the company. Abigail had done what she could, but he soon learned to run over her just like his father did. Telem had leveraged his position to be steward, but under Shemuel. Even as Shemuel gave orders, Telem had to figure out how to get it done in a better way without destroying the company. It was quite a dance Telem had worked out for himself.

The one thing Telem could count on, however, was the wine taking its toll on Shemuel. When he drank enough, he would want to be alone and disdain life. Any intrusion would result in a rage-filled attack. Telem looked forward to these times and put Shemuel in a solitary place to drink, pass out, vomit on himself, and sleep it off. He could squeeze two days of freedom out of these times.

The staff and workers in the warehouse had learned to act the right way when Shemuel was around, but when he wasn't there, they knew Telem would be running things to make it work out. He knew that it was only a matter of time before that would fall apart in his face. So, for the last few years, he had started setting things aside for himself. He had accumulated a tidy sum and knew where he could go, away from the grime of Lachish and his scummy son.

Shemuel had been married, but he had driven his wife away childless. He was alone with what servants he could keep. Many had learned how to steal from him and make a living from it. None were loyal to him; none liked him. He had his own house, his old one held memories of Lachish he couldn't stand; he let Abigail keep it. Telem made sure he had enough to keep the servants and the liter they used to cart him around. Everyone knew the actual boss was Telem.

Now Shemuel wanted more. It was too difficult to keep him in the dark and pacified. It was time for Telem to do something about it. He gained friends through the way he did business and started siphoning off transactions under his own hand. Abigail was taken care of. Peninnah was gone to her own household. All that was left was Shemuel. Telem restructured the income to bring some to Shemuel, but he knew that it would be frittered away until there was nothing left. He knew that Shemuel didn't know enough to come after him and take back everything. He soon had it all, leaving Shemuel with having to live within his own means. That would end in disaster.

When Shemuel finally figured out what was happening to him, it was too late. He drank more and more. He became much worse than Lachish had ever been.

Lachish had stayed with the Romans. Their drinking was legendary. He could usually find someone to inhabit for a while. One day the soldier he was in had been ordered to go to the suppliers and order more metal for the blacksmiths. He went to their normal supplier for iron and found it had changed hands. He went to the old owner to see if he could broker a deal better than he had before. He went to the man's house to barter with him there.

It was a beautiful house, a little run down and feeling empty, but it had seen many a good party. An old servant answered the door. "I am looking for Shemuel, the purveyor of iron stock. Is he home?" he inquired of the old servant.

"Right this way, sir," the servant said quietly while bowing. "I will alert the master of your presence."

The old man sauntered off into the back leaving him standing by the front door. He was used to waiting, that was the main thing they did in the Roman army. It was dark in the foyer with only one oil lamp to shed light on the interior. He could hear the man shuffling along to the back rooms and could faintly make out the voices. "A Roman soldier to see you, sir," he heard the servant announce.

"What about?" was the gruff answer with a raspy voice.

"He said something about iron, I believe."

"Okay, I'll be right there."

The servant returned with the message and then stood off a ways trying to blend into the wall. Soon, another figure was seen in silhouette down the dark hallway. It was not a large man, but one wrapped in a huge robe of black with scarlet embroidery and much embellishments. His undertunic was a darker blue made of expensive cloth. As he came into the light, it was obvious he was most the way toward getting drunk. His eyes were droopy and bloodshot. His speech was slurred and he was wobbly on his feet. He was unshaven and his curly brown hair was in need of grooming.

"I am Shemuel. What may I do for you?"

"Do you still provide iron for the Garrison here?" the soldier stood tall and straight so as to promote superiority. He knew it wasn't very long ago, he was as drunk as this man, but he couldn't let him know that.

"I have my sources. What do you need?"

"I have need of stock to make horseshoes and wheel bands, along with other projects. What kind of deal can you give me? The house of Telem seems to be able to supply a goodly amount, but it is a little high priced. What can you do?"

At the mention of Telem, Shemuel got indignant, in the way only a truly drunk man can be. "I can get you anything. And as much as you need," he spat out.

Inside the soldier, Lachish saw the merchant. He looked familiar for some reason, but couldn't place him. He had inhabited many people and couldn't remember all of them. But he did like what he saw. Here is a man who doesn't have to wait until the end of a shift to get drunk. He also looked like he had means to get good wine like Lachish had had before. The familiarity nagged at Lachish. There was something here but the need for the wine clouded his thoughts. While they were bartering back and forth, Lachish decided to leave the soldier and gravitate toward the merchant. This almost felt like a sort of home. This pleased Lachish as nothing had since he had died. He knew the merchant would be able to host him fairly soon considering the condition he was in presently.

The bartering became a little louder. The merchant was making promises he couldn't keep, and in his present condition, may not remember. The soldier thought he was getting a great deal here, thinking he was going to be able to go back and get credit for obtaining materials at a better cost. Both men thought they were getting the best of the other until they came to a conclusion and struck hands on the deal. The soldier left all pumped up with a delusion that didn't match reality, and the merchant went back to his room all cocky about duping a Roman. This deal wasn't going to work for either of them, but that wasn't Lachish's concern. He had gained a good prospect of experiencing this man getting drunk. Everybody lost today.

All seemed quiet. Each day had its surprises as life has a way of supplying. Shimon had stepped in stride with the happenings of life. Everyone had worked together to figure out where he was to live. The house of Baruch and Shimei was full. Uriah's was too. Elihu was the best bet since Ezra had built an additional room on Elihu's house for himself and Ruth. Hepzibah was gone with her new family leaving only Boaz at home. Hepzibah being a girl, she had established her own space leaving the boys to themselves. Now Ezra is gone into his own place in the house with Ruth, leaving his old room open. Shimon moved in. It wasn't difficult; he didn't have anything. They had to find or buy everything a man would need.

Shimon had a hard time figuring out how old he was. It wasn't about how many years since his birth, but how old his body felt. Raising from the dead healed all his diseases, aches, and pains. "Could I live another thirty years?" he thought to himself. "I need to know what to do with this life I have been given."

Kohath the priest had stopped by to talk. He wanted to talk to Shimon. They had a bond together, having both risen from the dead. It didn't take long to tell him about confession and belief. He had been filled in from the other priests about Jesus and the last three years, especially the part about the trial and crucifixion. They had whispered among each other about him coming out of the tomb since the soldiers had come to the High Priest telling about the light and the stone being rolled away. They came hoping the High Priest would smooth things over with Pilate since it was known and admitted that they had been unconscious on duty. The priests paid them to lie saying his disciples had come and stolen the body. Caiaphas himself went to Pilate to get the men off, which seemed to work. The priests had heard that Pilate was shaken with the news that Jesus was no longer in the tomb.

So when Kohath had come by, it was easy to fill in the gaps with what they knew. He was easily led into confession and belief. Shimon knew there was more to the story for them than they remembered, but it just wouldn't come to mind. They had heard there were others who had also been raised. Each story was someone who had a strong desire for righteousness when they died. Some had come to the Temple to tell their story. As they did, Kohath took them through the story of Jesus, ending with confession and belief. Shimon and Kohath had become a team, working together for these and others.

The weaving shop was making good money. Baruch and Susannah were set for their whole lives. Baruch was showing signs of getting older. It was hard on Shimon to know he was Baruch's father and was "younger" than him. The young woman that used to run the household was now a grandmother, and she was starting to show her age quite a bit. Shimon related more to Shimei, Uriah and Elihu. Technically, the shop belonged to him; he started it and established it a long time ago. So, as awkward as it seemed, he asked Shimei for a job.

He remembered the moves of weaving and was quickly doing many things. He did the menial, consistent jobs of making common cloth. That left Elihu and his apprentices more time to work on the fancy cloth and custom orders. He was soon pulling his weight at work, but his mind had a tendency to wander. After a week of doing nothing and a week of working the loom, he had an itch to get out and see people. The driving question in his mind was, "Why was I returned to life? Is there a purpose?" He didn't want to miss the purpose God had for him here. He found himself talking to God a lot. An idea started to form that he should be telling people about Jesus and what had happened to them when they believed. He was living proof. He shouldn't hide that in the shop. With a deep sigh, he went to talk to Shimei. Again.

They came up with a good solution for all of them. They let Shimon do what he had done before, delivering packages and orders that had been completed. That gave him the freedom to talk to people and get out in the community.

He had the freedom now to stop by the synagogue once in a while to talk to the Rabbi. Gershom always had interesting things to talk about, especially after confirming his belief in Jesus. That put a draw on Shimon to go by there fairly often. Three weeks after his raising (and Jesus's), Shimon went to the synagogue after delivering some packages to a few merchants nearby. The old building was pretty much the same as when he used to visit it many years ago, but a little bit older and some bit run-down. They had done a few repairs here and there, but it was virtually the same.

Skirting the main front room where the meetings were held, Shimon made his way to the back room where they had the scrolls stored and where the men sat and debated everything possible to debate. There were a few men in there, as usual, talking continually as he entered. They didn't slow down any perceptively but acknowledged him with a nod. They had many a discussion about him when he wasn't there and eventually a couple about his death and new life with him in the room. Now there was a lot of talk about the others that had risen. Shimon enjoyed stirring the pot with discussions about Jesus and the scandal of his so-called trial and illegal execution. Gershom knew he was just getting them riled up just to watch them spin. These events were still too current and there were raw nerves about it in the Jewish community.

Baruch and Shimon had come here the first week often, but now it was more sporadic now that Shimon was working again. He did, however, stop in to check with Rabbi Gershom on what was happening in the community.

Gershom was sitting at the far end of the group of men and stood when Shimon entered. He greeted Shimon warmly with a hint of mirth about the discussion that was raging. "Please, save me from this."

"My pleasure," said Shimon with a smile. Then went to the back of the shelves where the scrolls were stored. There were chairs there for the attendants to sit but were unoccupied for now. The two men sat, Shimon plopping heavily into the chair. "It's been a good day of deliveries, done a lot of walking already today."

"It does me good to see you enjoying your work," Gershom commented. "Anything exciting?"

"Not really, but people all through the city are still a little stunned. It is like they are numb or, at least, dull. It seems like a damper has fallen all over the city. It's as if everyone is waiting for something to happen."

Gershom nodded, raising his eyebrows knowingly. "Perhaps," he ventured, "Or perhaps too much has happened and they aren't over it yet."

"What have you heard? Are there rumblings from the folks about anything?"

"Levi's Aunt Martha was one of the ones raised. Her life is mostly different, but some things don't change completely. He is complaining that she is still trying to tell him what to do."

They both chuckled at that. "Maybe he should just listen. He needs all the help he can get!" That tidbit lasted them a few minutes of mirth.

"The thing that is on my mind is that one of Jesus's disciples came in the other day." Gershom got more serious as he continued, "Jesus has been seen by many people. This disciple, Surnamed Thaddaeus, one of the older disciples, comes in to read the scrolls. He told me that Jesus had shown himself several times to all sorts of different people. Sometimes he just vanishes once they know who he is." Gershom was speaking matter-of-factly as if he told people about this all the time. Shimon sat riveted on his words.

"Truly? How many?

"I don't know exactly; He said it was 'very many'," Gershom said with flourishing gestures. Shimon wasn't prepared for that information. His heart jumped up in his chest with a deeply emotional thrill and at the same time with incredulity.

"Where can these disciples be found?" Shimon turned this into a serious discussion. This was no longer passive conversation to him.

"I think Thaddaeus mentioned an upper room where they had Passover." Gershom was almost defensive.

"Elihu talked about a place like that. He knows where that is. Maybe we can talk to them directly."

Gershom held out a palm toward Shimon, "Careful. I heard they are trying to stay hidden somewhat. They are still concerned that the Romans are looking for them. There is a rumor going around that they stole his body from the guards at the tomb."

"That's ridiculous! How can these common men overpower a Roman guard unit?" Shimon was getting worked up. He had become emotional very quickly and it surprised Gershom.

"Calm down," the Rabbi said. "You don't have to get all excited over it. We've been the brunt of rumors before. We can handle this. So can they. Time will tell everything."

The men in the other room had heard the commotion and their discussion had slowed considerably. It was getting quiet in the synagogue and that wasn't always a good thing. "Go ask around discreetly. Ask Elihu. Just keep it down and be careful."

Shimon quieted down quickly, his eyes apologizing to his friend. "I will. This is big news. I had no idea. I should take this home," Shimon said. "Thank you so much. I will come by later and talk again. Be blessed." He stood preparing to leave. Gershom stood and embraced him.

"Be careful. Please."

Shimon gave him a reassuring smile and walked away. He walked through the group of men who were now mostly watching and gave them nods all around with a small smile and headed home with his brain churning away.

Shimon arrived at the shop just in time for the midday repast. Jerusha and Dinah were passing out morsels, bread, and water as everyone sat around to rest a while. Shimon nonchalantly sidled up beside Elihu who looked like he needed the break.

"How is it going?" Shimon asked as a way to start the conversation.

"Pretty good. Had to repair the loom this morning, but it has been working great ever since. And you?"

"Oh, doing well. Stopped by the synagogue today and talked with Rabbi Gershom." Shimon was acting as if it were just small talk, but Elihu picked up on something.

Turning to look closer at Shimon's face, he could see the twinkle in his eye. "Okay," Elihu said as he started the interrogation, "What's going on? You're about to burst."

Looking almost sideways at Elihu with a grin that gave away everything, he started with, "He told me that Jesus has been seen by many, many people. We could still see him around if we keep an eye out for him. He seems to have a plan. The other thing I learned is that his disciples are all staying in that upper room where they had Passover with Jesus, and they have seen him."

Elihu's eyes narrowed as he gave a look to Shimon. "You want to go talk to them, don't you?"

"Saw right through me, didn't you?" Shimon countered. Elihu could read that face like a scroll.

"You want me to tell you where it is."

"Well, yes," Shimon said. "And possibly go with me?"

"Ahhhh. Now I get it. You want to go have some fun, don't you? And you don't want to go alone." Elihu just looked at Shimon who had the look of a teenager asking permission to go do something slightly dangerous with his friends. He had never been able to resist his Grandfather. "Okay," he conceded, "We'll go as soon as I finish this project. It should take me another three hours. That okay with you?"

"Excellent! Do I need to talk to Shimei for you?" Shimon's excitement was infectious.

"Would you, please? It would be better coming from you." Elihu felt like a conspirator trying to get away with something. He knew they would never do something wrong, but they might do something that no one expected.

"Will do," Shimon said finalizing the deal.

"Maybe you should get your work done, too," Elihu told him. Shimon just nodded with an "of course" look. Then he leaned back against the wall and grabbed a morsel of fish and some bread, sitting there eating as if nothing had happened. Elihu just sat there shaking his head. Oh, how he loved this man.

Shimon went home after talking to Shimei. There were no deliveries for the rest of the day and it was cleared for them to seek out the disciples by leaving work a little early. As he got home, Keturah was just leaving to go to the shop. "Be blessed," she told him as she walked past. "The house is all yours. No one will be home for a few hours."

He blessed her and watched her for a little while as she walked toward the shop. He was thinking of how blessed he was to have the family he has. Getting to know everyone was a challenge and a joy. Elihu had quite a prize in this woman. Ezra was at work and Ruth must be shopping for the household. Life was always busy, so Shimon was appreciative for the chance to be alone and quiet.

The roof was normal for houses in Israel. It was flat and open with a canopy over it for shade. There were chairs up there for people to enjoy the breezes and sit for fellowship after meals. It was very quiet up here today as if the neighbors and everyone had gone someplace else. Shimon sat in the shade, removed his keffiyeh and leaned back just to meditate. Now that he had a plan to meet the disciples of Jesus, he could relax and wait, clear his mind and talk to God.

"Hello, Shimon." The voice came out of nowhere. Shimon's eyes darted to the direction the voice came from. Many things happened in an instant. Shimon saw a man sitting in the chair just three feet away, facing him. He was dressed in white, very normal looking, with medium length brown hair and beard. The man smiled at him. Shimon knew in an instant that he knew this man. He had seen him before. His mind was reeling as it opened up to memory he didn't have access to before.

"Jesus..." It was a statement of fact. He knew that he knew who this was and where he had known him from. It took him a moment to process the magnitude of these thoughts. Then slowly it came to him, this is the Jesus he had worshipped in Sheol. He slipped out of his chair and slid to his knees, bowing deeply before his King. "My Lord."

"Blessed Shimon, please sit and talk with me." Jesus leaned forward, extending a hand to him, helping him up and into the chair.

"My Lord, what do you want of me today. Just say it and I will obey."

Jesus laughed lightly. "Just to sit and talk a while." Jesus sat back in his chair, folding his arms across his body and relaxing. Shimon tried. He was quite overwhelmed and unsure of how to process everything.

"You have been a faithful servant for me for a long time. You were chosen to return to life. My Father knew you could be trusted to handle it. We also knew you couldn't be allowed to remember your time in Sheol for a while. You wouldn't have been able to handle it all. But now you are seeking me and growing in who you are. I will be directing my disciples to go to Galilee where I have critical things to do and to tell them. I want you to be here for them. They are being sent out to do the work of the ministry. You are here to witness to them and others of my love and grace. Follow their lead. There is a plan, but no one gets to know too much too soon. You will have to trust me. My Spirit is in you. Listen and obey."

Shimon sat there in complete awe. Receiving the Spirit of God is what happened to them when they believed. That made sense to him. "My Lord. How long am I to live? What do you want for my family? What..?"

Jesus put up his hand and stopped him. "It isn't for you to know the future. You will have to trust me. Do what you know and learn more. Trust and obey."

He got it. "Yes. I see," Shimon said in a near whisper. "You are the only one who knows the future. We must live for now."

"There are going to be many changes," Jesus said plainly. "I have taught my disciples what to do. They will remember. You need to show others you believe. Be baptized. They have been taught that. It is important."

"Learn to love as I have loved. You are blessed. You will not remember everything about Sheol. Just know there is a better place. You will come to me in the proper time. Now, be blessed."

Jesus stood up. Shimon stood with him. Jesus smiled and vanished. Shimon was left standing there on the roof alone. His heart burned within him, and his mind reeled trying to keep everything in perspective. He stood there until he finally realized what a massive gift he had been given to see and talk to the Messiah. Then he sat. The magnitude of this encounter hit him like a flood washing over him. He sat thanking the Lord God and weeping softly as he worshipped there on the roof.

Elihu led the way. Shimon was different this afternoon than he had been at midday. Elihu kept asking him how he was, but he only answered that he was fine. They were both looking forward to trying to find the disciples of Jesus, knowing that if they did they would learn much more about what had happened to them and what to do next. Shimon, however, had a faraway look and seemed distracted. When they stood in front of the building, Shimon perked up. He was standing on the edge of a cliff of adventure. Today was a day to remember.

They went to the door and opened it to a narrow stairway. They went up the stairs to a landing in front of a strong, wooden door. They knocked a few rapid knocks and waited quietly. They didn't hear much coming from inside until they heard someone asking who they were.

"My name is Elihu. I am a weaver. I am friends with Joseph of Arimathea. We were the ones who helped bury Jesus." That mention gained a little noise from within. A bolt was heard sliding and the door opened a little with a face staring at them from the crack. It was the young disciple that had been at the crucifixion.

"I recognize you," he said tersely. "Who is that with you?"

"He's my uh..." Grandfather wasn't going to look right. "He met Jesus once." It wasn't a lie. Elihu didn't know about this afternoon. He did know about the baby story, though.

"What do you want?"

Shimon spoke up. "I died thirty years ago, and Jesus sent me back from the dead to witness to you about him." The man reacted to that news, not knowing what to do with that information. The door opened further to another man standing there staring at them. He was a large man with an intense look, as if he were trying to look through them. His size combined with the full, long dark brown beard, thick, bushy eyebrows and suspicious gaze made him intimidating.

"We are not a threat and are alone," Elihu offered. "We just feel that we need to meet with you and exchange information. We have many questions and some answers." The men stepped aside and motioned for them to enter.

After looking down the staircase, the large man backed into the room and closed the door, sliding the bolt home.

"We don't know who to trust,"he said. "We need to be cautious. There is so much that has happened and we don't know what to do. Come in. Be at peace." Elihu and Shimon moved into the room slowly, adjusting to the lack of light. There were several people in the room. They were all extremely quiet. Everyone was watching them, waiting for them to say or do something.

The younger one from the door said, "I am John, this is Peter. These are all followers of Jesus. What is your story? You died?"

They all sat with Elihu and Shimon in the middle. Shimon tried to tell some of his story from the beginning, how he had prophecied over Jesus and Mary. As he said that, he heard a gasp over by the window. An older woman sat there staring at him wide-eyed.

"That was you?" she said.

"Yes, it was."

"You look much younger than the man who spoke to us back then. How is that possible?"

"I died the next day," Shimon ventured. "I was buried and went to live in righteous Sheol. I met Jesus again when he came there after his death. He brought me back with others when he rose from the dead. My body was healed and brought to life. I have been living with my family for the last few weeks. I have been trying to figure out why Jesus would bring me back with him. Today, he told me." Elihu's head snapped around to look at Shimon. Shimon looked back at him tenderly. "Jesus appeared to me today and made a couple of things clear for me. One of the most important is that we are not to know the future, but we are to trust him for it."

They were all looking at Shimon as if he were made of feathers and was ready to fly. Finally, John started laughing a little, and it grew until he was making quite the noise. Others had joined him while others did not look amused. "That sounds like Jesus alright. He is doing mighty things, and we don't understand them. All of us have the peace in us we felt when he returned. Instead of trusting that he gave us peace for a reason, we are getting more and more fearful. He has shown himself to many of us and many others also. When are we going to let God work? He will show us what to do at the right time."

Joining in their mirth, Shimon said, "When I saw him today, he was smiling and joyful. I don't think he is too worried about things. He mentioned being publically known as believers in him. He said you knew about being baptized. You will have to help us in that area, I know nothing about that except the ritual mikvah. Other than that, he wants you to go to Galilee and meet with him there. He has much more to show you and tell you."

"See? I told you so!" another man piped in. "I told you we were to go to Galilee soon. Remember? Even the women at the tomb said that. It's been just over a month since the resurrection. And here we are just sitting here. It took a little jolt from someone we don't know to jar us into obedience. And he had to come from the dead to do it!" Others joined in, including some of the women who remembered that is what they were told to tell everyone.

Elihu could tell they were divided. Some wanted to leave right then, but others, like Peter, were reluctant. Elihu didn't know why they were there. Things had changed. They came to get information about Jesus, and found themselves in the middle of controversy. The disciples weren't very much more informed than they were. The only thing they had to go on was Shimon had come back from the dead for a reason. He had put them on the track to watch for the Messiah, and they had. They were there for the crucifixion and had even been used of God for the burial, including the burial cloth. They had knowledge of Jesus being raised and had one of their own raised. Now they waited.

All but Shimon. He had met with Jesus today? Why didn't he say anything? Now peace and security emanated from him, a calm reserve.

Shimon stood. "We have brought to you what we were supposed to," he stated. "I feel we are just beginning a relationship with you folks. I think we are going to see God do great things together." He walked over to Mary by the window. "We have so much to catch up on since the last we saw each other. You were very young and I was very old. What an adventure we are living!"

She smiled at him and was obviously touched by his tenderness and memory. "Thank you for coming. I am so glad to have met you. Again."

"For me, it seems like only a few weeks ago. Your image is very fresh in my mind. I so clearly remember holding that baby in my arms. It seems that what I told you back then has come to pass, hasn't it?" Shimon knew they were going to be friends. There was so much to tell each other.

"We will be in contact with you all." Shimon addressed them as from a position of authority. "God put us together. There will be time to put all the pieces together. My family are believers. We want to be marked as such. Please, lead us in this baptism you know about. If this is something we are supposed to do as believers, we need to tell others about it. We can't if we haven't done it. So, please, allow us to be part of that when you do it. But for now, I think we will leave you in peace to decide what your next step is going to be. We will check in with you from time to time. My family and I will be here for you if you need anything. Please, if you can, keep us informed. We desire to be part of what Jesus is doing."

Bowing deeply to them all with his hand on his heart, Shimon signaled to Elihu they were leaving. John went to the door, slid the bolt and opened it. He was smiling at them and welcomed them to come anytime. Shimon thanked him for receiving them and they went down the stairs.

As they reached the bottom and went out into the street, Elihu said, "So when were you planning on telling us about today?"

Shimon just laughed. "I would have gotten around to it eventually." He started walking down the road with a light step and a grandson who was just shaking his head.

CHAPTER 8
Tying Loose Ends

The anticipation was driving him to distraction. Shimon had been patient. Much more patient than he thought he needed to be. It had been just over forty days since Passover. Pentecost was coming quickly. That was the normal way of the feasts to go. Do Passover, wait 50 days, have Pentecost. Passover had been disrupted, the old ways had been changed, traditions had been fulfilled and explained in ways that were mind-boggling. What could happen to Pentecost?

The disciples had been gone for a week. The upper room was still busy with the folks that hadn't gone with them. Only the Eleven had gone north. Shimon, Elihu, Ezra, and Shimei had become fast friends with those who were still there. They would drop in on them periodically. Shimon had become quite a part of them. He spent a lot of time with Mary. They were both of the old school, but weren't trapped in it. They both had a story to tell, and they told it to each other. Everyone was on edge a little as they waited for something to happen. No one knew what to expect or when to expect it.

Then, just as abruptly as they had left, the disciples returned. John was vibrant. There was a change in Peter; the self-indulgent moping had been removed. Something had happened to him and the Eleven knew what it was. Even old Thaddaeus had a new spring in his step. They all were calm and peaceful. This was a report worth hearing. They had come up the stairs to a group of anticipating eyes. Everyone wanted answers, but no one knew what questions to ask. "Welcome back." "How are you all?" "Where is Jesus? Did you see him?" All they could do was smile and gesture to relax and wait. All would be reported in due time.

Shimon was delivering a couple of packages to the south side of the city and was just approaching the shop when Phinehas saw him and ran to greet him.

"They are back! They are back!" he reported excitedly, grabbing Shimon's hand and pulling him toward the shop.

"Who's back? What are you talking about?" The frame of reference is usually preferred before the information is given.

"Jesus's people! They are back from Galilee!"

"Ahhh. Okay, okay. I'm coming." he said as he picked up his pace.

Coming into the shop, Elihu met him with a smile. "I see you've been informed."

"Oh, yes. By special messenger!"

"Ezra happened to be close and heard. He brought us the news just a few minutes ago. The shop is buzzing with questions. Do you have any more deliveries for the day?" Elihu enquired. "If not, maybe you could go down and see what is happening."

"I believe I am free to do so." Shimon was excited to get in on the news. He quickly excused himself and headed toward town.

They had all got into just calling it "The Upper Room." Joseph funded it so they wouldn't have to worry about it. The disciples and followers had pretty much gotten away from the fear of the Romans or even the Jews. Everything was on an even keel and people came and went with no one feeling particularly watched. Shimon entered easily and was greeted by several. He noticed most of the Eleven were there getting settled. The room was humming with conversations all over. This wasn't going to be easy to sort out everything. Shimon went to his normal place to check on Mary. John was there talking to her. They had become increasingly close since the crucifixion. Shimon was becoming one of the family.

"Shalom, John. Welcome back! How did things go up north?"

"Thanks. It is good to be back," John sighed. "We have had quite an adventure."

"We are all interested. Tell us all about it."

"We've decided to tell everyone everything at once. That way we all get in on it at the same time. We can share it all without anyone feeling left out. We will gather together tonight. That will have to do for an answer."

"I guess it will," said Shimon. "I'm looking forward to it. May I bring Elihu and Ezra and a couple more?"

"Certainly. They are part of this story, aren't they?" John took a deep breath. "I need to rest up some before, though. If you will excuse me."

Mary got up and excused herself also; she went to help the others with getting food ready for those who had returned. Shimon greeted a few others and left to get the family.

Quite a crowd had gathered. Shimon had brought back Baruch, Elihu, Shimei, and Ezra. They all crammed into the Upper Room after greeting each other, acknowledging their interest. The lamps had been set, and the room was smoky and dim with the flickering. It was a warm evening, so the windows were open hoping for a cross breeze. The anticipation was growing. Many were expecting Jesus to show up. The Eleven came together at the end of the room.

Peter stood, took a deep breath, faced the crowd and began with his booming voice bringing everyone into submission. "Thank you all for coming. We have had a very great time in Galilee. It wasn't what any of us expected and none of us expected the same thing." A look of concern briefly crossed his face and then was replaced with an expression of resolve. "To begin with, you all may know about how I had denied Jesus the night he was taken. That weighed heavy on me. I felt like I couldn't be trusted and didn't deserve to be part of his disciples anymore. I went north with the others feeling like an outcast and doubting that God would use my life. When we first got there, I didn't know what to do and felt useless, so I decided to go back to fishing. Maybe I would be able to pick up my old way of life." His eyes dropped to the floor. The room was silent.

"It was a miserable night of fishing. We caught nothing. I was feeling like a complete failure. I denied my Lord and now I couldn't even fish. The sun had just come up when we saw a man on the shore. He called out asking if we had any fish. I thought he was someone wanting to buy from us, but we didn't have anything to show for the night's labor. Then the man shouted to us to throw the net on the right side of the boat. At this point it didn't matter what we tried, so, why not?" He was getting into the story and was gesturing openly, as he usually did.

"So, we threw the net on the other side of the boat and, Wham, the net was filled! We could barely hold on to it. Then John said as he looked toward shore, 'It's the Lord!' I couldn't believe it! I grabbed my tunic and threw myself into the water, swimming as hard as I could! There on the shore was Jesus, smiling at me. I wanted to be with him so badly, but I didn't feel I deserved to be. I didn't know what to do. He had a coal fire started with fish and bread on it. The others towed the net in. Jesus told me to get some of the fish, so I ran to the guys and we pulled the net ashore. We had one hundred and fifty-three fish! And the net didn't break! We had a magnificent breakfast with Jesus." Everyone was clapping and really getting into the story with cheers.

"After breakfast, we were all fellowshipping and resting from the long night of work. Some guys came by and offered to buy our fish. That was excellent. We didn't have to do anything with them. Well, we kept a few." He truly looked embarrassed as if he had been caught. "They Jesus looked at me. He said to me, 'Shimon, son of Jonah, (which is the name I went by before I met Jesus), Do you truly love me more than these?' I knew what I had done. I had no right to be close to him. So, I told him, 'Lord you know everything. You know I am fond of you.' His face showed the pain of the break of our relationship. 'Feed my lambs,' he told me.

"Then again he asked me, 'Shimon, son of Jonah, do you truly love me?' I said to him, 'Yes, Lord, you know that I am fond of you.' 'Shepherd my sheep,' he told me. I didn't understand everything he was telling me. Then he said, 'Shimon, son of Jonah, are you even fond of me?' It hurt like a knife to hear him ask me that way the third time. Then I told him, 'Lord you perceive all things. You know that I am fond of you.' He looked at me without any judgment. He tenderly smiled at me and told me, 'Feed my sheep.' He was giving me the opportunity to express my love for him after the denials I had committed. I wasn't strong enough. Then I realized he didn't want me to lie to him but to tell the truth of what was in my heart. He loved me with all my weakness and failures. He forgave me and my denials." By now it was hard for him to be understood since he was crying while he spoke. The emotions were deep throughout the room. People were remembering their failures and the things they had done wrong. People were looking within themselves to relate to what Peter was saying.

"That's when I realized the other thing he was trying to tell me," he said as he composed himself somewhat. He had used my former name, not the name he personally called me, so I would see that there isn't anything for me in my past life or career. I am a different man now. He also took away my old profession. I am no longer a fisherman for fish. He made me a shepherd of his people. That is why I am telling you all this. We are to share our experiences so everyone will benefit from them." The Holy Spirit within them was working with each person as they heard from Peter. There was a new dynamic at work in their lives. This was a time of great learning for all of them.

Peter sat down. There was a moment of silence in the room. James stood up after a while. He was becoming a leader in the group. "Thank you, Peter. That was the beginning of our time with Jesus. He told us many things, most of which we didn't understand, but we know that we will someday. What we did understand, though, is that we are being put in service to those who are believing into him. We have a message to give to those around us about the crucifixion, burial, and resurrection of Jesus. He died for our sins so we can be whole and pure. We are just beginning to understand some of these things. But the thing he told us that is to be our guide from now on is this: the commissioning of us to do what he did. He told us, 'Now that you are going, make disciples of every sort of people. Baptize them deep into the name of the Father, and into the name of the Son, and into the name of the Holy Spirit. Teach them to observe everything I have told you to do." As he spoke, his eyes drifted up until he was looking over the heads of the people and apparently gazing out into the distance. "Then he told us, 'Pay attention to this, I am with you always, even to the end of the age."

The people were staring at him blankly. It was occurring to some of them what was being said, while others were completely at a loss. The Eleven were deep into thought as they remembered what was said, knowing what was coming.

"Then he told us to wait in Jerusalem until we received the promise of the Father. None of us understood what that would be. We will, however, be obedient to it. Then he raised his hands over us and spoke such wonderful blessings." James faded off for a minute as if he was still seeing it happen. "Then, he started lifting off the ground while he was still blessing us. He faded out of view in a cloud and we saw him no more."

With that, the people gasped. They were waiting for news about where Jesus was and when he would be among them again. Now they heard that it wasn't going to happen. They weren't going to see him in the physical anymore as they had before. No one said a word. This news hit them very hard.

Mary let out a soft sob. Her son had left. Shimon put an arm around her. James continued, "That is why he told us he would be with us until the end of the age. He isn't gone, he is here with us all the time. He wants us to continue his work. His Spirit is in us. Remember, he told us that he would give us the Holy Spirit and the Holy Spirit would remind us of all the things he had said. He would lead us into all truth. He told us he would never leave us, nor forsake us. He is truly here; not in body at this time, but definitely here. We all can talk to him, and the Father, and the Holy Spirit anytime we want. If that is true, when we all go our separate ways, he will be with all of us. We have just expanded the work many times over. We just have to wait for the Holy Spirit to teach us how. That is why we must wait in Jerusalem. Something is coming. We must be patient."

The Eleven all were in agreement. They were nodding their heads, speaking agreement and coming into unity. That jelled the crowd into that same spirit of agreement and solidification. Then Mary let out an exclamation of surprise. Everyone turned to her. She looked up at them with a smile on her face in excitement. "When I calm myself and listen," she said quietly, "I can hear him and feel him. He is here!" She looked at Shimon putting her hand on his arm, "Can't you?"

That took Shimon by surprise. It took him a few seconds before he awoke to the fact that she wanted him to try. So he stopped doing anything, closed his eyes and spoke his name, "Jesus." He knew instantly Jesus was right there waiting. He felt the peace and joy he had felt before in his presence. Looking back at Mary he confessed, "Yes. Yes, I can." The room had a different atmosphere suddenly. Others were giving it a try with the same results. They were soon all feeling the presence of Jesus.

Elihu knew that the Jesus he had seen crucified and that he had believed into not too long ago, was standing right in front of him, even without a body. He giggled and turning caught Ezra's eye. Ezra burst out laughing. Shimon knew his family had again encountered the Lord Jesus.

This set them on this path forever. And he knew there was more to come.

After a week, things settled into a routine. There was nothing to do. Shimon and family went back to work. The Eleven stayed pretty close to the upper room. No one wanted to cause any attention to be drawn their way. All they knew was they were supposed to wait. So, wait they did.

Shimon made deliveries. He encountered the people who had been raised from the dead, making sure they knew everything that had happened. He had become fairly close to many of them, having deep, lengthy discussions. Kohath, the priest, had been reinstated into the work of the priesthood since they didn't know how old he was anymore. They didn't know when the fifty-year mark had hit for him to be disqualified. Shimon's discussions with him had stirred something in both of them to be able to remember little things from Sheol. They couldn't tell anyone else, but they had a good time talking to each other. The name Malachi still struck a familiar chord with both of them.

John had never been to the weaver's shop. He was excited to go because of the mission he had been given. As he came into the shop and stood there waiting for his eyes to adjust to the lack of light, he was recognized by Elihu.

"John! What a pleasant surprise! What brings you to the weaver's shop?" Elihu stepped out from behind his loom and stepped to greet their guest. "In the market for more table cloths?"

"No, no. Nothing like that," he said with a defensive smile and his hands motioning the blocking of what was coming to him. I have come to bring some news and ask for a favor. Is Shimon here?"

"Uh, I'm not sure," Elihu said as he looked around. "I never know when he is here or not. He is in and out all the time." As he was speaking Shimei came in with a load of goods. He saw John and brightened up considerably. "Shimei, have you seen Shimon? John is looking for him."

"Greetings. Welcome to our shop." As if he were looking for something he lost, he stated, "He should be back by now. He makes unscheduled stops during the day. He is pretty hard to keep track of. Isaac, have you seen Shimon?"

Isaac was just coming in from the direction of the house. "Yes. He is with Baruch in the courtyard. Hi," he said to John as he noticed who it was in their doorway. John nodded at him smiling.

"Well, there you have it," Shimei concluded. "He is right this way."

"Actually, I am here for all of you." John put a halt on all activity by saying that. They all were looking at him now with shared inquisitive looks. "If you would be so kind, I want to tell him and all of you at the same time. I think it would save a lot of time."

Shimei was the boss, so he responded first. "Okay. Isaac, get Uriah and Ezra and meet us in the courtyard, please. Gentlemen," he spoke with a sweeping gesture of his arm inviting them all to head toward the courtyard.

They all arrived as a parade flooding from the house, quite interrupting and surprising Shimon and Baruch as they sat across from one another in conversation. "What's this?" said Shimon and then recognized John. "Oh, well we have a guest!"

John came through and presented himself to Shimon and Baruch. Shimon stood to greet him, Baruch was the elder and didn't need to stand.

"What do we give the honor of your coming to us this fine day?" Shimon asked their guest.

"I am here to bring some news, and I wanted to speak to all of you if I could."

"Certainly." Shimon motioned to a spot at the end of the courtyard where he could stand and address everyone. The others had come in from the shop quite filling the courtyard. They were all listening attentively.

"A couple of days ago, Shimon came to the Upper Room and announced that Jesus had talked to him. We were all very pleased at that, but part of it caught us off guard. It hadn't occurred to any of us that we should baptize anyone after their encounter with giving their lives to Jesus. He had taught us to baptize and so did John the Prophet that preceded Jesus. We had never guessed why we were taught that in the first place. Now it makes sense. It is an act that pronounces to everyone that we are uniting ourselves to his death, burial and resurrection. We will be marked as followers of our Lord Jesus, the Messiah."

All of them were stunned into silence. They had no idea what to say to that. "Therefore," John continued, "we are inviting you all to come with us tomorrow to the pool of Siloam for baptism like we did at the beginning of his ministry. What do you think?"

They were all speechless. They were looking around at each other waiting for someone to say something. Finally, Shimon took his place as the head of this family. "Uh, this is more than I had expected or even dreamt about," he stammered. "What an honor! We will gladly accept this most gracious invitation." He could see the faces of those around him in complete agreement. The smiles told him they were very pleased. "What time?"

John was enjoying their response. "We were thinking about the third hour, about this time tomorrow. Does that meet with your approval?"

"As if you needed our approval!" Shimon said. "We will be there."

"It isn't only your family we want there," John said directly to Shimon. "You know who had been raised and the ones who have believed on Jesus since the resurrection. Can you get the word out? We want them all to be part of this."

Shimon felt like they had given him a mission to accomplish and it fulfilled something in his heart about doing something for the greater good. His heart swelled with joy and pride as he took on this mission. "I would be so honored to do that," he said beaming, holding his hand to his heart. "It will take some time to find everyone, but, if I get started right away, shouldn't be a problem."

"Great!," John concluded. That should about do it. We look forward to seeing you all at the Pool of Siloam tomorrow morning.

He wasn't kidding. Shimon left almost immediately after the meeting with John. So much for any deliveries today, there were many people to find all over the city. His first stop was the synagogue to see Gershom. It was very pleasing to Gershom to hear about the baptism. Shimon asked him to help. If they split up the city, they should be able to get ahold of just about everyone. Gershom went west and north. Shimon had the south and east of town.

He went to the temple and found Kohath who was extremely excited about this. They found a few folks they needed while they were at the Temple. The next place was the market. Several people were there they were looking for. Now they had hit the biggest public places; it was left to go to individual dwellings. That was the part that took the most time. Some were home; some weren't.

Shimon was getting a little tired and frustrated. He stopped for a while to sit in the shade and rest. It occurred to him he wasn't being wise about this. Bowing his head where he sat, he started praying, "Lord God. I am sorry for doing this in myself. I can't do this. You know where everyone is and how to find them. I need your help. I believe it is your will for them to come tomorrow, so I need to tell them today. Please, help me find people and to talk to the ones you want me to talk to. Thank you for your love for us."

He was learning he wasn't alone anymore. He had the Lord with him all the time. The thing he had to learn was to remember that and talk to the Lord. It would make things much more fulfilling.

Once he had that in mind and put in the Lord's hands, he took a deep breath and stood up ready to continue. Although, now it felt like there was a plan and he could trust the Lord for it. This was so different than the life he had lived for so many decades. This is much better.

He made it through his territory and contacted everyone he knew about. He went back to the synagogue to check on Gershom. He was getting very hungry and tired. He had covered a lot of territory.

Entering the synagogue, he headed to the back room. As he entered, he saw Gershom sitting with his sandals off and his feet up on the table. Shimon laughed at seeing that and related to the attitude being displayed. "Wear you out, did it?" he quipped as he sat down across the table from Gershom.

Gershom snickered a little. "I'm not used to walking all that much anymore. People come here to see me. I'm exhausted."

"How did you do?"

"I got everyone I knew of. I'm sure they will invite others they know about. I know I am going to bring my wife and son. How many people do you think that will be?"

Shimon took a breath as he contemplated the answer. "Hard to say. I think it's about eighty folks or so. It will be quite a crowd for Siloam. The pool isn't that big. But I don't know much about this baptism thing. I am aware of the ritual mikvahs, but I'm not sure they are the same thing. I guess we will have to learn from the disciples." He was thinking and he got quiet. Then the thought occurred to him and with a quizzical look at Gershom, he asked, "You're a Rabbi, don't you know about this stuff?"

"I was wondering how long it would take you to come to that," he said as he shook his head. "I went out to the Jordan to see what everyone was talking about when that Prophet, what was his name? Oh, yeah, John was baptizing out there. I watched and listened. It made sense about washing away your sins by faith with actions to follow, but I didn't see how it was something I needed to do. Now I wish I had learned more. This faith in Jesus is different than he was preaching. I guess I will learn more tomorrow."

It was a rather small pool, very long but quite narrow. It was only about thigh deep and the poor would come here to bathe. It had stone steps on both sides allowing access from all directions. The upper end was a tunnel coming from the Gihon spring. This was the best source of water for quite a ways and was used by most folks in the southern end of Jerusalem. The stone steps made for easy benches so many could see what was happening.

The Eleven stood at the north end where the water came out of the tunnel. They could be seen and heard by anyone from that place. They waited as people were coming from all over the area of Jerusalem. Shimon, Baruch, and family were there in force. It was becoming increasingly difficult for Baruch to get around. Shimon thought it interesting that he would be there to help him. Nothing, though, was going to stop him from being here. His three sons were there with wives and sons and daughters and spouses and kids; in all there were 22 members of his family present.

Others were joining them. Kohath and sons and wives, Gershom and his wife and son, Levi's Aunt Martha who had been raised and her family of four, were all there in anticipation of what this meant. By the time they started, there were around ninety people present.

James stood up and quieted the crowd. He had shown himself to be a good leader. He was with Peter and John as the ones that were closest to Jesus. He spoke with a calm assurance and a strong voice. "Thank you for coming today. It is a very important day for me and the other disciples that traveled with Jesus. This day is one that will help us become what Jesus called us to be." He took a breath as he remembered some of the things they had been told. He could feel the presence of the Holy Spirit as he continued.

"We had been taught to baptize at the beginning of our days with Jesus, but we didn't know where it would lead us. Jesus continually reminded us of his future, but we didn't catch that either. We were caught completely off guard by his trial and execution on the cross. It was devastating. Our future was gone. We were left with nothing but emptiness. Then came the resurrection from the dead! We have never recovered from that. And may we never!" He received some comments from the Eleven for that. The rest of the crowd was getting onto what was said. Shimon was wholeheartedly wrapped up in the words.

"Then, the night after he raised from the dead, Jesus came to us. He gave us the Holy Spirit and our lives were changed forever. Since that time, we have been meditating and wondering about everything we had been taught. We were still completely puzzled about what we were to do. Jesus showed himself to several people, by last count about five hundred people have seen him. Through those contacts, we were instructed to go to Galilee. There we met with Jesus and were commissioned to do his work throughout the whole earth, starting in Jerusalem. We still have no idea how to do that. He told us to stay in Jerusalem until we receive the promise of the Father. We are waiting for whatever that may turn out to be. But in the meantime, it had come to our attention about baptism." Jacov nodded at Shimon with an acknowledging smile. Shimon returned it with a little bow.

"Which brings us to today," James continued. "We are going to start with the Eleven. We will baptize them first and then they will carry on the ministry by carrying it to the rest of you." He had to get the order of it out of the way so he didn't have to think about it anymore. Now he was free to explain more about it.

"When we baptized in the Jordan a few years back, we were shown how. It didn't make sense, but it does now. Before, we were doing something that seemed like a ritual we had seen done before in the ritual mikvah of cleansing. The idea then was to be completely submerged in water to show we are completely submitting to the cleansing of our sins by repenting. Some did it every day, knowing it didn't wash away anything. We didn't feel differently afterward, only wet. Then Jesus died, was buried, and rose from the dead. That is exactly what happened to us as we died in him. He died as our substitute. He took away our sin. This water of baptism is a show for everyone to know that we are forever linked to Jesus's death, burial, and resurrection. We are marked by others to be associated with Jesus from this day forward. It is a symbol of our death in him. We are raised to be in his service forever!" James had increased his fervor steadily as he went along. The crowd was snatched up in his message. Each of them felt the power of what was said. "Are you in agreement to this?" He looked around the crowd as he brought it home for each of them.

Shimon stood staring Jacov in the eyes. "Yes, I am! I want everyone to know I am a believer in Jesus the Messiah and what he has done for me!" Baruch stood with him and the entire crowd started standing in agreement one at a time until everyone was standing.

James was overcome with emotion. He raised his hands to heaven with his face tilting up and his eyes closed. "Lord God Almighty. We are here in your presence to be obedient to your word. Bless us as we walk this out before you."

It took a moment for anyone to do anything but pray and submit to the Holy Spirit. James opened his eyes and looked over to the Eleven. "Peter. Will you come here and baptize me, please?"

Peter was having trouble getting a grip on his emotions. His new calling was very recent and something he was trying to wrap his mind around. Now he was being called out to start a new ministry. He was humbled beyond words. He stepped into the water and walked to the center as James stepped in and came to him. Peter held James with a hand on his chest and a hand on his back. "My brother, James. Do you now give testimony to all those around that you are bound to Jesus the Messiah for the rest of your life? Do you acknowledge that you are showing your death, burial, and resurrection with him to live for him and him alone?"

James closed his eyes as tears streamed down his face. "Yes," he spoke with a trembling voice choked by tears. "I do!"

As he lowered James backward into the water, Peter said, "Be baptized, my brother, in the name of Jesus." Peter lowered him completely into the water and raised him back up to stand. "You are now linked to Jesus for your entire life. Be blessed!"

James stood there overwhelmed with joy as he worshipped the Lord God for bringing salvation to men. As he opened his eyes, he turned and gave Peter a huge hug with great enthusiasm. Peter was surprised for a second and then participated in the hug and the laughter that ensued.

James stepped to the side around Peter and grabbed him. "Are you ready?" Peter was surprised again, but only for an instant.

"Absolutely!"

James spoke out very loudly, "Peter have you taken Jesus and the salvation he bought for us as your own?"

"Yes, I have!"

James had a little trouble taking the big man down, but got him under control and put him completely under the water and groaned trying to get him back out. After some effort, Peter stood before them all. He was beaming in delight. He needed this.

After a short time of celebration, James and Peter took some of the other eleven and began baptizing them. James took his little brother, John, and that was intensely personal for them both. They saw the value of keeping it in the family.

As each one was finished, they spread out down the pool and made a line of people baptizing people. Shimon went to James. He wanted to do it for his family. They lined up behind him and it was a deep time of great personal involvement, bring the things of the Holy Spirit into the family. There was shouting and laughing as they all celebrated the beauty of what the Lord was doing in them. Eventually, everyone was wet.

There were people watching from the steps, wondering what was going on. If they listened, they would have heard it all. These people were telling everyone they were part of what Jesus did. The name of Jesus was being promoted and heralded to the people.

Shimon and his family walked back to the shop. Everyone was dripping, but the dry Israeli air was drying them off fairly quickly. They were laughing and carrying on with each other as if they had just come from a party where wine was flowing. It was still before midday, but that didn't seem to matter. This was a day to remember.

CHAPTER 9
Use of the Cloth

Jerusalem was getting crowded as normal as Pentecost was coming up. It is the feast of the Spring wheat harvest. The Eleven had called people to come and pray with them, as many as could. Since most were taking the day off as a feast day, they had garnered quite a group. This is also called the Feast of Weeks, since it was a week of weeks since Passover; seven weeks and this is the day after making it the 50th day. The men of the Shimon family had decided to come to the Upper Room to pray with the Eleven. They had gone early since they tended to be early day type people anyway.

It had been a week since the baptism. Gershom had told Shimon that several of the Eleven had been to the synagogue regularly to look through the scrolls. They were trying to find references to things Jesus had told them. The one that surprised Gershom was Peter. He was the least likely to spend time studying the scrolls, but he had become the most energetic and spent the most time with the scrolls. He seemed to be looking for something in particular, but Gershom couldn't get him to talk about it or ask for help. Peter appeared to be getting more and more introspective.

The day of Pentecost, Peter was with the others in the Upper Room, but he was more to himself. He wasn't the usual loud and boisterous person he had been for so long. Something was on his mind; he was serious and focused.

John welcomed Shimon as they came in. Shimon went to Mary and greeted her warmly. He sat next to them being friendly and casual. John and Mary were usually together, so joining them was normal for Shimon. He had felt all day that something was going to happen, but he had no idea what it might be. They had arrived an hour after sunrise. People were coming in by two's and three's, filling the Upper Room. Everyone had to make their way through crowds of people from everywhere; the city was very busy today.

James stood to talk to the people who had come. "We asked you to come today because it is the Feast of Weeks, the celebration of the Spring harvest. We wanted to spend time in prayer. There is a great need for the world to be harvested in so many ways. We all seem to be wandering without direction. We are waiting for the promise of the Father, like Jesus said. We don't really know what that means, but our hearts yearn for the Father to work among us."

As he spoke, he looked around the room and saw that those who came were in agreement with the purpose here. There were new faces and old faces, but everyone was in unity. He continued, "Please, let us pray together for what the Father wants. Each one pray to the Lord God of Israel to work in us today. Let's lift up His name and worship him together."

Each person focused their attention to praying. There were pockets of people crying, pleading, or reciting Psalms. The atmosphere of the room was peaceful with individuals imploring God. Every once in a while spontaneous worship would break out. This extended time didn't weigh heavy on anyone; they just continued to pray.

Then, as if a dam burst, there came a sound that was nearly deafening. It was like a roaring sound that permeated everything. It hit the room with force, flooding through with a swirling power as if it were on a strong wind. It took people's breath away leaving them in awe of the intense power. As they looked around trying to figure out what was happening, small flames of fire appeared at the ceiling, falling on them, but not like any fire they had ever seen. It didn't burn anyone or cause any fear. Each flame fell on a certain person, one at a time. As the flame came to a person, it only landed on their head, growing as it hit, until everyone had one on them. The flames ignited a force inside them. They spontaneously burst out in praise, telling of the mighty works of God in excited and forceful terms. They were soon shouting their praises in focused worship to the Lord God.

It being a warm day, all the windows were open. The people in the streets heard the sound of the forceful wind. It drew them all toward the building. As they approached the building, they could hear the people in their praises.

One of the men told those close to him, "I hear him in my native language!"

Another one said, "I do, too!"

Peter noticed the crowd outside growing as they came to see what this sound was. He motioned to the Eleven. "Come. These folks want to know what is happening. We need to get out there."

They went to the stairs and, still in their ecstasy, went out to the landing at the bottom. Most of them were still speaking their praises, but each person they came close to, heard them speaking in their own personal dialect they were born to.

One man close said in unbelief, "He is talking in perfect Parthian. How is this possible?"

The man standing next to him, looked at him as if he were crazy. "No, he isn't. It is flawless Egyptian!" The word was spreading through the crowd. They were amazed.

"How can this be? They are dressed like Galileans! These aren't educated men! How did they learn all these languages?" The crowd was trying to put this in context, and it wasn't working.

Finally, someone said, "This must be alcohol speaking. These men are just drunk!"

"What? Since when does wine give you new languages. All it does is make you slur your speech. What are you talking about?"

What everyone heard though, was great deeds the Lord God had done and praises to His name. Others were coming out of the Upper Room, spilling out into the street speaking as they had never spoken before. The crowd was getting mixed up, some in wonder, others in mockery. The wine theory was promoted by the mockers.

But standing up with the Eleven, Peter lifted up his booming, bass voice and spoke out to them, "Men, Jews, and all those living in Jerusalem, let this be known to you, and listen to my words. For these are not drunk, as you imagine, for it is only the third hour of the day." He stepped up on the landing so he could be heard better. The mockers had been answered and something kept them from continuing.

"But this is that which has been spoken by the prophet Joel, 'And it shall be' in the last days, God says, 'I will pour from My Spirit on all flesh, and your sons and your daughters shall prophesy;' 'and your young men shall see visions,' 'and your old men shall dream dreams.' 'and also I will pour out My spirit on My slaves and slave women in those days,' and they shall prophesy. And I will give wonders in the heaven above,'" he stretched out his hand to point out the loud sound coming from heaven. "And miraculous signs 'on the earth below, blood and fire and vapor of smoke. The sun will be turned into darkness, and the moon into blood, before the' 'coming of the great and glorious' 'day of the Lord.'" He paused for them to let the meaning sink in a little.

Looking directly into the eyes of those hearing, he continued, "'And it shall be that every one who shall call on the name of the Lord will be saved.' Men, Israelites, hear these words: Jesus the Nazarene, a man from God, having been approved among you by works of power and wonders and miraculous signs, which God did through him in your midst, as you yourselves also know." Peter was now being very pointed about what he was saying. He saw Pharisees and Priests among the people in the crowd. "The One given to you by the before-determined purpose and foreknowledge of God, you having taken by lawless hands, having crucified him, you killed him. But God raised him up, loosing the throes of death, because it was not possible for him to be held by it." He could see that it wasn't only the Jewish leaders who understood they were part of his crucifixion. Many of these men were in that crowd that day. The word about Jesus had spread.

Peter was now grasping the scripture he had been digging into all week. He was prepared. "For David said as to him, 'I always foresaw the Lord before Me, because he is at my right hand, that I not be moved. For this reason, my heart rejoiced, and my tongue was glad; and my flesh also will dwell on hope, because You will not leave my soul in Sheol, nor will You give Your Holy One to see corruption. You reveal to me paths of life; You will fill me with joy with Your face." The words were having quite an effect on the crowd. Peter could see it in their faces. Now was not the time to stop, but to press in.

Taking a deep breath, be proceeded, "Men, brothers, it is permitted to say to you with plainness as to the patriarch David, that he both died and was buried, and his tomb is among us until this day. Being a prophet, then, and knowing that God swore with an oath to him that of the fruit of his loin, as concerning flesh, to raise up the Messiah to sit on his throne, foreseeing, he spoke about the resurrection of the Messiah, 'that his soul was not left in Sheol not did his flesh see corruption.' This Jesus, God raised up, of which we all are witnessed. Then being exalted to the right hand of God, and receiving the promise of the Holy Spirit from the Father, He poured out this which you now see and hear. For David did not ascend into heaven, but he says, 'the Lord said to my Lord, sit at My right hand until I place those hostile to you as a footstool for your feet.' Then assuredly, let all the house of Israel acknowledge that God made him both Lord and Messiah, this same Jesus whom you crucified."

The effect was amazing. It was nothing anyone expected. The look on the faces of the people around them was near terror. They had seen with their own eyes and heard with their own ears the power of God. Now this man told them it was their fault for crucifying the man called Jesus who just happened to be the Son of God! And he was alive again! Now they were being held personally responsible! The conviction of their sin went through the crowd like a wave. They had no defense against this.

One man standing close to Peter caught his eye. The man said in despair, "What are we to do?"

Another cried out, "How can we change that?"

Peter looked them straight in the face addressing them, but in a way to address everyone. "Repent and be baptized, each of you on the name of Jesus the Messiah to remission of sins. And you will receive the gift of the Holy Spirit. For the promise is to you and to your children, and to all those afar off, as many as the Lord our God shall call."

The first man said to Peter, "Yes. I want to do that. Will you help me?"

"Me, too," another said vehemently. Many were speaking the same things as they started coming to the Eleven.

Peter saw there was a problem. They didn't expect people actually to receive what they had to say. Now they were. What do we do now? Peter looked at James with a "now what?" look. James stood up beside Peter but was looking at the Eleven, not the crowd. "Spread out," he told them. "Take as many as you can and explain to them how repentance works. If they do repent and seek Jesus for salvation, take them to Siloam or up to Bethesda and baptize them. We have our work cut out for us. Try to keep track of how many and possibly who is baptized. They are marked as one of us as soon as they do that. Go! May God be with you all!"

Peter knew others were trying to understand what was happening, so he stayed in the same place and talked to as many as he could. As they would submit to acknowledging their sin and trusting in the blood of Jesus to cleanse them, he would send them to one of the pools as he saw the other disciples heading out to take people there.

James knew there was more to be done. He moved to the stairs and went up them at a good clip. As he reached the door to the Upper Room, he was met with many faces, wondering what to do. Raising his hands to calm them and gather their focus, he told them, "Friends. You have been with us for a while and have prayed with us. Today we have experienced the Holy Spirit coming on each of us. He is doing a mighty work that we are all called to be part of. He will guide you into doing what you need to do. Right now we have a huge crowd of people that are asking about our Father God and the salvation Jesus bought for us. Please, let God direct you to whom you need to speak and what you need to say. We will need all the help we can get to get done all we need to today."

The faces all started gelling into resolve. Each one saw what they needed to do. It was time to get it done.

"So, go. This is the work Jesus has given us. May we be blessed in the doing." James's words were like igniting a fire in them. They gathered into small groups of people who had an interest in doing similar things. Many went down to help outside. Some talked to people; others helped move them to where they needed to be, others still escorted them to one of the pools for baptism. Each of them, however, found themselves praying as they worked and very often it was in a language they didn't understand. Sometimes it was a language someone there needed to hear and could understand in their own tongue, but sometimes it was just an intimate language between that person and the Lord.

Everyone was involved somehow, and it took the rest of the day to do what had been started early on. It was close to sundown when Shimon and company made it back to the shop. As they approached the door, there was Jerusha standing, watching for them. She was visibly relieved to see them coming. "Oh, there you are," she sighed. "You left early, and nothing was heard from you the rest of the day.

We were really wondering. I sent Phinehas to find you, and he came back saying there was a huge crowd gathered and all sorts of things happening. He didn't find any of you."

Shimei smiled at her as he got up close and gave her a big hug of greeting. She received it and after a few seconds backed off a little and looked at her husband closely. "What's happened? What is different about you?"

He smiled at her again trying to give some assurance. He took her hand gently with both of his. "We have had quite a day, my dear." He took a breath to tell her but realized there was too much to tell. "Why don't we just go in and have some supper. We haven't eaten all day, and there is so much to tell you about."

She looked at him and then turned to examine the others. It was obvious they had all changed somehow. There were peace and joy with a calm confidence all over them. "This has got to be good," she thought to herself. "Then come on in. We have everything ready."

They all moved slowly into the family area where things were all set up. Ruth, Dinah, and Tamar were bringing in food and drink as they entered. Isaac was greeted quickly and quietly by Dinah, but Ruth almost bowled people over trying to get to Ezra. She wasn't used to him not telling her where he was. Uriah decided to go home; the family was waiting for him there. Keturah was in the kitchen with Boaz bringing in firewood. Shimon came in the door and stood by the door watching his family. Baruch hadn't come today; he wasn't feeling well. He and Susannah were in their room waiting for the family to come home.

Shimon was trying to get his thoughts together. How was he going to tell this to the family? So much had happened. It had only been forty-seven days since he rose from the dead. How does one even register all that in their brain? But here he was; watching as his family came together after the incredible blessing they had seen today. Was it all a dream? What blessings had come his way. He just observed and tried to keep from crying with joy.

They had dinner with everyone laughing and eating. It was a little more boisterous than normal. The men seemed like they were merrier and less inhibited. They almost acted as if they were a little drunk, but none of them had been drinking. The women watching them were very pleased with what they saw and also quite perplexed. Baruch was also interested, seeing how the others had somehow been changed. He was getting caught up in the merriment along with the children. Finally, after dinner was served, eaten and nearly cleared, Shimon took a good long breath and said, "Well, I guess you are all wondering what happened to us today."

That did it. Everyone quieted almost immediately, paying rapt attention. Shimon laughed at how quickly that happened, seeing every eye on him.

"We have been waiting for something else to happen, especially since Jesus told the Eleven to wait in Jerusalem for the promise of the Father. Today we went to the Upper Room to pray. There were over a hundred of us in there. So we started praying. That's what they called us to do anyway. We did, but it wasn't long after that something big happened." They were all hanging on every word.

"We heard a sound," he continued softly as he built the mystery of the story. "It was incredibly loud, coming from above us. It sounded like the room was filled with a very strong, powerful wind. But there was no wind! Then, suddenly, flames of fire appeared at the ceiling spreading all over the room, but it wasn't burning anything. Then the flames dropped down on all of us until every single person there had a flame on their head!" He paused to let that sink in. Then growing his narrative with gestures and raising his voice he went on. "As soon as the flame touched me, my whole body tingled, and I felt like I was going to be lifted off the floor! My whole body and soul were filled up with the presence of God as if he had taken us and dunked us completely into the Holy Spirit!" As he said that, he noticed every man who had been in that room this morning looked like they were experiencing it all over again.

"I knew we were filled to overflowing and I couldn't just sit there doing nothing. I had to worship my God. As I opened my mouth to praise Him, a language I had never heard before came out of my mouth! I was astonished! It sounded weird, but felt wonderful! I was speaking without understanding what I was saying. But I knew it was of God and about God. I didn't want to quit. I looked around and that was happening to everyone around me!" Each of the other men was speaking agreement and shaking their heads, wiping away tears. The room was filled with wonder and joy.

"I really don't know how long it went on like that, but a commotion was stirring outside, so I made it to the window. Peter and the Eleven had gone down to the street. It seems that everyone heard the noise of the wind and then heard all of us talking all at the same time. I found out later that the men of the city all heard us and understood us in their own native tongue! How does that happen? This is certainly something God was doing."

"Then Peter began to speak. It wasn't like anything he had ever done before. He proclaimed Jesus to the crowd and quoted the Prophet Joel about how the Spirit was going to be poured out and then told the crowd that this is the fulfillment of that prophesy! This was the promise of the Father! He poured out the Spirit on us today!"

Shimon scoped the room at the conclusion of his story to see everyone completely caught up in what he was telling them. He was experiencing a great deal of joy, and his body language and facial expression showed it.

"The Eleven had us help them as the crowd received what was being said to them. Peter had invited people to join us by believing and repenting of their sins. He told them the proof of their repentance was being baptized and being marked as a believer in Jesus. So, the rest of the day we were helping the Eleven baptize all those who came. It was around three thousand people!" He knew that was the total the Eleven had decided on as the counts from both pools came in. "We are no longer a small band of people hiding our beliefs. We are now known to the people of

Jerusalem! It is time for us to stand out and let people know who we are and what we believe."

The little crowd of his family was excited and clapped and spoke out their agreement. It was quite a rally they were having together. Shimon had never been a public speaker, but he could feel the Spirit working in him. He was becoming more than he had ever known possible. It thrilled him in a very unexpected way.

As the applause died down to everyone just laughing with each other, Baruch asked a question that quieted the room. Others had this same question, and now it was out there waiting for an answer. "What about the ones who didn't go today? Was that the only time the Spirit will be poured out? Are we not able to to get in on this?"

"I asked John that very question," Shimon responded to him firmly, yet quietly. "He said Jesus had told them that when the Spirit was given to us as it was on the day of resurrection, that the Spirit would remind them of what Jesus had told them. John remembered that Jesus told them the Father would give the Holy Spirit to anyone who asked Him. We came to the understanding that anyone who asks for this immersion into the Holy Spirit will get it! I wanted this for the rest of us. It is now open to any of you who wants it!"

The joy Shimon had felt was now flooding the room. "If you want it, all you have to do right now is ask Jesus for it. He will baptize you in the Holy Spirit. That is what John the Baptizer said he would do. So, who here wants it?" Baruch burst into tears of anticipation. The wives all were jumping in on this. The younger generation was jumping right in. Phinehas looked like he was coming out of his skin with excitement. Those that were praying were being filled as they received the Holy Spirit on them. There were people speaking languages that no one knew all over the room. It was a night to remember. The family of Shimon, the weaver, would never be the same.

The next day, Shimon went to the Upper Room after his rounds to report what had happened to them. John and Mary were there together. The place was next to chaotic with all the people doing many, many things. Shimon got John's attention finally and calmed him down for a minute to ask what was going on.

"We are not prepared to deal with so many people and what all happened yesterday. We have a throng of people who want to know everything. We don't have enough people to go around to explain it, so we are having to do it in groups. We don't even know what all happened and why. We are just getting glimpses of Jesus's teachings."

"Are you getting any reports in about this continuing on others? Are more being baptized in the Holy Spirit?"

John's shoulders dropped and a look of resignation covered his face. "Oh, yeah. It is happening everywhere. God is doing a mighty work, and we aren't able to keep up with it. What do we do with three thousand people? And the number is growing all the time!"

Shimon just grasped John's shoulders, looking him in the eye with the calm assurance that comes with age. "Relax. God wouldn't do it if he wasn't going to help us get it all done."

John looked as if he had been slapped. "You are so correct. Our discussion last night among ourselves brought us the understanding to a degree. Jesus told us that we would have the power to heal, cast out evil spirits, basically everything He did because of the power of the Holy Spirit in us and on us. It is so hard to remember that. There is so much to get used to; so much to learn."

"What we need," Shimon said, "is to spend some of that time praying. I am sure he wants us to ask him for help and guidance. Don't you think?"

With a sigh, John bowed his head a little. "That is why we need men with wisdom. Maybe we should make that an integral part of what we do. I will bring that to James." Then, after a quick breath, John looked up at Shimon. "Is that why you have come today? To bring us into line?"

"No, but if that helps…" he said with a smile. "Actually I wanted to tell you that our family received the Holy Spirit last night. It comes to all who ask, just like you said. We will never be the same. Is there anything else about it you know? This is all so new to us."

"Not really. This is new for us also, remember? We think it is how the Holy Spirit equips us to do what we need to do."

A little laugh off to the side attracted their attention. Turning, they found Mary laughing at them good-naturedly. "What's so funny?" John asked her.

"God is doing such amazing new things and we find ourselves right in the middle of it without knowing what we are doing. It sounds like Him, though, doesn't it? He brought the Messiah to a fourteen-year-old to bear and raise, who didn't know anything about that either," she said. "I think He enjoys doing this to people!"

They all three were tickled at that. John finally stated, "That is why we need to pray more, huh?" They nodded to each other in agreement.

John took his new tidbit to James and Peter, who immediately saw it was the correct course of action to take. James relinquished the "take-charge" attitude he was gaining. "Let's send word to each of the Eleven that we must take the time to pray with each other. It is a little chaotic to give a place right now in here," he surmised. "Let's spread it out some."

"We are already trying to spread out the breaking of bread to various houses so the burden isn't in just one place," added John. "We could do the same for prayer and fellowship."

Peter came into the conversation, adding, "We could also go to the Temple for prayer times. It isn't far. Maybe our prayers can help affect the religious leaders so they will see us as the followers of Jesus and accept him. We need to do things in the sight of the priests and Jews."

"Good point. Peter!" James saw that he wasn't the only one who had to come up with answers. He had been feeling the burden of things come on him. Now he was noticing that these ideas were being given to people by the Holy Spirit. He felt he could relax more and trust in the Lord to lead people into the various ministries that were needed. "Let's get everyone together this evening and talk this through. We need to organize and not forget to hear from God."

"It's getting close to the ninth hour prayer at the Temple," Peter noted. "John, do you want to go with me to the Temple? We can get started by getting into prayer right now."

Peter and John left for the Temple right away so as not to miss the time of prayer. As they approached the Temple, they were coming to the stairs leading up to the front gate. There were many people milling about and heading in and out of the Temple. There was one man, though, that stuck out in Peter' mind. A beggar.

This man was lame in both legs, having been born deformed. His family carried him to the Temple stairs every day. His income was a major part of the family resources because of the obvious visual deformity. This wasn't an act; he really needed to beg. He was well versed in how to get people's attention and knew how to capitalize on it when someone looked at him. He saw Peter and John coming and watched to see if they would look at him.

Peter saw him, and something happened inside of him. Compassion, like he had never felt before, hit him without warning. It made him catch his breath a little and he felt deep within him that God was in this moment. He couldn't take his eyes off the man. John saw what was happening and looked at the man intently to see what was going on.

The beggar saw they were looking at him. He knew he was about to receive something from them and brightened his face towards them. "Alms," he said as he stretched out his hand toward them.

"Look to us," Peter spoke firmly. The man was totally expecting money now. His heart on fire, Peter took the man's hand, startling him. No one had touched him before. "We don't have any silver or gold, but what we do have, I give you. In the name of Jesus Christ the Nazarene, stand up and walk!"

Power surged through the man's legs like lightning. He gasped loudly and looked down in time to see both of his feet snap around to the proper alignment. The muscles started growing on his calves. He flexed his feet back and forth, up and down. He watched them as if he had never seen feet work before.

Peter hadn't let go of his hand, but started pulling him up. The idea of standing was completely foreign to him, but now it was breaking through his consciousness. Is it possible? With a little effort, he started to stand. He realized he wasn't going to fall and there was no pain. He stood upright to his full height, still looking with wonder into the eyes of the man holding his hand.

When he was standing on his own, Peter let go. The man had full understanding that he had been healed. He was now able to walk like any other man. He bent his legs, testing the theory. Seeing that everything was as if he had always walked, he took a few steps. That worked! He bounced from one leg to the other, cautiously at first, then more and more enthusiastically. Soon he was jumping up and down, taking huge leaps into the air. He wasn't silent about it, either. He was shouting, laughing, hooting, yelling at people to look at him, and screaming that he had been healed.

Many people around recognized him as the beggar that had sat at this gate for years. Amazement filtered through the crowd, drawing them closer for a good look. Peter and John were thrilled. They understood that God was using them now in a way like He used Jesus. They were beyond happy.

They didn't want the attention on themselves, necessarily. They wanted the attention to be turned to the Lord God of Israel who healed this man. The man was telling everyone about God and praising him and was throwing the name of Jesus around. It was now known what was happening.

Continuing on into the Temple, Peter and John were trying to just go on with the mission they were on to go pray. The man, however, had other plans. He wouldn't let them go. He went with them. These men had a connection to God. He wanted to get in on this and let everyone know what had happened to him through this Jesus.

They made it to the top of the stairs and tried to go in, but couldn't make it into the gate. They were pressed on by the crowd that had gathered. Peter stopped and turned to meet them. He felt the Spirit just like he had yesterday as he spoke to the crowd.

"Men, Israelites, why do you marvel at this one? Or why do you stare at us, as if by our own power or godliness we have made him to walk? The God of Abraham and Isaac and James, the God of our fathers, glorified His child Jesus, whom you delivered up, and denied him in the presence of Pilate, that one having decided to set him free. But you denied the Holy and Just One, and asked for a man, a murderer, to be granted to you. And the Author of Life you killed, whom God raised up from the dead, of which we are witnesses." Peter was now looking at the individual faces in the crowd. He was speaking to people whom the Lord God loved. He wanted them set free. He saw the intent of the Lord.

"On the faith of his name, this one whom you see and know was made firm by his name, and the faith which came through him gave to him this complete soundness before you all. And now, brothers, I know that you acted according to ignorance, as also did your rulers. But what things God before proclaimed through the mouth of all His prophets that the Messiah should suffer, He fulfilled in this manner. Therefore, repent, and convert, for the blotting out of your sins, so that times of refreshing may come from the face of the Lord., and that He may send for the one before proclaimed to you, Jesus the Messiah, whom Heaven truly needs to receive until the times of restoration of all things, of which God spoke through the mouth of all His holy prophets from the age past." Peter was building again. He was speaking with more conviction and power.

"For Moses indeed said to the fathers, 'The Lord your God will raise up to you a Prophet from among your brother, One like me; you shall hear him according to all things,' whatever he may speak to you. And it shall be that of every soul, whoever should not hear that Prophet shall be utterly destroyed from among the people. And also all the prophets, from Shemuel and those following after as many as spoke, also before announced these days." Looking at them as if speaking to each individual, he concluded with saying, "You are sons of the prophets and of the covenant which God appointed to our fathers, saying to Abraham, 'Even in your Seed all the families of the earth shall be blessed,' Having raised up his child Jesus, God sent him first to you, blessing you in turning away each one from your iniquities."

As he was speaking, the rulers of the Temple saw the crowd gathering and got there in time to hear what Peter was saying. Priests along with the Temple Commander and those from the sect of the Sadducees stood off to one side of the crowd listening. The Sadducees were upset because they were announcing that Jesus had been raised from the dead. They preached against the resurrection in any way. This was directly against them, and they knew it. They stirred up the Temple Commander, who was over all the Priests in the Temple, to do something. He made his way through the crowd, who separated in front of him to let him pass. He had with him his contingency of guards. The Sadducees stayed well back in case the crowd got rowdy.

The Commander spoke to Peter with a loud, commanding voice. "You there! You can't stir up a crowd like this in the Temple. You will have to come with me. You will stand before the council for what you are telling the crowd. You are speaking against the Jewish rulers." They were taken in for the evening; the council wouldn't be in session until morning.

They took Peter and John, but they had to take the man that had also been healed because he wouldn't let go of Peter. They went into the Temple area under guard and left the crowd just watching.

One of them, however, ran off to tell the other disciples what had happened. Thus confrontation and healing had started.

Reports were being brought back to Satan. He couldn't be everywhere but he had eyes and ears spread all around. This report interested him deeply. They had been stirring up the Jewish leadership as much as they could. Now they have something started that will give them great effect against these new believers. Maybe now they can start wiping them out, stopping this thing at the beginning. Satan went himself to see this action. He directed various spirits to fester in the leadership, keeping them on edge. This is where we will concentrate our efforts. Religion just became the greatest tool in his hand to destroy these hated followers of his great enemy. "Here is our weapon to cut them off", he thought. A glimmer of a plan formulated in his mind. "They will not be able to withstand the heat of public hatred." His gloating was infectious, it fanned the flames of the realm of Darkness.

CHAPTER 10
Stretching the Cloth

"They've been arrested!" That woke up the room. Someone was running up the stairs yelling, trying to get anyone's attention. The remnant of the Twelve that was there jumped up to intercept the bearer of such news. James was in the back of the room and was now scurrying forward.

"Who's been arrested?" James inquired of the young man running in out of breath and wide-eyed.

"Peter and John," he announced. "They were at the Temple. They healed the man who sits at the gate. Then Peter started preaching to the crowd. It upset the Temple Commander. He had them arrested and taken into the Temple." He was speaking much faster than the people could absorb it. His voice was high pitched and squeaky.

'Calm down. Peace, peace," James said reassuringly. "Are you sure? Did you actually see it or just hear about it?" He had his hand on the young man's shoulder holding his attention.

"I saw it. I was there. It was amazing! The healing was a full miracle. It caused quite a stir," he said to James as if they were the only ones in the room. "But it was his preaching that made the Jews look bad for crucifying Jesus. When he told them Jesus had been raised from the dead, they got real mad."

James was thinking. What should we do now? He couldn't say that out loud, it would have drained the faith of most of the people there. They were new at this. "Thank you for telling us. Get a drink of water and rest. We have to talk about this." He nodded at a man standing close who took the young man for some water. He turned with a concerned look on his face. "There isn't much for us to do right now. We don't know what is going to happen. We have had an effect on Jerusalem, and we can't expect everything to go unchallenged. What were we talking about this morning? We need to pray more? I guess that is where we are right now, isn't it?"

Watching all this happen, Shimon stayed by the side of Mary. None of them had ever been through something like this before except when Jesus was arrested. That scene was heavy on the minds of the Twelve.

"The last time we didn't know what to do about it. But back then we didn't have the Holy Spirit in us like we do now," said the disciple named Andrew. "He might be my brother, but he is the one God spoke through yesterday. I would have to assume the Lord is using him again. You are right. We need to hold him before God in prayer."

The others were quick to agree. James looked at him and it appeared he had made a decision. "Perfect Andrew. Would you, please, take whoever wants to join you and take that back corner over there? That is the prayer area from now on. Let me know what you all hear from God. I will join you as soon as I get some of these matters cleared up I am dealing with."

Mary stood up with some considerable effort and went to join them in the corner. Shimon helped get her there, but didn't stay. He returned to James.

"I know it was my idea for more prayer, but I feel I need to go to the Temple and find out what I can. I am well known there. I should be fairly safe."

James looked at him for a moment, then saw it was no use to argue with him. "Go ahead. Don't get arrested, okay? Bring back anything we will need to know. Be blessed."

He had gone and learned everything he could at the temple, which wasn't very much. Shimon had stayed until it was dark before he made it back to the Upper Room. His report was that there wasn't anything to report. He left them there and went home tired. It had been a long day.

The next morning, Shimon went to the Temple to check on what was happening. There was quite a stir. Word had been sent out that they had arrested Peter and John. The High Priest, Annas, and his father-in-law who was the previous high priest, Caiaphas, brought in many of their family, elders, and scribes. It took a while to get these together, so it was getting close to the third hour of the day. This time wasn't lost on Shimon; he knew it was the same time the Holy Spirit had come on all of them on the day of Pentecost. It was also the time they crucified Jesus. After all had gathered, they brought Peter and John to the Royal Stoa, the place just off to the south of the Temple itself where the Sanhedrin met and conducted business.

Shimon walked in as if he belonged there, moving past most people until he had procured a spot on the right of the proceedings, next to the wall, to not stand out conspicuously. He realized he wasn't alone. Many people who weren't of the council had come also. Since this was in daylight and not like the illegal trial of Jesus, it was open to the public. There were witnesses this time. It was obvious to Shimon that it wasn't comfortable for the High Priest and company.

Placing Peter, John, and Mesha, the man who had been healed from being lame, in front of the semi-circle of raised stone seats where the council sat, Annas stood and addressed the crowd. "We are here today to deal with a disturbance that occurred here yesterday." Turning to Peter, he asked with a booming voice, "By what sort of power, or by what sort of name, did you do this?"

As they were standing before them all, Peter, John, and Mesha were just three men seemingly in trouble. When asked that question, Peter felt the power of the Holy Spirit filling him as He had done yesterday and on the day of Pentecost. He knew he was speaking for the Lord God before these men. With boldness and clarity, he spoke to them as one who had authority.

"Rulers of the people and elders of Israel, if we are being examined today on a good work of an infirm man, by what this one had been healed, let it be known to all of you, and to all the people of Israel, that in the name of Jesus Christ the Nazarene, whom you crucified," as he looked directly at Annas, "whom God raised from the dead, in this name this one stands before you whole." Peter put his arm around Mesha resting his hand on the opposite shoulder.

"This Jesus is the Stone counted worthless by you the builders, the One who has come to be into the Head of the Corner; and there is salvation in no other One, for neither is there any other name under Heaven having been given among men by which we must be saved!"

Annas understood the accusation that had been leveled at him and the council. He clearly saw they had been caught in something bigger than they had thought possible. This Jesus incident won't go away. Now there are more doing what he did. Looking around at the crowd, he knew he was under scrutiny. This had to be handled carefully.

Looking back at the council for some kind of support or indication of how to proceed, he saw they weren't sure what to do either. The boldness that this man had was remarkable. It was obvious he wasn't an educated man. He was a commoner, from Galilee by his clothes and accent. Then recognition set in. These men had been with Jesus. And everyone knew it.

Then he noticed that the man with them wasn't one of the disciples of Jesus. Another moment of revelation set in. This was the man who had sat at the Temple gate for many years! He was standing! Annas was at a loss for words. A deep inner panic was rising up within him. There was no denying the man was healed; he was standing right there. Everyone knew him. Annas had just been accused of killing a man God raised from the dead. He knew he appeared guilty, and there didn't seem to be any way to come out of this predicament. He turned to the council for answers, but they didn't appear to have any either. They needed to discuss this.

"You men, stand outside for a while. We need to deliberate this situation." Annas dismissed them with a wave of his hand and turned his back on them while facing the council. Peter, John, and Mesha slowly strolled out as the crowd gave them leeway. Peter had a confidence about him that could be seen by anyone.

The council crowded in as they talked together in a conspirital hushed tone. Annas asked Caiaphas, "What do you think we should do? We need to be careful with everyone watching."

Caiaphas was very serious in his answer. "What may we do to these men? This is a notable miracle that occurred through them. It is plain to all those living in Jerusalem. We are not able to deny it."

Annas knew Caiaphas was right. "We can threaten them. We have to stop this here. We can't let this spread any further into the people," he said with a dark bite in his voice. "This is getting out of hand. It should have stopped with the crucifixion. They have to know we won't let them use this name any longer." The nods around the group signaled agreement. Annas was set in his decision. He knew he had great authority, not just in the Temple, but in all of Israel.

As the council separated and returned to their seats, Annas spoke out, "You men, come back to the front." The crowd parted again letting them walk back in. They didn't look like men who were about to receive judgment for doing something wrong. They held their heads high and Peter was smiling. They came to the front and stood there for a minute. Annas was taking a minute to establish his control and authority.

"We have decided to let you go. However, you are not able to speak at all, especially in this name of Jesus. You cannot teach others on this name. We have spoken!"

Peter snickered a little. "Whether it is right before God to listen to you rather than God, you judge," he said in a voice that was bright and clear. "If you speak for God, then you would know how this was done."

Bolstered by the Spirit of God and the words of Peter, John spoke up, "We are not able to not speak what we saw and heard. It isn't just what we say; it has been seen by all these people. Your authority over this name doesn't exist."

Annas' face turned bright red in anger. He knew he had to be very careful how he responded, but said to them, "Under penalty of punishment we command you not to use that name in Jerusalem any longer. Now leave!"

Peter still had the little smile on his face. He bowed a little bow from the neck with his head tilted slightly. John and Mesha followed suit. The three turned and the crowd let them through again as they walked out with their heads held high in an air of victory. They found themselves in the large flat area between the Temple and the Royal Stoa. Everywhere they turned the people were smiling at them encouraging them to stand strong.

Mesha was beaming, still staying very close to Peter. Every now and then he would let out a little yell of praise accompanied by some jumping around. The people around him would join in and glorify God for the healing they had witnessed. These folks were being drawn to the name of Jesus by the Spirit of God and the healing they had witnessed. There was real power there, and the people knew it.

Mesha stuck with them, even though he needed to go back home. He hadn't been home since the healing. His family heard all about it when they came to help him home after his day of begging, but he had been taken in arrest with Peter and John. That night he had heard about Jesus and faith in what he had done. It was a night of experimentation for Peter and John as they helped him in his belief and the new birth experience. Then they talked at length about the baptism in the Holy Spirit as it was new to them also. So when they were called to stand before the Sanhedrin, all three of them were firm believers. It was hard for Mesha to leave them, even though now he had no idea what he was going to do for a living. Here he was at forty years old with no craft to use except begging, but he also had a new relationship with God he had never known about before and things were certainly different.

Shimon worked his way through the crowd and joined himself to their band of men as they headed back to the Upper Room. Their discussion was about what they had seen and how to walk in this new kind of life. They had so little information. Every move was new. They had to figure out how to get things done and what to do with what they had.

They were very involved in the discussion and didn't notice what was happening around them as they made it back to the Upper Room. People had gathered to see the heroes from the Temple. As they approached the Upper Room, they finally saw that people were staring at them and smiling. They were becoming well known.

James was out front to greet them. "Welcome back!" he said as he clasped their hands enthusiastically. "Out having adventures, are we?"

John just laughed as he embraced his brother. "It certainly wasn't planned!" he quipped. "It seems we need to be prepared for everything all the time. Remember how Jesus told us that we would do everything he was doing? Well, here we go. We had better be prepared."

That statement got through to Shimon. "He is right," he thought. "It isn't just about going to the Temple or the synagogue. And it's not about one person doing it, but everyone. It's about all of us bringing the Holy Spirit with us all the time everywhere." That revelation captivated his thoughts. It would continue to think about it for a long time.

They all went in to give a report. John stood up in front of them and told of the threats they had received. Instead of making them afraid, the opposite effect happened. They all started praying and praising. In unity, they prayed as if they were one.

Being a leader among them, James prayed as their representative. Lifting his hands and face to heaven, he spoke their heart to God. "Master, You are the God who made the heaven and the earth and the sea, and all things in them, who through the mouth of Your servant David said, 'Why did the nations rage, and the peoples meditate foolish things? The kings of the earth stood up, and the rulers were assembled on the same day against the Lord, yea, against His Messiah.' For truly both Herod and Pontius Pilate, with the nations and the peoples of Israel, were assembled against Your holy child Jesus, whom You anointed, to do whatever Your hand and Your counsel before determined to be done." His voice cracked in the middle of the depth of emotion pouring out of his heart to God. With tears streaming down his cheeks, he continued, "And now, Lord, look upon their threatenings and give to Your slaves to speak Your Word with all boldness, in the extending of Your hand for healing and miraculous signs and wonders to happen through the name of Your holy child Jesus!"

The entire room shook with the power of God, as the Spirit of God filled them all. They were given great boldness to do the works of heaven. They were touched deeply and a bond was established between them. They knew they were all at the crossroads of what God was doing on the earth.

Discussions became praise reports at the dinner table for Shimon and his family. It had been a few days since the arrest and release, and the prayer meeting. Signs and wonders had regularly been happening among them all. Every day it was exciting to hear what was happening around the city. The number of folks associated with this new movement was now around five thousand. People had started opening their homes to folks who didn't have much. Many were giving large quantities of money to the disciples to help take care of those who came. Logistics of care had become a major concern to the Twelve.

But for Shimon's family, they had been preparing for such a thing for a long time without thinking about it. They had always taken care of each other, sharing whatever anyone had with the others.

Each of them was seeing how the Lord was using them differently than the way he used others. Ezra found that he believed in healing and would touch others and pray for them quickly with amazing results. Elihu had a heart to help folks and make sure they were taken care of. Shimon discovered he had an inkling to bring wisdom to those who needed to know what the Lord was telling them and had deep compassion for them. He also felt a certain amount of authority. He had witnessed one of the Twelve casting an evil spirit out of someone, and it pleased him in a way he couldn't explain. Shimei had organizational matters flowing through his head all the time. It was very interesting to them how they all seemed to be empowered by the Spirit, but it was for different things and in different ways.

When they got together, they were interrogating each other about how things went with them and what the Lord was showing them. Even though they had these other interests, they still had a business to run. When they listened to the Spirit, they had plenty of work and ways to get it all done, plus the work they were doing for what they now called "The Assembly of Called-out Ones."

Shimon had the opportunity to take the Spirit out into the community more than the others since it was his job to go out into the city to deliver fabric and such from the shop. He was witnessing the works of God as others were out doing the acts the Twelve taught them to do. He saw how the entire city was being touched in some way. He also saw how it made many people, especially the city and Temple leaders, quite upset. This sect of those who follow the Messiah was shaking up the old city of Jerusalem. It would never be the same.

He was delivering some new table coverings to a rich man one day when he felt the Spirit telling him to pray. He felt that when he was entering a place of danger or a place where things were quite affected by evil in some way. He came close to the front door and stopped to look and listen for a while. "Please, help me, Dear Lord. Open my eyes to see and protect me from what I may encounter here. I am dependent on you, Mighty Spirit of God." Taking a deep breath and letting it out slowly, he then knocked on the door. A servant opened the door to ask who he was. "I am Shimon the weaver. I have a package to deliver to the master of this house. He asked to see them when they were finished."

The servant beckoned him in and told him to stay by the door while he announced him to the master. Shimon kept praying under his breath while he waited.

"Good day, master weaver," the voice came from a tall, well-built, older gentleman in a simple but expensive robe. This man didn't need to promote himself; he knew who he was and what he did. He knew he had the money and power of his company, but he didn't need to lord it over anyone. His bearing was without doubt. "Welcome to my home. My wife will be very glad to hear these are finished and ready." Shimon bowed and handed him the thick and heavy package.

"I am so honored that you would have us make these for you," Shimon said with a quiet assurance.

"My name is Telem. I usually let my servants deal with these kinds of everyday situations, but I must confess, I have an ulterior motive." Shimon reacted to that with his head coming up to watch the man. Telem then dismissed the servant and motioned for Shimon to come deeper into his house. "I have heard of this sect that has overrun the city. Many things have been brought to my attention. I have heard of healings and miracles. My workers are quite abuzz with the tales."

They made their way to a large room filled with pillows and table set around in very tasteful surroundings. "Please be seated," he spoke smoothly, waving with an open hand to the table closest to them. There were several bowls of fruit and cakes set out with some cups for wine. "I need to ask you some things. I heard you were part of this sect of the Nazarene. Is this true?"

Very glad he had stopped to pray earlier, Shimon thought very quickly on how to answer. "Yes, I am." He didn't offer any more information yet until he had more to go on. "What may I do for you?"

"There is someone in my life that needs help. I can't help him. I was hoping you could." Telem had deep emotion in his voice. "Many years ago, I worked for a man who was rich and had built a very strong company. He died suddenly and his widow elevated me to be the steward of their house. I have made a very good living and took care of the widow and her family the best I could. However, her son has become a very big problem. Could you meet him and see if there is something you could do for him?" Telem was emploring Shimon with eyes brimmed with tears.

With compassion fairly bursting out of his heart, Shimon knew what he needed to do. "Certainly," he said as he yielded to the move of the Spirit. Telem's head looked as if it had collapsed under the load as he slumped in relief.

"I am so glad. I have always wanted to help him, but had no way of doing so." Raising up his head, he continued, "He is here. Can you see him now?"

"I will do what I can. Let's go to him." They both stood up and Telem moved deeper into the house with Shimon following, praying with every step. They entered a room in the back of the house. There folded up on a large pillow lay Shemuel. He was disheveled and smelled of urine and vomit. There were several bowls and jugs for wine laying around. As they approached, Shemuel looked up at them.

His face was blank and clouded. His eyes were vacant, barely making out the forms of the men who had come to see him. Telem spoke to him gently but firmly. "Shemuel. This man has come to help you. Will you please listen to him?"

Shemuel scowled at Shimon. "I don't need your help," he slurred. Shimon was not seeing the man in front of him. Instead, he was seeing the spirit that was in him. It was as if he could see past the physical face and see the face of the being that inhabited him. He could discern the mocking attitude of the spirit as if it were saying, 'He's mine; you can't have him!'

The Spirit of God rose up in Shimon, filling him with courage and authority. "Look at me." The evil spirit focused intently on Shimon. "I command you in the name of Jesus the Messiah to come out of him! You cannot stay! Leave him and depart from here!"

Lachish had found a home, as much as a spirit can. The longer he stayed in this man the more he got to know him. When he saw Telem it all started making sense. No wonder this all seemed so familiar. This host is his own son. It didn't change much. This man he was inhabiting loved the wine and had the money to get it. It wasn't like the poor men or soldiers he had inhabited before. This was familiar and close, as much as living in continual pain could allow. He fiercely fought to keep this place and control this Shemuel as much as he could. He enhanced the desire to get wine with all he had. It didn't matter that the wine was killing his son. Time and natural affection didn't matter to a dead man. All that mattered was the intense desire for the feeling of getting the wine.

Shemuel finally wasn't able to live on his own. They had come and gathered him in, putting him in this room. It didn't matter to either him or the man he was in that those around him were so deeply hurt by his actions. It was only the wine. The wine. The wine.

Then here comes something different. Lachish could discern the difference between a departed spirit and the living. Then came the day he met that being that shone like light was coming from every part of his being. He kicked Lachish out and out he went. That being was different and not anything to fight; he just obeyed.

Now another being had come into his presence. He wasn't just living. He didn't just have the slight glowing aura all living had. He had light shining out of him. The light hurt Lachish. He fought viciously not to run away. Then something happened that surprised him. This man commanded him to leave. A force he couldn't explain, nor resist, hit him. The pain was excruciating. He had to leave and leave right now!

Lachish found himself outside the house with no host. He had been violently extracted and thrown outside. He spun around to look at what happened and there standing in a position of protection stood an angel looking at him. He was larger than any demon he had ever seen and the light coming from him continued the pain. Lachish didn't take another second to leave the area. He went a ways off and stopped. He longed for his former host and to be housed in that place again. His emptiness was astounding and consuming.

Shemuel suddenly was able to focus on the men standing in the room. He was aware of his surroundings. He could smell the urine and vomit. He felt dirty and was faintly disgusted with his condition.

He recognized Telem who was standing there with his mouth open. The other man he didn't know, but he could feel that he was able to be trusted. There was something different about this man. "What is happening?" he asked, trying to get his voice to work.

"This man is here to help you," Telem said matter of factly. "And he has. How do you feel?"

"I feel good. I am very tired. And hungry. And I smell very bad." Telem couldn't remember when the last time he had seen Shemuel completely sober. He turned and called for servants who had been waiting close to the entrance. He had told them not to be around. He didn't know what to expect. Now he needed them. They came running.

"Help him. Get him cleaned up and fed." They came in and helped Shemuel stand and supported him as they took him out to clean him up. "Clean up this room, too. Let's make it presentable again." He let the servants in to start doing what they were supposed to do. He walked back to the main room, Shimon followed his lead. His head was swimming with thoughts about what just happened.

Telem went straight to the pillow he had been in before. Shimon then noticed the air he had with the servants was completely gone. This man was shaken badly. As Shimon sat next to him, he saw Telem had his face in his hands and was weeping. "It has been so difficult. I am so glad you could do something for him. Can you explain what happened?"

"I can tell you about some of it, but I'm not sure about it all myself," Shimon admitted. Have you heard about Jesus and how they had crucified him the day of Passover?"

"Yes, I thought it was a bunch of rumors and political wrangling. I have to work with the Romans. It really shook things up at the praetorium. I couldn't verify anything I had heard. I thought he was some kind of itinerant preacher that made the Temple Jews jealous. I try to stay out of those kinds of things. It doesn't help business to have an opinion around the Romans."

"Well, the crucifixion wasn't the most important thing. He rose from the dead. That is important."

Information like that is a little hard to take. Telem stared at Shimon. "What? How do you know?"

Shimon just smiled. "How do I tell him what I know?" he thought to himself. "I know because I talked to him afterward." He could tell Telem was having a hard time with this. "I know it is difficult to hear this and believe, but God is working again in Israel. He has given us His Holy Spirit. That is how I was able to cast out that spirit that was inhabiting your friend. It is time to understand that the spirit realm is as real as the physical. But the only way to get access to it is to repent of your sins. Jesus died as a sacrifice for us. If we will come to him and know we are sinners, he will receive us and give us life. He will forgive us. We can have a whole new life in him."

Telem was hanging on every word. The Holy Spirit was drawing him in, convicting him, showing how his life was filled with selfishness. "I need that," he said quietly. "Will you help me?"

"Absolutely. He is listening right now. Let's talk to him." Shimon helped Telem come to Jesus and give him his life. What they didn't see were the angels who were spinning, shouting, dancing, praising and making quite a spectacle in the spirit realm all around them as a new life was redeemed.

The news was taken to Telem's family. He also shared it with Abigail and Penninah. The only one who didn't want to hear it was Shemuel. He just felt like he was an outcast again. Everyone else got it, but he didn't want anything to do with it. He was happy just being clean and walking around in society again.

It had been a couple of days before Lachish tried to see if his former host had been ruined for him. Coming around again, he found the house and the inhabitants in the physical were changed. There was a different atmosphere. Then he saw the living who were in the house. They weren't normal living like he had been used to for so long. These didn't just have the simple aura the living normally had. They had more. Their being vibrated a frequency that hurt him. Some of them had a stronger force coming from them; they were covered in the light, and it hurt to get too close.

He was just about to give up when he saw his son leaving the house. He floated in close to check him out. He didn't have the extra glow, only the normal living glow. He was clean and it bothered Lachish. He knew the way Shemuel could be. He could see the longing in his eyes and the desire of his heart. He could feel the vibration of wine lust coming from him. Lachish longed for it again with a hunger that was all consuming. He was thinking how to make this happen.

He knew he was a spirit that was focused on wine. He also knew there were other spirits that were focused on things even more than he was. If he can bring in some others that would influence his host for even greater activity in that kind of function, his need would be supplied easier. He needed help.

He flew out to the wine places he had used before. He went in and found Beor. With him were several other spirits working at inhabiting some of the common drunks. Lachish flew close. "I have a plan," he told Beor, "I have a good host with money."

Beor looked at him suspiciously. "Why help me?"

"Because it helps me and we can all get something out of it. All we need to do is influence him to get back in the wine. This will work for us." Lachish enticed them with his plan. They had heard of this and some had done it before, but it wasn't open for use very often. Here is their chance. The greed and lust that filled their souls was also the key to using and abusing them. It seemed to be working. "We are dry. This doesn't do anything for us. Let's go."

They agreed. Unity isn't difficult among them because they all have the same narrow focus of lust. Lachish led them out on a search for Shemuel.

He wasn't hard to find. He was standing outside the market area staring into the booths and people milling around. He wanted wine, his body craved it, even though he knew it wasn't going to work to go back to it. The family was overjoyed that he was different. He may be different on the outside and some different on the inside, but he knew he was still attached to the wine. His body shook for it. He was standing there sweating, his tongue and mouth parched.

The spirits all saw what Lachish told them was true. This man just needed a little shove and they were all in. Lachish went close and whispered to his mind, "A little wine wouldn't hurt anything. Just enough to take the edge off." The little shop on the right side, down a little ways, sold the kind of wine he really liked. He could almost taste it now.

The other spirits floated around his head making an atmosphere of desire. Shemuel could feel the bag of coins that hung from his belt. He knew he had the money and there wasn't anything to stop him, really. First, there was a little tremor in his leg and then a very small step. The next step was a little easier and a little larger. Time was imperceptible as each step grew a little quicker and soon Shemuel found himself heading to the wine shop with a steady beat of his steps.

He entered and bought some of the wine in a very nice jar. It wasn't like he had to have gallons of it right now. He only wanted just enough to feel better. He was very amiable with the shopkeeper, smiling and greeting him politely. He had what he wanted and he proved he could interact with people with no problem.

He stepped lively with his treasure back to the house and into his room. No one saw him. He was alone. He picked up a small cup with the intent of only having a few sips, just to stave off the trembling a little. In a little time without Shemuel acknowledging the passing of time, he had drunk the whole jar and was feeling quite well. He stumbled to the storeroom and found a few more wineskins full of some very good wine. Taking a couple of them back to his room, holding them so no one would know he had them. Soon he passed out in his room completely under the influence of the wine.

The spirits were reveling watching the process. As they waited for him to pass out, they were all totally concentrated on his every action. They closely watched every cup that went to his lips. Their anticipation was intense. As soon as he passed out and the aura opened, they scrambled into him.

Lachish didn't know what each of the spirits had for a focus, he knew it entailed wine, but he didn't know if there was something else. He soon found out. When Shemuel began consciousness again in the morning, they were all speaking to his mind. The first and foremost area of thought was the wine, but there was violence present. There was the influence to steal. Lachish was almost shocked at the severity of what was being promoted inside his son.

As the household woke up and began their daily routine, a servant came to Shemuel's room to tell him that breakfast was soon to be ready. Shemuel looked like he had been dragged behind a chariot. He was craving the wine again and his body felt terrible. The servant could see the signs and left him alone. He went up to the master and reported what he had found.

Coming down to Shemuel's room, Telem could tell it was bad. His heart sank. He wasn't going to have this in his house again. He had no idea how to help him this time. Until Shemuel wanted the help, it wasn't going to be good.

Telem made arrangements that day for a little place down by the wine sellers for Shemuel to live. There was a small stipend for him and a servant that looked in on him from time to time.

Shemuel was different. He could feel it. He had thought he was driven to have wine before, but now it was much more intense. He had no idea how that could be true, but it was. He was bitter at Telem for taking over everything. As he sat in his rooms, he knew he had everything he needed. He had been rich before. Now he had enough, but only just enough.

His attitude had now changed. He had thoughts of violence that he had never had before. He had always been a fairly quiet drunk. Today he was getting mean. He was no longer nice to the wine merchants. He got his wine and left. He had gone back to his place and sat there indulging himself in wine and bitterness. Everyone was against him. They couldn't see how they treated him. It was all about him in his little universe of Shemuel.

Day by day steadily marched on. He had gotten into a fight with another drunk who had bumped into him on the street and the violence exploded out of him on this man. It felt good to lash out. He knew he had hurt the man and that felt good, too. They had pulled him off and stopped him from going too far, but it didn't stop the feelings. He had also been having sexual inclinations; he was losing his inhibitions toward women.

Inside him, Lachish was experiencing more feelings than he had ever had in someone. It was driving him, making him want more and more. The wine and the feeling that came with it was strong. The only problem was, it still didn't satisfy. Time had ceased being a factor a long time ago. The additional spirits that had come into this man with him were causing him to want other things, not just wine. The host was getting more and more out of control.

One night he had gotten violent at some men, lashing out with venom at them. He had been knocked down and kicked in the head. It hurt so much, and only wine could make the pain go away. He bought some wine with the last of his stipend, went home, and proceeded to drink it all. He laid across his bed and passed out in an awkward position on his back; his head pushed down into his chest. He vomited, filling his airway, and he wasn't aware of it at all. He asphyxiated there in an inglorious display of wretched abandon.

Lachish knew his host had died. The man's spirit left his body in an expulsion.

Shemuel found himself standing in his room totally aware of his surroundings. He turned to see a body slumped in the bed. He knew the clothes and knew it was his room. As he watched, a being crawled out of the body, a disgusting person, covered in vile filth. The being snarled at him and floated out toward the street. Then came another and another. They had shown violence and degrading displays of behavior. Each one looked at him with disdain and floated away.

The last one was an emaciated being that looked at him in disappointment. Lachish stood there looking at Shemuel. "I had such high hopes that you would last longer," he said to him. "Now you are one of us." The hurt and pain on his face were blatant. Now the disappointment of his son beoming like him in perpetual longing hit him deeper than he had anticipated. "You were supposed to be better than me. I gave you everything."

The recognition hit Shemuel like a club. "You are my father." The bitterness welled up from within him. "I never knew you," He said with venom and hatred. "Now what do we have? What is this existence?"

Lachish answered quietly, "This is what we chose. There is no hope for us anymore." He turned and left, slowly and sadly. Shemuel had no idea what just happened. All he could do was follow as he tried to understand this complete emptiness he felt. Their existence was fraught with loneliness. Shemuel wandered out trying to figure out what his life was like now, longing for some wine.

CHAPTER 11
Making the Garment

"What are we going to do with all these people?" Andrew started the impromptu meeting in a close panic. The Eleven had gathered to discuss that very question, but each was coming from a different point of view.

There were so many that needed to be fed. Housing was becoming an issue with people being kicked out of their homes for not adhering to traditional Judaism. Others just had nothing and were newly brought into a family of people like they had never been. And there were the widows that no one was taking care of, even though the Law of Moses was there to make sure they did.

They had many people who had given up all they had to bring it to the Eleven. One couple tried to lie to the Holy Spirit about what they had given and died on the spot. That shook the rest into seeing the importance of doing things with honesty and integrity.

There was so much to do. Teaching and prayer had become increasingly important, but there didn't seem to be enough time to do either of them. The logistics of dealing with over five thousand people was daunting, to say the least. The Eleven were getting exhausted. They needed to figure out how to get more things done.

Along with that, the miracles, signs, and wonders were happening more often. With each one, two things happened: more people came to faith in Jesus and the established religious leaders were getting more furious. This group of believers was catalyzing the whole city.

Shimon still was having contact with many of the poor of the city. He had continued his practice of bringing food and clothing to those he ran across that needed it. It took a day of his week. Shimei knew that day wasn't one for work; it was Shimon's personal ministry day. One day, he helped a few people who were lame and crippled to lay out in the sun. Peter was just walking back to the Upper Room from the Temple where he had been teaching at a gathering by Solomon's porch, on the east side of the Temple grounds. Many people gathered there every day to hear teaching and to be healed. As he passed this small group of sick people who didn't have anyone to help them come to the meetings other than Shimon, his shadow passed over them. The first one yelped, "I am healed!" as his pain disappeared and his leg straightened out. Peter was deep in thought and didn't relate the noise to himself, so he continued walking. The second one's head snapped up as his disease disappeared. The third one saw what was happening and watched Peter' shadow come across him and then watched his legs gain size and strength. He started weeping in joy immediately.

As he stood at the end of the group, Shimon's mouth dropped open in shock. It wasn't what he was expecting or even believed could happen. He had prayed for each of them without them being healed and now they were. This was the answer to his prayers, but God was working how God wanted to and not how Shimon had expected him to work. His emotions went from stunned shock to complete elation by the time Peter got close to him. Peter acknowledged Shimon with a smile and a nod and then with a quizzical expression. Shimon had to point out what had just happened. Six people had just been healed by Peter' shadow. No one was more surprised than Peter. No one knew how to respond, either. This was extraordinary, even for these days.

Word got out. People were lining the streets with sick folks waiting for Peter to walk their way. Peter finally understood why Jesus had told people not to tell anyone about their healing. It didn't take long before he couldn't go into the towns for the crowds. Now it was difficult for Peter to get anywhere.

Shimon didn't help. When he found others who were stuck at home, he helped them go to where Peter was going (he cheated because he basically knew where Peter was going to go) and set them strategically in the path. It tickled Shimon no end to do this. Peter would look at him in mock rebuke but they both knew it was God and not either one of them in control of the situation.

These proceedings perturbed the Jewish leadership. The sect of the Sadducees had been gaining power and prominence. They didn't believe in such things as healing, resurrection, angels, or anything of a supernatural flavor. They used Judaism as a means of personal gain. They could see the priests were starting to fall in with this new sect. The Pharisees also were coming around to the followers of Jesus. They took it upon themselves to keep Judaism pure. They were losing control over the people. They knew they had to do something.

Annas, the High Priest, was still reeling from the rebuke from Peter and the healing that had happened at the gate. Now they were healing people in Solomon's Porch! He roused up the Sadducees, trying to determine what to do. At the close of one of the days, they had all the Eleven in one place. They were coming out of Solomon's Porch at the end of the meetings there. The people had dispersed and they were alone as they were discussing matters that needed to be handled. They suddenly found themselves surrounded by Temple guards. The Commander told them they were under arrest by order of the High Priest for teaching heresy. They were taken to the prison which was outside the Temple grounds to the southwest of Jerusalem.

As they were being taken, a couple of them had started to resist. James motioned to them to be calm. "Now is not the time for resistance," he told them. "Let's see what the

Lord is doing. There is a plan; we just don't know what it is yet." They all felt the peace that came with that wisdom and each conceded to let things happen.

The prison was dark and smelly. There was an outer enclosure with a locked gate and guard. Inside that gate, they were taken inside the building where there were cells. It wasn't a clean place; they had to use a corner for a toilet. There was a small window that allowed a speck of light into the cell. There were torches on the wall outside the cell that cast limited light but seemed to fill the air with smoke. Straw had been thrown on the floor. All they had were their own cloaks to wrap up in. They were given water and dry, hard biscuits for dinner. Normally men thrown in here dispaired of life or future. That didn't happen to these men.

They knew there were guards who would look in on them from time to time, so they also knew they were uninterrupted to talk and pray. James took the opportunity to lead them in prayer. The peace of God fell over them, they all knew God was present and they were quite safe. Safe enough that they talked and prayed and eventually fell asleep one at a time. They spent the night in quiet rest, laying on the straw wrapped in their cloaks.

While it was still dark, James was awakened by a gentle nudge to the ribs. He opened his eyes to see a man standing next to him who was glowing like a candle. The man smiled brightly and said, "Good morning. It is time to wake up. There is much to do today." James stirred and stood up to face the man. The Eleven all woke without being groggy (which was very unusual for Levi). The angel next to James spoke to the men. "You must go and stand in the Temple and speak to the people all the words of this life." He stepped over to the door and opened it without a key. The Eleven all brushed off the straw, adjusted their clothing, and readied themselves. The angel started walking down the hall to the front door, leading them out. The Eleven didn't say anything; they just followed quietly.

The front door also opened. The guards didn't see them. They could see the guards, but it was as if they were blind. They crossed the yard to the gate and the angel opened it for them and stood by it, letting them walk freely out into the street. Jochanan spoke to the angel as he passed, "Thank you." They stood there for a second smiling at each other as if they were old friends. John stepped away as the last of them cleared the gate. The angel closed it silently and walked back into the prison. The Eleven headed to the Temple like they were told.

They arrived there at dawn. The shofar was just being blown and there were many people there for the morning prayer time. When the people saw the Eleven coming in, they gathered to them and soon there was teaching going on in Solomon's Porch.

Satan stuck close to the head leadership of the Jews. This is who he wanted to influence the most. He pumped up their hearts with pride, feeling they were right and doing a good thing to get rid of these interlopers. There were many demons who were affecting the others on the council.

They were working this new angle. They hadn't been able to stop Jesus or even Lazarus but these men were ripe to be lead. Their focus was to stop this before it got too big. It was already bigger than they wanted it, but now they just had to work harder.

Annas and those close to him started their day early, getting everyone they could to come to the Royal Stoa to interrogate the Eleven. As they arrived, they were very confident they could put this thing to rest once and for all. They situated themselves in the prominent benches and called the guard to retrieve the leaders of this renegade sect from the prison. They sat in their smug and superior way so as to intimidate those who were brought before them.

The guards came back running to them without anyone with them. The Commander ran to the front and bowed to Annas, talking out of breath. "Your Honor. We went to the prison to get the sect leaders and they weren't there."

Annas' head snapped up in command, demanding an explanation. "We went in," the Commander continued, "and all the doors were closed and locked. All the guards were still in place and hadn't seen anything all night. But there isn't anyone in their cell!"

Annas stood up walking to the Commander with a completely baffled look on his face. "Are you sure?"

"Absolutely. We looked all around for them. They aren't there."

One of the servants who was bringing in water and cakes for the council heard them talking. "I beg your pardon, but who are you looking for?"

Annas and the Commander both looked at the servant with the look that spoke: "Why are you talking to us?" The Commander said to him, "The followers of Jesus."

The man looked a little confused. "Well, the men whom you put in prison are in the Temple, standing and teaching the people. They are right now in Solomon's Porch. They are right over there." He pointed with his finger as if they didn't know where Solomon's Porch was. Both of them followed his finger anyway, looking out across the Temple grounds.

Annas broke the Commander out of his thoughts. "Go get them!"

"Yes, sir. Right away, sir." He bowed quickly and sprang off picking up his guards on the way.

Bursting into Solomon's Porch, the Commander saw the men with different groups around them teaching the people. Crying out loud to them all, he shouted, "What are you doing here?"

Peter was the closest to him. "Ahh, teaching? What does it look like?"

"The Sanhedrin is calling for you. You are to come immediately!" He grabbed Peter' arm, trying to maintain an air of authority. Peter was quite a bit bigger than the man and wasn't moved by the gesture. The Commander realized he was being watched by a good number of people who were getting upset at his actions.

"Okay," Peter said to him. "We are coming." The Commander knew he was being obeyed, but he wasn't completely in control. The other guards had spread out escorting the Eleven to move. They went slowly out of Solomon's Porch and, surrounded by guards who were starting to fear the crowd around them, they walked across the ground to the Royal Stoa.

As they entered, they could see Annas sitting in the main seat incensed. The Eleven were calm and unhurried. Peter, James, and John stepped up to face him without fear or intimidation.

Annas stood up, still trying to intimidate them by standing higher than them. He spoke directly to Peter since he had been the one he had talked to before. "Did we not command you by a command that you not teach in this name? And, behold, you have filled Jerusalem with your doctrine and intend to bring on us the blood of this man."

Speaking in a firm, controlled voice, Peter spoke up. "It is right to obey God rather than man? The God of our fathers raised up Jesus, whom you seized, hanging him on a tree. This one God has exalted as a Ruler and Savior to His right hand, to give to Israel repentance and remission of sins." Pausing for a moment, Peter looked around at the other men seated in the positions of authority. "And we are His witnesses of these things, and also the Holy Spirit, whom God gave to those obeying Him."

His words affected each of them. They felt their guilt, and it didn't feel good. They knew they looked bad before the people who had followed the proceedings. There were scowls and frowns shared between them as they sat there listening. No one could refute these words.

Then a man stood up to address the council. They knew him well. He was Gamaliel. He normally lived in Tarsus, but was in town for some meetings. He was a very prominent teacher, a Pharisee, who discipled young men into the strictest lives of the pharisaical sect. He was held in high regard by the council and the people. "Please, put these men outside for a while. I wish to speak to this council alone." The Eleven stepped out quietly and the people were also put out so the council could talk in private.

Gamaliel stood in front of them all, gathered his robes, paused for effect directly looking at each of the men. "Men, Israelites, take heed to yourselves what you intend to do on these men." He let that warning sink in before continuing. "In the past, do you remember when Theudas rose up, claiming himself to be somebody, to whom was joined a number of men, about four hundred, who was done away and all, as many as obeyed him, were dispersed and came to nothing." He could see that several of them remembered that time.

"After this, Judas the Galilean rose up in the days of the Registration. And he drew considerable people after him. Yet that one perished, and all were scattered, as many as obeyed him." He had sounded like he was making a lecture to students. Then he turned serious and stepped closer to the group, his words becoming more intense. "And now I say to you draw away from these men and permit them; because if this counsel is of men, or this work, it will be destroyed. But if it is from God, you will not be able to destroy it, lest even you will be found to be fighters against God."

The council saw the wisdom in what he said. They couldn't argue with him, they really needed an answer. This seemed to be the wisdom they sought. They all agreed, but with a stipulation. Annas said some kind of move needed to be made so they would know who had the authority. Agreement was reached one more time. All Gamaliel had to say was, "Do what you think you need to. I just hope you don't regret it someday."

They had the men brought back in. Annas was resolute, but limited. He had the men stripped down to their waists, and a flagrum was brought in. There were no walls between the Royal Stoa and the Temple ground, so everything could be seen, but not heard. The men were flogged. They were given three lashes each. They were allowed to dress again.

Annas spoke one last time. "I am commanding you again not to speak on the name of Jesus." As soon as he said it, he knew they would not obey him. He knew he was dealing with something much bigger than he had dealt with before. He let them go.

The Eleven left. They also knew something big had just happened. They knew the leadership of Judaism no longer had authority over them. They were listening to a much higher authority. They rejoiced that they were deemed worthy to be dishonored on behalf of the name of Jesus.

It did nothing in restricting them. They continued doing what they knew to do. They were teaching and preaching the good news of believing into Jesus the Messiah in the Temple daily. They were going out ministering to people house to house. They were more focused than ever.

Even with all that happening, the work wasn't any easier. Some of the widows started complaining that they were being overlooked in the daily giving out of food. Word got to the Eleven and James had enough. He knew they never had the time to get everything done and the pressure was becoming too great. He talked to the Eleven and they came to a consensus. Calling the greater multitude together they addressed them all.

"Men, brothers, it has come to our attention that things are being overlooked in the daily workings. We are being called out from teaching the Word to serve tables. We can't do everything. We have realized we don't have to. It is time for others to take leadership and take on some of the responsibility. There simply isn't enough of us to go around. We are getting worn out.

"We want you to search out among yourselves people who you have seen doing the work, men who are trustworthy. Find men who have a good testimony and are known among you. We will appoint seven of them to be part of our leadership. That will free us up to teach and minister the Word of God."

Word spread like wildfire. People were to be added to the Eleven to work. Out of over five thousand people, they were going to place only seven. The list was fairly long. Shimon was on that list.

People had seen him working and how he took to leadership. All those he worked with looked up to him, respecting him and who he was. The only problem was, he didn't want it. He felt it would bite into the time he spent with the poor and would restrict the things he liked doing.

He continued working for Shimei and going out touching lives of people he came across. That is what gave him joy.

Soon a list of men was narrowed down to seven who were well trusted and well known among the congregation. The work began to smooth out and soon there was a way of bringing up things that needed to be done and it would be attended to. One of those men was a young man named Stephan. He was one of the Hellenised Jews who had moved in from Greece when he was but a child, hence the Greek name. He was well known and well liked. His biggest strength was his energy and enthusiasm. He was always busy, happy, and helpful.

He also couldn't keep very quiet. He was always talking and discussing theology. Many times it turned into debates, especially with people from other countries. He was trying to convince them of the good news of Jesus so they could take it back to their home countries. It didn't take long before they were seeking him out.

He had been involved in many miracles and wonders. He argued with the synagogue leaders about Jesus who didn't already know him. Soon he became a point of dispute. Either you loved him or despised him. Those that despised him conspired to get rid of him. They went to the elders and scribes accusing him of blasphemy against Moses and God. Quite a large controversy was stirred up, to the point of them arresting him and dragging him before the Sanhedrin.

This time, however, Shimon saw them take him. He knew the arrest wasn't right but had no idea what to do for him. Instead, he followed them into the Royal Stoa and before the Sanhedrin. He worked his way closer so he could hear what was going on.

Annas, the High Priest, was presiding over the proceedings once again. Next to him, and being his right-hand man of support, was Jonadab, a Sadducee of influence. He had become one that Annas listened to for counsel in many ways. His twisted way of thinking had been steadily increasing as a force in Annas' everyday dealings. He sat behind Annas like a snake, watching everything and everyone. His hatred for the followers of Jesus was well known.

Gamaliel wasn't there any longer. He had gone back to his city of Tarsus thinking they had sufficiently decided not to do anything about this sect and let God work it out. With him gone, Jonadab was able to steer things toward a more direct approach. Things were just getting started over Stephan.

Shimon was intently scrutinizing the council, hoping for dismissal like they had done last time. His eyes fell on Jonadab and he decided to watch him. Jonadab slyly caught the eye of some of the men around in the crowd. They were obviously followers of his who were there to do his bidding. He nodded at one of them, setting a plan in motion.

As Annas called for order, this man stepped forward, "Most honorable Annas. I have heard this man speaking blasphemous words against this Holy Temple and the Law of Moses." His voice rang full among the people present. "We have heard him," he swung his arm in the direction of some of his friends standing there who nodded in agreement with everything he said. "He does not cease saying that this Jesus the Nazarene will destroy this place and will change the customs which Moses delivered over to us. This sect will destroy our very heritage and the fabric of life in Judaism." Those in the crowd, who were ready, were yelling agreement, stirring up the rest of the people.

Stephan stood there quietly, listening to the false charges. It was obvious none of it had any effect on him. He looked up, calmly glancing at the Sanhedrin members. Everyone he put his gaze toward, reacted. Their faces would register some kind of knowing and they would quietly stare at him. Shimon watched them change. He was amazed at it, so he looked over at Stephan and saw what they were seeing. His face had an expression of peace and confidence that showed authority and power. If he didn't know better, Shimon would have thought it was the face of an angel.

Annas stood directly in front of Stephan and asked him, "Are these things so?"

Taking a breath slowly, Stephan started telling them the history of Israel, starting with Abraham being called out to come to this land. He told of the covenant Abraham received about the land. He told of Isaac, James, Yoseph, and lingered on Moses. He told how Moses was called and how he went into Egypt and brought out the people. He went into detail about the mount and God giving him instructions about the Tabernacle. He jumped to Solomon building the Temple and what God said about it. Every member of the council was hanging on his words.

Then a change came over Stephan, subtle at first, but building. He was getting through to them. He could see his words having an effect. "But the Most High does not dwell in temples made by hand, as the prophet says, 'Heaven is My throne, and the earth a footstool of My feet; what house will you build Me,' says the Lord, 'or what the place of My rest?' 'Did not My hands make all these things?'"

He paused to take a breath, but it was obvious something else was happening in his heart. Stephan' eyes zeroed in on the council members. He made eye contact with them as individuals and began to speak the words of the Holy Spirit to them. "Oh stiffnecked and uncircumcised in heart and in the ears! You always fell against the Holy Spirit. As your fathers did, you also did." The words came at them like knives. Stephan wasn't speaking in a mean, condemning voice, but the power behind it was palpable. "Which of the prophets did your fathers not persecute? And they killed those before proclaiming concerning the coming of the Just One, of whom you now have become betrayers and murderers, who received the Law by the disposition of angels and did not keep it."

There was total silence in the room as each of the council stared at him. Conviction hit them collectively. They all knew they had been exposed and accused and he wasn't wrong. They began responding to him as people do who have been laid bare before people. They couldn't truly defend themselves, but they looked very bad in the eyes of the people. The only course of action they had left was to attack the messenger. They spat venomous slurs against Stephan, trying to put him down so they didn't look so vile.

The center of their attention was on Stephan, but he was no longer focused on them. The Holy Spirit came over him and touched him deeply. He raised his eyes as they were opened to see into the spirit realm. He said out loud to no one in particular, "I see the heavens having been opened, and the Son of man standing at the right of God!" No one knew what to do about that. It enraged them all since they were the ones God would show things to, not these renegades!

Jonadab saw his chance and incited them to rush him and take matters into their own hands. "Take him down! Get rid of the blasphemer!" Others cried out so they couldn't hear Stephan any longer, some of them with their hands covering their ears. They all rushed the front to take Stephan and stop him from any more convicting words.

Standing off to the side, Shimon was bumped out of the way. He was having a very hard time understanding what was happening. Things went from a deeply spiritual experience to mob rule in an instant. He stood there with his mouth open in utter amazement and stunned inaction. The crowd took Stephan, leading him out of the Temple grounds going south, out of the city.

The crowd gained in numbers as they went. The main instigators, however, were still the members of the

Sanhedrin. People could see this was an official function since they were leading it. Shimon just tried to keep up without being trampled.

As they reached a place where the road took a sharp turn, they threw Stephan onto a bare spot. The crowd moved around so they would have a good view of the action. The council stood to one side as they oversaw what was happening. Each of the council picked up a stone. They had to throw one to be a witness to its legality, even though they had their underlings who would actually be doing the heavy part of it. They took off their outer robes to be able to throw the stones. There was a young man standing there who had come to Jerusalem very recently and was known as an ardent, radical Jewish zealot they called Saul. They all trusted him to take care of their robes while this duty was being accomplished.

Standing in front of them, Stephan knew he was going to be killed. He knew the Lord Jesus was standing there to receive him. One of the men threw a stone that hit him in the chest, spinning him around with the force of the blow. He turned back toward the council grimacing in pain. Another rock hit him and then another. They were coming fairly quickly and the pain was building. Then one stone hit him on the side of his head, letting blood splatter behind him. He fell to the opposite side. Managing to roll to his front, with stones hitting him on his back and side, he cried out as he got to his hands and knees, "Lord Jesus, receive my spirit." Another stone hit him squarely on the forehead, knocking him on his back. With the blood pouring from his head, running down his face he made it to his knees. He cried out as loud as he could, "Lord, do not make this sin stand to their account!" His face went limp, his arms fell dangling at his side and he fell forward on his face as his spirit left his body. Stephan was dead.

The stones kept coming for a while to make sure it was finished, but the anger from the mob began to dissipate. Each one came and received his robe back from Saul who stood there justified as if they had done something righteous and glorious. Stephan' body was partially buried under the pile of rocks. When it was all over, the only ones left were the followers of Jesus as they silently came and removed the body from the pile of stones. The mood was somber indeed.

Lachish had learned how different types of departed spirits could actually work together to get as close to what each one specifically wanted. Being one who followed alcohol closely, he found spirits of sexual lust liked to party to get their participants to lose inhibitions. He saw how wine increased the ability to get people more violent, so the spirits of violence were sometimes very good to follow. Spirits of greed, food, self-indulgence, and all forms of hedonism could be used in combination to try to fulfill the others. It didn't take long outside a host to find another, but many times it was in conjunction with another form of spirit.

There was a growing problem, though. There was a growing number of people who no longer used the spirits or did what the spirits liked. These people were the ones who glowed more intensely than the other living ones. It was painful to get too close to these new ones. Lachish soon despised these people. They were causing problems wherever he went.

He could see the demons working hard to try to destroy these followers of the One known as Jesus. The demons just called him "The Son." Even Satan didn't know what to do with these people. He thought he had won when he killed The Son. Then the unthinkable happened! He rose from the dead! Then he gave the Holy Spirit to the men around him. The Spirit went to others, making them a new kind of being. Another thing happened that was beyond his ability to think. The Holy Spirit was no longer just in people. He was on them, giving them the kind of miracles that The Son had. Signs and wonders were happening all over the place. These new beings shined light that was painful to be around. The forces of darkness were reeling. They didn't know what to do or where to go from here.

Many departed spirits just wanted to leave the area, go find somewhere there wasn't these kinds of folk. The demons were ordered by Satan to keep as many as they could to cause as many problems as possible for these "believers." Lachish saw that the demons were trying to stir things up against these believers. They were trying to influence the leaders to hate the new folk so they could be destroyed. The spirits of violence were watching closely and were agitated to the possibilities. Lachish knew where these were working were those who would also be getting into the wine. It was a time of turmoil for everyone, demons, departed spirits, Jews, and believers alike. That kind of atmosphere lent itself to be good for the dark realm.

Lachish knew there were some who were close to the leadership of the Jews who were the unworthy types. There was always that kind of people around. There was something about people who did things in secret that increased the intensity of the experience. It was good to be around them if you were a spirit. They were easy to feed from.

Lately, believers were brought before the council. For the most part, nothing big happened, except some of them were flogged. The anticipation, however, was that something big was in the works. He was hanging around with some of the violent spirits as they watched as demons roused up the council against this new man. He was one none of the demons or departed spirits liked to be around. He was powerful and very discerning about what he was dealing with. Then he was arrested. The attitude of the dark realm was one of offense, working to destroy him. He was young, impulsive, and would eventually get into trouble.

It was a major confrontation between the light and the darkness. The Sanhedrin was being heavily influenced by demons and departed spirits. Lachish could see how forcibly the spirits were working, darting in and out around them. All the spirits spat vitriol at the young man shining in front of them. They couldn't get close, but they could hiss at him from afar.

There were several in the crowd who were light-bearers. There also were many who were inhabited by the spirits in the crowd. It was a complete mix, but there was only darkness among the council. As the proceeding advanced, Lachish saw the dark spirits trying to whip the council into a frenzy. There were several religious spirits pouncing on the members as their indignation grew against this man. The intensity of violence was incredible.

The young man spoke. The Spirit of God shone out of him in great power. It reached out and touched members of the council in conviction. The spirits screamed into the ears of those on the council. Everything was ready to explode. The spirits yelled at the young man, trying to speak through those they were with. A very forceful demon grabbed a certain leader and directed him to contact other spirits in the room. It was obvious that there was a concerted effort to take down this young man.

The frenzy expanded until it flooded over. When that happened, the last vestiges of restraint were snapped. The council rushed the young man joined by those in the crowd whipped up by the spirits. They grabbed him and took him out of the Temple grounds to the outside of the city. There they proceeded to get undressed and stone him. The spirits of violence were having a wonderful time, fully expressing their hatred and destruction. They still couldn't get close to the young man, but they could help direct the hatred from the council and those under their hand. The crowd helped feed it all.

Then, the young man opened himself to see in the spirit realm. The pain the spirits felt was intense. They screamed at the ones they inhabited to put an end to it. "Kill him! Kill him!" The flurry of stones showed who was obeying them. The young man died.

His spirit came out of his body in full light. He stood there shining like the sun. Then manifesting directly in front of him was The Son, Jesus himself! The young man stepped forward and Jesus hugged him with a long, tight, and tender embrace. The sky was filled with angels and the spirits of darkness were stunned into inaction. Then Jesus turned and led the young man as they lifted off the ground fading into a brilliant flash of light. Then the light, The Son, the young man, and the angels were gone.

The crowd dissipated. The spirits of violence were left for a few seconds stunned and inoperative. Then they turned on each other and left; kicking, biting, slashing at each other. There was some, however, who stayed beside another young man who had stayed by the clothes. The people who had the light on them, stayed until the crowd left and went to the body of the young man who had died. They took his body. Their light didn't diminish. They hadn't lost. They had a victory they couldn't explain.

Lachish watched. It was a mystery to him what had happened. He sought the crowd of darkness. They weren't hard to find. They were stunned and unfulfilled in what they had witnessed. Many of them wanted to dull what they had seen with wine. Lachish had his pick of who he would inhabit tonight. Nothing felt like victory to him. Not now. Not ever.

CHAPTER 12
Dressed in Light

The death of Stephan profoundly affected Shimon. He was there. He saw the whole thing. Now he was kneeling beside the body lifting stones away, unburying him. Shimon got blood all over his hands as he held the head of this precious young saint of God. They turned Stephan over. Shimon saw how his face was so peaceful. He was in a very good place. There was no grieving here. They all felt the peace as it permeated the air around them.

News had been spread as they had taken him out of the Temple grounds. Word got to James, John, and Peter that this time was different. They had taken Stephan out of the city. Many disciples ran just in time to fight the crowd as they were coming back into Jerusalem. They made it out to the scene of the stoning as the body had been completely freed. They ran up to see what had happened and slowly knelt. Each touched the body. Shimon took off his robe and they wrapped the body in it. Very quietly, they carried the body back to the Upper Room until they could figure out where to bury him.

Someone took word to Stephan' family. They came to get the body. The family was stunned that something like this could happen in Israel. They had always been good Jews who had been participants in the synagogue. How could the Jewish leadership let something like this happen, let alone be the ones who did it? There would be a funeral procession in their family as soon as the body could be prepared.

The effect on the body of believers was also profound. They knew they were supposed to be grieving, but it just wasn't happening. They found that dying in Jesus was different. It wasn't the end; it was the beginning. Judaism had preached that for a very long time, but it had new meaning now. Death seemed to lose its grip on people in Jesus. There was so much more than just this life.

Now the message of eternal life had a ring of truth to it. They all understood that they might die because of their belief in Jesus, but that was okay. The finality of death wasn't final.

Shimon went home. He wasn't sad, but he was deeply thoughtful. As he walked into the shop, others could see something was up. Shimei met him just inside the door with a few new packages to deliver. He stopped short seeing Shimon come in with no robe and blood all over his tunic. "S'ba! Are you all right?" he gasped with deep concern coming out of his voice. He dropped the packages on the floor grabbing Shimon by the arms, checking him over. The immediacy of his tone got the attention of many others. Work came to a standstill.

Elihu and Ezra came scrambling from behind their looms. Shimon held up a hand reassuring them, "I'm okay, I'm not hurt. This isn't my blood." The same question was coming from every set of eyes in the room. "It is Stephan' blood. They just stoned him to death this morning."

That statement made everyone take a step back trying to wrap their minds around the meaning. "What? Stephan is dead?" Elihu plied his question as a way of trying to comprehend the seriousness of it all.

"The Sanhedrin did it themselves," Shimon said rather absent-mindedly. "He was accused of blasphemy." One of the workers produced a stool. Shimon sat down, looking at his hands. He had only wiped the blood off his hands before coming home. He could still see Stephan' face as he held him. The peace still affected him. "I saw it all happen. I went into the Royal Stoa and saw them put him on trial. His face shone the presence of God. He answered them and then told them their sin in the situation with Jesus. They couldn't handle it." He trailed off as he was seeing it in his mind. The images were burned in as if they were playing again. He caught himself as he realized they were all staring at him. He took another breath and continued.

"They took him out of the city on the road to the south and stoned him there. There was nothing we could do."

Shimei patted him on the back gently, trying to console him. Shimon saw what effect his words had on them. Every face was filled with sorrow. Shimon snatched them back suddenly, "No. No. It isn't like that! It wasn't a defeat. It was a true victory!" They were all taken by surprise. This isn't normal. "He was taken into heaven in the arms of our Lord Jesus. He died for the cause of salvation. It showed us all that this isn't the end. We are not just in this world with all its problems. We are citizens of heaven! We are looking ahead, not back. It was of the highest honor for Stephan to give his life for the sake of Jesus!"

Everyone was staring at Shimon as if he had lost his mind. This was new thinking for them. They had never considered this before. Now that someone had died for Jesus, there was a new path for them all. Nothing was holding them here. Everything was forfeit. It was going to take a while for them all to come to this way of thinking, but it was now planted in their consciousness. The seed will grow.

Elihu was the first to respond. "Well, I didn't expect that!" He chuckled at Shimon with a smile. Shimon looked at him with a gleam in his eye. "Can there be joy in the death of someone?" Elihu asked. "We of all people should know death isn't the end. Look who we have sitting right here!" The attitude around the room softened up. They all knew this was serious, but it wasn't final. This could happen to any or all of them. What is the cost of this life in Jesus?

"Come on, S'ba," he said as a conclusion of the matter. "Let's get you cleaned up. We all need to hear the story, but I think you need to process it a little." Shimei nodded at Elihu. Shimon stood up and the two of them went on to the courtyard. The rest went back to work even though they knew work was going to be somewhat interrupted for the day.

As they entered the courtyard, they saw that Baruch was sitting out there. He was surprised at the sight of the blood, but they were both smiling. Explanations were in order. Elihu intercepted the inquiry. "We are okay. No one is bleeding right now. We are going to steal a tunic from Shimei and get cleaned up. We will be right back." They went on through to Shimei's room and knocked first. No answer assured them that Jerusha wasn't there. They went on in and found what they wanted and Elihu left Shimon to change. Elihu went back to the courtyard and sat with Baruch as they waited. Elihu told him what little he knew so they were all even when Shimon returned wearing a tunic from Shimei's room.

Sitting down across from Elihu and Baruch, he took a breath. Elihu told him Baruch was caught up with the rest, but it wasn't very much. Shimon smiled a little knowing smile. It was going to be difficult to express what he was thinking.

He told the details of the trial and the stoning as best as he could. He had times where he stopped as he was reliving it in the telling. He told how his robe had become a temporary shroud. Elihu interjected that they could supply a real shroud for the burial. The facts being covered, Shimon began to share what he was feeling about it all.

"When I found myself in that tomb the day Jesus was raised, I had no idea what to think about it all," he said introspectively. "I couldn't remember what had happened after I had died. I just found myself naked, cold, and healed of all my pain. Why me?" His brow furrowed in deep thought. It was a question he had asked himself and God many times. "For what purpose was I brought back? When I held Stephan in my hands, I saw the peace in his face. I knew at that point that this life is indeed fragile at best. There is more. We are actually heading somewhere. This is just a journey. Death isn't the end of the journey, just a door to the next passage. I am certain we are supposed to learn all we can about Jesus and the life he gives us here. This is a time we are given to grow in our relationship with the Father. We must apply what we have to this life."

They could see he was wrestling with his own thoughts trying to put things in the proper place of understanding. "I don't know," he said as he dropped his head in resignation. "I don't think we will understand it all in this life. I guess the best we can do is trust Him and live each day as if it were our last." Then with a little twist of the head in consideration, "And our first." He looked up at the others who were just trying to follow his wandering thoughts. The look on their faces was of ones who were struggling to follow. It tickled Shimon who started laughing at them. "That bad, huh?" That broke their concentration and they reacted with their own laughs.

"It appears we are going to be trying to figure this out for a while," Shimon finally said. "We had better get on with our day, shouldn't we? We will have to let the Lord sort this out for us."

The days following the stoning of Stephan were different than they were before. The people were getting jelled into a unified front of people with something in common. They all knew they could be killed at any given point. They weren't lackadaisical about what they were doing. They did things on purpose for a reason. No one was flippant. They were much more given to worship and prayer. When the Eleven taught, people listened as if their lives depended on it. And soon it was proven true.

The man named Saul headed up a program started by the Jewish leadership determined to exterminate the sect of Jesus. The believers were calling themselves "The Way" after Jesus's word that He was the way, the truth, and the life. Saul went from house to house searching out members of The Way. He was dragging them to prison as heretics and blasphemers. Life was getting tricky for those who followed Jesus. Many left Jerusalem. There were, however, those who stayed and continued the work.

Shimon and his family were counted among those who stayed. The Eleven also stayed. They weren't arrested because of the social pressure, but the people under them were open game. Shimon taught his family to be wise and to listen to the Holy Spirit when they were out among the people. There was still around a thousand people in the congregation of The Way.

Arguments popped up fairly often in the Temple. The priests were tending to follow The Way. Many Pharisees also came to be part of them. The Saducees, however, were vehemently opposed. They proposed their theology that there was no such thing as resurrection or angels. They had taken God out of their theology, replacing Him with rituals and traditions. The division was whether or not there was a relationship with God. They contended that it was through their interpretation of the Law that people were kept in line and that they could assure their cultural hold.

Trying very hard to keep away from those kinds of arguments, Shimon found himself going to Solomon's Porch when there was teaching happening, but going to the Temple was asking for trouble. There were people there who were watching for members of The Way for the sole purpose of starting something. It kind of broke his heart to have the Temple taken away from him since it was such a large part of his life for a very long time. The synagogues were being split between those who were traditional Jews versus those who were followers of Jesus. It depended on what the Rabbi was teaching that determined their flavor. Shimon was very glad Gershom was one of the ones who taught Jesus and told of his death and resurrection.

Kohath was one of the priests, but he had been raised from the dead. Life was getting difficult for him. He moved to Joppa where his daughter lived. He wasn't as strong of a personality as Shimon. The family kept their eye on Shimon.

Ezra was also one to keep their eyes on. His zeal had grown over time and he had become quite an influence in the Way. He had been considered as one of those to take care of the daily administration of the congregation as was Elihu. They had both learned of their personal expression of their faith in Jesus and how to minister. They had to watch how they did things, knowing Saul was out there trying to mess things up.

On a few occasions, as people were arrested, someone would try to defend their family or friends. Things got dicey and some people were killed. The congregation would come together to help with the burials. An attitude was rising up among the believers to try and fight back, but James and Peter knew where that went. They taught the people how to be peaceful and not resist, but to trust in the Lord. The last thing they wanted was an armed uprising. The Eleven kept the teachings going with consistent prayer and worship.

With the pressure put on the believers and how they were responding, it wasn't going the way the Jewish leaders had hoped. More and more people converted to The Way. Soon it was spreading throughout Israel. It was more than one man could deal with it. Saul tried. He was sent by the council to cities close by to bring the believers back for trial and imprisonment. It wasn't easy; they were running out of space.

Jonadab had become a force to be reckoned with. His position just under the High Priest was powerful. Being a Sadducee, he didn't care for the Law and being close to God. All he wanted was rule and authority. He used what he could get to enforce that rule. He was one who sent Saul out and helped him do what he needed to do. Saul was a Pharisee, taught under Gamaliel. The one thing they had in common was their hatred for these believers in Jesus. Saul was willing to be under Jonadab as long as he was still able to do what was in his heart to fight for the purity of Judaism. Saul's zeal was what Jonadab would use to get his own agenda done. It was painful for Saul to see his fellow Pharisees taking the Way. It fueled his rage.

They had determined in the congregation that it would be worthwhile to keep an eye on Saul. When he went to other cities, they were freer to do their activities. They kept a small network of believers who would keep track of Saul's whereabouts. Young Phinehas was part of that squad. He would bring home news on a regular basis. He would report to his father, Yitzaq, what they knew. Yitzaq would report it to the rest of the family. The shop was a hotbed of believers who were a tightly woven group. Some days they would close the shop doors, gather in the back to pray and worship. It was a good time, but they knew they had to be careful.

Shimon was still the one to be out among the community. He still took care of bringing food and clothing to the poor. He was very careful who was around and how he spoke. He listened to the reports of Saul's whereabouts. That determined the extent of his activities. What he didn't understand was that Saul wasn't the only problem.

There were men who were loyal to Jonadab who had no compunction about doing things that weren't quite legal or even moral for all that. He had this group to help him accomplish what he needed to do to gain control over people. He was always amazed at what men would do for a little money under the table. If he could find men, like Saul, who would do things he wanted because of their own personal drives, he would use them. If not, he could always buy men to help him.

He also liked to go to the Temple, as that was where he could keep his hand on the pulse of the city and the religious community. He was there watching when an argument broke out between one of his disciples and a man from The Way. They were down by the Gate Beautiful. The Sadducee was attempting to debunk the ideas of this believer in Jesus. Jonadab moved stealthily to within a distance for him to hear what was being said. His disciple, Rekem, was mocking the believer named Asher, a young man who was new to The Way.

"Why do you follow someone who was proven to be a criminal?" Rekem said. "They crucified him!"

"He was innocent of any charges! They put him to death illegally!" Asher was getting red in the face. "The criminals were those on the council!"

Rekem's face showed the proper indignation in the light of the accusation. "If that were true they would have been brought up on charges. It is the holiness of the council that keeps this nation from falling into chaos. These renegade preachers should all be crucified."

"The proof was that he didn't stay dead! They killed him for crimes he didn't commit," he spoke with vehemence. "He rose from the dead the third day! He was seen by many people."

Unnoticed by anyone, Shimon was slowly coming in to try to calm Asher down before something bad happened. He was just walking by on a delivery when he heard the loud voices. He recognized Asher and moved in to quiet things down.

"There is no proof of that," Rekem said, as if his saying it settled it. "If he raised from the dead, where is he?" Sweeping his hand around the vista of the Temple. "No one here can point him out. He's dead! There is no such thing as resurrection. We know this."

Asher was enraged by that statement. How can he say such things? Many people saw the Lord. "Of course there is resurrection. Where do you get that there isn't any? Remember the man thrown into Elijah's tomb? He came back out alive!"

"It was Elisha's tomb, not Elijah's. You don't even know the scripture! That was just a story made up to scare the armies into obedience."

Asher was just about to explode in anger. Shimon put a hand on his shoulder. "That's enough, Asher," he said calmly. Asher spun to see Shimon, barely registering he had been spoken to. Seeing it was an elder of the Way took the fight out of Asher. He just stammered trying to put words together.

Rekem could see he was winning that fight by just getting Asher angry. He pressed on. "No one can prove any resurrection. Ever!"

Feeling the defeat of a debate, Asher fired one more volley. "I can! This man right here died and is alive again!" Speaking to Shimon, he said, "Isn't that true? You were dead and buried in a tomb. But now you are alive. Right?"

Shimon was taken by surprise. Trying to find a way of answering, he stuttered, "Well, yes, but that isn't... I mean... stop this argument. You need to calm down."

Rekem then focused on Shimon as he could see a small crowd gathering. "What does he mean you were dead? That's not possible."

His obnoxious attitude piqued Shimon's emotions. "I was born before the Roman occupation. I ran my business here through Herod the Great's reign. I died before Herod did. I was placed in our family tomb. Thirty-three years later, the same day Jesus came up from the grave, I received life and have been living here in Jerusalem since. I am living proof that there is such a thing as resurrection! Just because you don't have the intelligence to see the truth, doesn't mean we have to prove anything to you. We are done here."

Shimon grabbed Asher by the sleeve and fairly dragged him away from the Temple. He couldn't believe he let that upstart Sadducee get him riled up. Asher knew he was in trouble as the iron grip Shimon clamped on his arm meant business. "I'm sorry. I'm sorry. I didn't mean any harm. He got me all turned around."

"I know. I'm not mad at you; I'm mad at myself for getting into the very argument I was trying to get you out of." He stopped and looked Asher in the eyes with a very stern expression. "We can't afford these arguments. It just opens up their chance to do something against us. Understand?" Asher was sufficiently cowed under. "Look. I know you were just trying to do what is right in defending

Jesus. He doesn't need your defense. You need to learn to listen to the Spirit when to talk and when not to." Shimon took a breath and let it out heavily. "We both got too emotionally involved back there. May the Lord God help us do better in the future. Okay?"

With a fully contrite attitude, Asher agreed. "I will do better."

"I know you will. Go and be careful." He patted Asher on the arm. He watched Asher walk away. He felt bad. "Oh, well. Lord, be with my emotions just like you need to be with that young man's emotions. We all need you and your presence." He continued on the street, still needing to deliver the package he had.

"That man is dangerous," Jonadab conceded to himself. He became acutely aware that a person who had actually been dead and raised would be quite damaging to their theological cause. Seeing Shimon walk away, he knew something had to be done.

As he went back into the Temple, he summoned his head servant. He knew this man would do whatever was asked of him and do it discretely.

"Shimon, the weaver," he spoke softly. "Do you know him?

"Yes, I do. He is all over the city. Does a lot with the poor."

"Well, that isn't what brings him to my attention. He says he has been raised from the dead. That makes us look bad before the people. We can't have any of that if we are going to influence the crowds. He is shifting opinion away from us and that is bad. Do you understand what I am saying?

His man just nodded compliance a couple of times, looking into the face of his master for complete meaning. "What do you propose we do about it?

"We? I can't be seen with him. I expect you are fully able to do what is needed without my help. If he has been brought back from the dead, he needs to be returned." Jonadab narrowed his expression to his lackey. "Do you understand my meaning?"

A small smile and bow, he looked Jonadab in the eyes, "I certainly do. Leave it to me. Do you have any preference for the method or circumstance?"

Jonadab thought for a second, stroking his beard. "Don't make it open. We don't need the attention and we don't need another Stephan on our hands. Quietly. Privately. Quickly. And soon. Any problems with that?"

"No, sir. Leave it to me."

"Good," Jonadab said as he leaned close. "One more thorn removed from our side."

The family had gathered for a meal together. They needed to discuss what to do concerning the congregation and the number of people leaving. Shimon sat at the head of the table as normal. It was usually the place of the eldest, and technically that was him. He had been born one hundred and sixteen years ago, but he had been away for over thirty years. Baruch was aging quickly and was not moving very well anymore. He looked a lot older than Shimon, it was tricky trying to figure out how old Shimon looked and acted, but he was the elder in the family.

Even Shimon had a hard time thinking about these things. It wasn't normal. How long is he going to live? Should he get married again? That thought dazzled his mind. There was no way he was going to do that, but he was able. He had thought about getting together with one of the women who had been raised, but it made him dizzy contemplating all that. No, he had enough wives to contend with in his mind. Something deep within him made him feel closer to the women he had been married with, as if he had just seen them and they were happy. He shook his head trying to get his thoughts back under control.

There were times he would see things in this memory and have no idea where it was that memory came from. He was reading the scrolls at the synagogue about Abraham and it seemed like he could actually see him and felt like he knew him. That was absurd! He had a warm feeling when he read Malachi and couldn't figure that out, either. He knew he was an anomaly, but the more he tried to figure that out, the less it made sense. Many times, as he would find himself thinking about it, he would just take a deep breath and tell himself to get back to work.

Here with his family, he would have memories of them a long time ago and would try to reconcile the images in his mind. Baruch was a vibrant, powerful man. Elihu was the small grandson he adored. Now they are both older and their lives have been spent without Shimon in them. He was so proud of how everyone had turned out. They had something even greater in common; they all loved Jesus.

What a time to be alive! The birth of a whole new culture. They were on the foundation of this great building that would be the way for God to come into lives and changing things for eternity! How fantastic!

All that was true, but inside Shimon, something else had been gaining ground. He saw how Stephan had died. He saw the beauty of going to be with Jesus. There was a yearning to go home that he couldn't define. Going home was the exact expression to him. He felt out of place here, like his time was past and it needed to be in the hands of the new generation. How often he would question God about why he had come back and what his purpose is. He had been instrumental in the Eleven getting what they needed and going further. He had done his part. He was feeling as if his part was soon done.

The meal had commenced. The joy of everyone laughing and carrying on like they did sparked a deep satisfaction in Shimon's heart. They had made full contact with the outlying close relatives. Chaim and Naomi, Esther, Rahab, Tirzah, and Hepzibah had all been completely brought up to date as best as possible with the goings on of The Way. It was obvious that God was doing a special work on the planet right now, and it was good to be a part of it. The persecution had, however, put a real face on the condition of the world. Not everything was perfect and full of flowers. People were now dying for the cause. It seems that the time of great grace was coming to an end. There was darkness looming ahead. Shimon knew it was only a matter of time before the family was afflicted with sorrow and pain.

Ezra had come to bring news of the coming and going of Saul. He was away right now and the congregation was feeling peace for a season. Activities had resumed for the most part with the public teachings still happening. The Jews knew they couldn't afford a straight out confrontation in public, yet. But there would come a time, they believed, when this sect will be driven out. The believers, however, had seen that every time there was a push against them, more people would come to Jesus. This wasn't working for the Jews.

Shimon sat back and listened to the conversations around the room. He was impressed with how much the women entered into the discussions and how thoughtful they were. He could see the foundation had been laid in the family. He wasn't needed anymore. He wanted them to take their rightful place.

Baruch sat next to Shimon. They had built quite a friendship since Shimon came back. It wasn't like father and son; it was more like comrades with a lot of history in common. Baruch had become all his father had wanted for him. Now Baruch was getting to the final stages of his life and it had been a good life at that.

"What do you think, Baruch?" Shimon asked him. "What should we do as a family? Should we relocate or stay in Jerusalem? Break up and go to different places or try to stay together?"

That was the crux of the matter. Baruch had been giving it a lot of thought. The emotions of being away from family ached deeply in his heart. He also knew, however, that the Lord might have different plans.

"It doesn't matter what I think," he surmised. "I know my emotions and what I want may be very different than what the Lord needs us to do. I want everyone to be together and without pain. That isn't very reasonable, is it?"

Shimon chuckled. "That is exactly how I feel. We don't have much say in the matter, do we?" Now that his thoughts were being framed by the spiritual realm and not just the physical, he knew they were not always going to see things the way they were before. Everything is about eternity. What happens here and now is only working toward something a lot bigger and a lot more important. We will all be together forever. There is a price to be paid for living right now. "The greatest thing we can do is help each other be the believers we need to be."

The discussions were scattered and varied. Finally, Shimon got everyone's attention. He stood to talk to his family. They all got very quiet. There was no joking or even interaction. This was time for Shimon to talk. They listened.

"We have been given a massive privilege. We have followed Jesus through his entire life in some way or another. Some of us were there for his miracles and teachings. We have been a part of his family and disciples. We were there when he was crucified. Even greater, we were there when he rose from the grave. We now have the privilege to see the birth of The Way, a body of believers. We have experienced the receiving of the Holy Spirit and the baptism of the Holy Spirit. We have seen and experienced miracles, some through our own hands. We have been together through it all somehow. God has placed his hand on this family since the birth of Jesus until now. I was even brought back from the dead." He shook his head, smiling at the vastness of that statement.

"We have nothing to complain about. We should be totally willing to do whatever the Spirit asks of us. Soon, he will be asking a lot. Some of us here will probably be given the privilege to die for him. The rest will live for him. Both will be a sacrifice and an honor." The

room was full of the Spirit of God. They could all feel His presence.

"I want to tell you all how much I love you and am honored to be called part of your family." He choked up, his eyes filled to overflowing. "I don't know how long we have together, but it has been wonderful to have seen you, get to know you, and see how Jesus has filled your lives. I worship the Most High." His eyes closed with the tears streaming down his cheeks, his face lifted up, as were his hands. The room joined him in worshipping the God of the Universe. As his worship subsided a little, he continued by saying, "Thank you all. Continue to be in our Messiah. Do what he calls you to do without fear or wavering."

Lifting his hands over them, with his palms down, he spoke firmly and passionately. "I bless you today with peace. I bless you with joy. I bless you each with full relationship with our Lord Jesus Christ. May each one of you know his voice, his hand, and his face. May you walk with Him continually throughout your lives. You are mightily blessed. In the words the Lord gave our priests in the scrolls: Jehovah bless you, and keep you. Jehovah cause His face to shine upon you and be gracious to you. Jehovah lift up his face to you, and give you peace. I declare before you today: You are all blessed!"

There wasn't a dry eye in the room. The Spirit of the Living God was touching each of them in a very sacred and profound way. This family was blessed. No matter what else happened to them from this day forward, they knew they were blessed.

Elihu found Shimon in the courtyard after everything had been picked up. This place was special to him ever since he used to stand out here with his grandfather many years ago and pray. Shimon was deep in thought. Elihu had to break in. "S'ba? Are you okay?"

Shimon jumped as he was startled. "Oh, yes. Better than okay. I am blessed." He smiled as he watched Elihu sit close by. "I used to see you in this place praying with me as the shofar blew in the Temple every morning." Elihu smiled as that was what he was thinking about also.

"I wanted to thank you for the blessing tonight," Elihu spoke tenderly. "It meant a lot to me. I know it will follow all of us for a long time, no matter where the Lord sends us or what happens to us. What are you feeling?"

"Me?" Shimon was surprised at having the focus put on him suddenly. "Why, I am so blessed. I was just thinking about how my life has turned out. This isn't anything like I thought it would be, but it is everything I have ever hoped for. I feel completely fulfilled in my life. It is like the reason He brought me back from the dead has been accomplished. I am satisfied."

This admission from Shimon hit Elihu hard. "What does that mean?"

"Oh, nothing, really. It is just a good thing to have this kind of clarity in your life. At least once before everything gets crazy." He snickered sitting back looking up at the stars he could see poking through. "I really do love you, Elihu. You are special."

With the tears at the ready, Elihu knew there wasn't much he could say. "I love you, too, S'ba. You are very important to me. I lost you once, and God gave you back. Thank you for pouring into my life." They sat there silent and just loving each other's presence.

Keturah came out looking for Elihu. "We need to get home. Are you two coming?"

"Be right there," Elihu answered. Looking at Shimon, he said, "Are you coming?"

"Soon. Go on without me. I know my way home." Elihu stood, stepped over to Shimon, bent down and gave him a very tender hug. Nothing was said, but much was communicated.

Now that he was alone again, Shimon just talked with his Lord. "Thank you so much for him. Each of these is precious. I put them in your hands, my Lord. That is the best place for them." His mind went to Stephan. "I pray we have the grace to die like he did." The thought of Stephan leaving in such a way and knowing that he went directly into the presence of Jesus, struck him again. The beauty of it was indescribable. As he contemplated it all, he couldn't help but express his heart.

"I just want to die."

Today was a day for seeking out some of the poor and helping them. Shimon loved these days. He had been doing something like this for eighty years or so (with a thirty-year break to be dead). It did his heart good to see the faces of those he helped light up with a smattering of hope. He loaded up a bag with food and some blankets. Soon he was on his way into the Northwest quadrant of Jerusalem. There were many very rich people up there with a lot of poor in between.

It was mid-morning as he came across a man who was crippled in his feet. He was older and as Shimon approached him, he had a look of 'are you really going to talk to me?' mixed with 'you are going to regret talking to me.' Shimon could tell he was extremely lonely and as he got closer he understood why. It was the smell. He had sores on his legs that were oozing fluid. The picture jogged his memory about another beggar he had known so many years ago. This time, however, he had more to give.

"Hello, my friend," he said gently and brightly. "How are you doing today?" He went steadily closer to the man, trying to disguise the look of repulsion he must have had on his face. "Would you like some bread? Do you have a blanket?"

The man received the bread hungrily with gratitude beaming off his face. "Thank you so much," he said in between bites. It was obvious he hadn't eaten in a while.

"Look, my friend, I know some people who can really help you. I can help you get over to them if you want." Shimon pleaded with him with concern and compassion. Very few had ever spoken to this man that way. "Here is some water, to help wash down that bread." He handed the man his water skin.

"You would take me somewhere to get help?" He was clutching the rest of the loaf as if someone would try to take it away.

"Certainly. Let's get you up and I will take you over there." Shimon put an arm around him and lifted. Together they came right up and were standing together. "Can you walk?"

"Some. If you don't go too fast. That is my stick."

"Great! Let's get moving. We are going to the end of this alley and turning left. Do you have anything you want to take with you?"

The man pointed weakly. "That's my bedroll and satchel. That is all I own." Shimon took it by the rope that held it together and slung it over his shoulder.

"Very good. Let's go." Now they were established, they shuffled down the alley with the man leaning heavily on his stick. Shimon was having a hard time breathing, but was muscling through.

As they walked, the man talked a lot. He hadn't had anyone to talk to for a while and was going to make the best of it. "I am scared that I am going to die and no one will know. I have been alone for many years. My Rebekah died several years ago."

"My wife was also named Rebekah and she also died a long time ago." Shimon thought having this in common would comfort the man some.

They turned the corner and were slowly making progress up the street. There were more people on this street, but when this man came close, they moved away rather quickly.

"Actually, I am afraid to die at all," the man said shakily. "I don't have long to live and I am afraid there is nothing for me after."

Shimon noticed that a certain man started walking fairly close to them from behind. He didn't let that distract him from his conversation. "I knew a man who rose from the dead. He was the Messiah. Anyone who believes in him will have a new life here and the promise of a life with Him forever. His name is Jesus."

"I've heard of him!" the man exclaimed. Is it true that he came back to life?"

"It is true. I, myself, have talked to him." They stopped walking as the man turned to Shimon to look him directly in the face.

"You did? There is hope after death?"

Shimon laughed a little as he said, "There is hope. In fact, I also died. Thirty years later, God brought me back to life." The man was slack-jawed staring at him.

"Then die again," the voice said as the man behind Shimon produced a knife and lunged at him. Shimon sidestepped quickly, but not enough as the knife sliced an open gash along his ribcage. The assailant recovered, not knowing exactly what to do. This man was supposed to die easily.

Shimon looked at him as he pulled his hand away covered with blood. "Why are you doing this?"

"Your telling people you are alive again is causing problems," the man snarled at him.

Indignation hit Shimon. "Then I will tell more people about how Jesus is the Messiah and He gives life to anyone who believes in Him!" His voice raised to the point that he was almost preaching to the people around. The assailant couldn't allow that and lept forward one more time, plunging the knife deep into Shimon's belly. Shimon's face showed the surprise and shock of the attack. All his strength left as he collapsed on the street.

The beggar cried out, "Murder! Murder!" as the people around spun to see the scene. The assailant turned and tried to run, but a man nearby grabbed him, causing him to drop the knife. Soon there were three men holding him. The beggar dropped to the street, unable to help in any way. A woman nearby ran to Shimon pulling him up on her lap as she knelt on the street. She was one of the congregation and immediately tried to comfort Shimon.

The men who had the assailant looked back at Shimon on the ground. Shimon looked at them and raised a hand. "No. Let him go. God will deal with him. He isn't the one at the top. Someone sent him. Let God expose them." The men were baffled, but they slowly let him go. The assailant looked at Shimon and the look in Shimon's eyes burned into his mind like a hot iron. He pushed aside the men and ran.

As Shimon looked, he saw Jesus walking through the crowd toward him with a huge grin on his face. Shimon felt his pain fade away. He stood to greet Jesus. They hugged an intense embrace. Shimon finally let go and stepped back a little. Something caught his eye. Looking down he saw a man lying on the ground covered in blood. He looked closer trying to recognize him. The clothing gave it away. His face lit up with full realization and he spun around to look at Jesus.

"Yes, my faithful servant," Jesus said, holding Shimon's face in his hands. "You have died again. This time for good." Shimon saw them now. Angels all around for as far as the eye could see. He was finally home. Oh what a beautiful new adventure laid ahead of him.

Epilogue

Things got complicated for the assembly of believers after that but, just like most things in life, that's the beginning of growth pangs. The young man Saul had an encounter with Jesus Christ while he was on a mission to persecute believers. He was turned by that miraculous time and became a major part of the future of the assembly. He changed his name to Paul to show that change and God used him mightily.

The family was stunned at the death of Shimon. The congregation was also. There were more deaths happening all the time. Persecution of the followers of Jesus was heating up. It wasn't surprising, though. They knew this was coming for quite a while.

Baruch felt all his determination to live drain away. He died the day after Shimon. Shimei became the head of the family in Jerusalem and had a double burial to attend to.

Elihu was making the same fancy weave for a tablecloth for Joseph of Arimathea to replace the one used for the burial cloth for Jesus when word came of Shimon's death. They all felt it was appropriate to use it for Shimon's shroud. They knew this one wouldn't come back. Elihu felt it was a fitting tribute to this man they had loved that had died many years ago and came back to bring the good news of Jesus, to be buried in a shroud like His. He made another one later that actually was used as a table cloth.

It was quite a large turn out for Shimon's burial, almost as large as Stephan's, which was remarkable since there were so many fewer believers in Jerusalem. No one dared disturb them. They were glad they had repaired the tomb so quickly after Shimon had left it being made alive. They now had need of it rather quickly. They placed Shimon on the shelf where he had lain before. They placed Baruch beside him on a stone platform they made. There was crying, but mostly the atmosphere was one of joy and anticipation of eternity. They had very little grief.

Chaim and Naomi opened their substantial house for believers to meet. It grew to be quite a force in Joppa. Uriah and his wife and sons moved there to help. Josiah eventual became the leader of the assembly there. Elihu helped as much as he could, but it was Ezra who became a leader under James until James' death by sword. He then was a great support to Peter and the others who kept the group in Jerusalem. Shimei and Elihu kept the business running and were significant in meeting the needs of so many in the congregation. They remained faithful and consistent in the gathering of believers.

Shimon experienced the new place called heaven. Malachi greeted him as he entered.

Appendix

Scriptural evidence for departed spirits.

In this book, the character of Lachish is a man who dies and finds himself living without a body and subject to the addictions he had while living. I have been asked about this phenomenon and if there is scriptural evidence of that happening. This is one of the reasons I wrote these books, is to explain in story form how it works.

Sheol

Sheol is the Hebrew word for the place of the dead. The word for it in Greek is Hades. Hell is not to be populated yet. Death and Hades will give up the dead in them, they will be judged at the Great White Throne Judgment and cast into the Lake of Fire which is Hell. Until then, the dead are kept in Sheol or Hades until they are brought to hell.

This isn't going to be an exhaustive study of Sheol or Hades, just a reference to point the way to those who would pursue that endeavor. It is tricky to determine where Sheol is exactly, because we tend to think on the physical plane only. When a body dies, that part of the person that isn't physical lives on, but in a different environment. The physics of the physical realm don't work since they are no longer physical. That means they are living in the soulish and spiritual realms. Whatever sin was their focus, it still is, even to the point of being their torment (or fire, if you will). They are on the earth, not able to interact physically. Since they are still souls and spirits, they abide in that realm and can interact on those levels. Where? On the earth, in the earth around the places where they are drawn because of the frequencies of their sin.

What that realm would be like is one thing I attempted to describe in my books. Just the fact that the departed spirits can interact with living people is astounding. We cannot see them, but they can see us and the things that are happening around us. They have no power, authority, nor ability to harm. They are an influence with the attachment of their addiction and the need to try to fulfill it.

Departed Spirits

We are told in the law, not to converse with the dead (Deut. 18:10-13; Lev. 19:31; Lev. 20:6, 27; Ex. 22:18; Isa. 8:19-20). Saul called up Samuel and did talk with him, but it cost him dearly (1 Sam. 28:3;20; 1 Chr. 10:13-14). It is not for us to contact them or interact with them, except to cast them out.

Departed spirits are not demons. Demons are fallen angels and have that power, but only within limits. This also is not an expose about demons and how to deal with them. Departed spirits are humans who no longer have a body. They are under the torment they put themselves under as living humans. The only hope they have is if they received the salvation of Jesus Christ. If they died without knowing Jesus, they are in this torment forever. There is no salvation left for them.

As shown in the book, those who had faith looking forward to salvation were in a different portion of Sheol made for the righteous. They were in that holding place until Jesus died and purchased eternal salvation. He went there as a man who died. He became our sin and therefore went to unrighteous Sheol only long enough to pay the price of sin. Then He went to righteous Sheol and preached to the spirits in prison (1 Peter 3:19), giving them the salvation they were looking forward to. He then took them to heaven, emptying righteous Sheol forever. Now, when someone dies knowing Jesus, they go immediately to heaven. Those who don't know Jesus will still go to Sheol, or as the Greek calls it, Hades.

It is what the unrighteous departed spirits do that is the mystery. We are not left without knowledge or information. Now we will look at those scripture to examine the evidence.

Proverbs 2:16-19

These will deliver you from the strange woman, from the foreigner who flatters with her words, who forsakes the guide of her youth and forgets the covenant of her God. For her house leads down to death, and her tracks to the departed spirits. All going in to her do not return, nor do they reach the ways of life.

This passage tells us that in the place of prostitution or sexual fornication, the departed spirits are there, those who have died. The question of why is prevalent. When a person (especially men) ejaculate, they open their souls to all manner of things. It is supposed to be there for a husband and wife to open themselves to each other for them to be one flesh, getting closer and closer. When sexual sin happens, it opens the person up to the deviated spiritual realm. Departed spirits can then attach themselves to that person with the desire to feel the illicit sexual feelings again. When we purpose to do what is known sin, we open ourselves to things we don't know about. This is true in all these passages.

Proverbs 5:3-6

For the lips of a strange woman drip honey, and her palate is sweeter than oil, but afterwards, she is bitter as wormwood, sharp as a sword of mouths; her feet go down to death; her steps take hold on Sheol, lest you should meditate on the path of life, her tracks are movable, you cannot know them.

The warning is quite explicit. Death and Sheol are there. No wonder sexual sin is so devastating.

Proverbs 7:24-27

Now, then, listen to me, O sons, and attend to the words of my mouth: Do not let your heart turn aside to her ways; do not go astray in her paths. For many are the wounded she has caused to fall; and plentiful all her slain ones. The ways of Sheol are in her house, leading down to the rooms of death.

The ways of Sheol leading down to the rooms of death are in her house. The story is unfolding, and the signs are quite visible to those you want to see.

Proverbs 9:16-18

The simple one, let him turn in here; and to the one lacking heart, she says to him, Stolen waters are sweet, and bread eaten in secret is pleasant. But he does not know that the departed spirits are there; her guests are in the depths of Sheol.

All four of these passages tell us about sexual deviancy and the consequences of participation. Ignorance will not save a person. The enemy loves this. It doesn't take a demon to get someone to give up their life. Departed spirits will help enhance someone into an addiction they have no way of fighting without Jesus Christ.

This makes it difficult for me to write about this subject as a novel. I can't write a story about sexual attachments without it being effectually pornography. That is the main subject about it, however, in the Word. I had to have the antagonist have an addiction to show their function in Sheol and interaction with the people who are still alive. Sexual sin isn't the only way they work. We have more evidence.

Proverbs 21:16-17

The man who wanders out of the way of prudence shall rest in the congregation of departed spirits. A man who loves pleasure shall be poor, he who loves wine and oil shall not be rich.

Any sin that opens up our soul to addiction is viable for departed spirits to work. Alcohol, drugs, anger, rage, violence, rape, murder, the list isn't short, all of them lend to behavior that is addictive in nature. Anything a departed spirit had a problem with in life that captured his focus and attention will be something he is still yearning for after death. That should be a wakeup call for people, if they only knew about this, but I don't hear people telling those around them about the true dangers.

Is there any evidence in the New Testament? Yes, there is.

Luke 11:21-26

When the strong one, having been armed, guards his dwelling, his goods are in peace. But as soon as one stronger than he having come, he overcomes him; he takes away his armor on which he relied, and deals out his arms. The one not being with Me is against Me. And the one not gathering with Me scatters. When the unclean spirit goes out from the man, he goes through dry places seeking rest. And not finding, he says, I will return to my house from where I came out. And coming, he finds it having been swept and having been decorated. Then he goes and takes seven other spirits more wicked than himself, and entering he dwells there. And the last things of that man become worse than the first.

What makes this interesting is that it doesn't specifically say demon, but unclean spirit. When a demon is cast out, he just goes. What determines a "dry place" for a demon? However, if this is a departed spirit who has been associated with a live person to help feed his addiction, however remotely, and is cast out, "dry places" makes sense. He will wander looking for another person to inhabit. If he doesn't find someone, he will try to return to the host he had before. If he finds it not occupied by the Holy Spirit, he will take it again. If he brings seven other departed spirits with him, they will help enhance this host to doing even worse than he had before. The original departed spirit will definitely be benefited by experiencing the damage happening to the host in more severe ways.

How can a demon find worse demons to inhabit someone? Demons are just demons. However, a departed spirit can have more addiction or more severe addiction or additional issues. The original spirit knows that if he brings others that are more perverted, he will get more of what he wants from the experience. There are always worse ones. This makes more sense.

Conclusion

In my ministry dealing with men addicted to pornography and other sexual problems, I have encountered several who have had spirits that were pushing them. The most interesting thing about departed spirits is that they don't have any authority. They are there because the person opened themselves up to them by their deviant activity. Departed spirits have to leave when discovered and commanded to depart. They don't argue or give problems, they just leave. The reason we need to know about them is so we can best defeat them and help others be set free.

ABOUT THE AUTHOR

Lee Eddy is a Bible teacher with over 50 years of experience, including pastor, missionary, seminar leader, and ministry developer. His ministry, Face to Face Healing Ministry, as set many free from addictions and interpersonal damage. He has written several teaching books and manuals including the Great Romance Marriage Course, Rocksot Teaching course, Pure Man course, and Advance Pure Man. With his wife of 46 years, Roxanne, he has raised 3 children. They live in Colorado and are continuing using and developing ways of bringing others into freedom.

Made in the USA
Middletown, DE
26 May 2021